Timeless

by

Kathryn Amurra

Heart's True Desire

Timeless

Cover Art by *Lea Schizas*

The Wild Rose Press, Inc.
PO Box 708
Adams Basin, NY 14410-0708
Visit us at www.thewildrosepress.com

Publishing History
First Edition, 2025
Trade Paperback ISBN 978-1-5092-6035-5
Digital ISBN 978-1-5092-6036-2

Heart's True Desire

Published in the United States of America

Dedication

To my mother and father, who were partners in all things and whose love created a perfect feeling of home that I carry with me always.

Prologue

In the last decades of the Ottoman Empire's rule in Bulgaria, there lived a jeweler in one of the biggest cities in the country. This man, a widower, had a daughter and a son—twins—and he loved them more than anything else in the world. On the eve of his daughter's wedding, the man wished to give his daughter something special to remember him by. He found a rare stone in his collection that he had obtained in a trade with another jeweler from the Orient years before, and he proceeded to make the girl a necklace. As he fashioned the chain and the mount for the stone, a thought occurred to him. He could not give his daughter such a gift without giving something to his beloved son, as well. So, he carefully cleaved the stone to obtain two similarly-sized stones. With one, he finished the necklace for his daughter. With the other, he made a ring for his son.

After getting the blessing of the parish priest on the gifts, the man grew to believe that the necklace and the ring embodied his unconditional love for his children. And just as he would do anything for his son and daughter, he believed the necklace and the ring now had the power to do anything his children asked.

Soon after, the son also married. Together with his wife, the two left Bulgaria and crossed the ocean to make a new life for themselves in America. Time passed, and their family grew. The couple's oldest daughter had the same adventurous heart as her parents, and when she turned twenty, she announced that she would not marry the butcher's son, to whom she had been promised. Instead, she would travel to the southern states and make her own way in the world.

On the night before she was to leave her childhood home, her father took her aside and showed her the ring his father had given him years before. He told her that whatever she asked of the ring, it would grant to her because of the power in the stone. He warned her that she could only ask for one thing, the thing she most desired. So long as she kept the ring, she would keep that which her heart desired most. Once she gave the ring to another, however, she would no longer have the stone's power in her life.

Embracing her father, the girl took the ring and kept it safe, knowing that someday its power would be needed.

Chapter One

Charlotte, North Carolina
Late January, Modern Day

The halls were quiet as Erin shut down her computer and pushed away from her desk. The darkness outside the floor-to-ceiling windows of her posh uptown office, along with the fact that she was the last person left on the thirty-seventh floor, made it feel like midnight even though it was only six o'clock. She hated the short winter days.

Reaching for her laptop, Erin paused, debating whether to shove the thing into her bag so she could do some work over the weekend or not. It wasn't as though she had any plans for the next couple of days, but it still irked her to give the law firm more time than it was due. She shook her head as she turned away, leaving the laptop where it sat. That kind of attitude wasn't going to get her to partner, and a year ago she would have cared.

Already overheating under her heavy winter coat and scarf, Erin slung her leather work bag over her shoulder and hurried from her office to the elevators.

Minutes later, she was bracing herself against the frigid night air as she stepped out into the icebox that was Charlotte, North Carolina, in the dead of winter.

Withdrawing an ungloved hand from her pocket,

Erin fished around the loose papers in her work bag for her phone as she hurried down the sidewalk, heading for the parking garage. As her fingers wrapped themselves around the cold plastic case of the phone, she realized what she was doing and stilled her hand. Letting the phone drop back into the bag and shoving her hand into her pocket once more, she bit back the tears that were already forming.

It had been a year, and still, her first impulse as she walked to her car was to call her mother and talk about her day. Sometimes Erin couldn't stop herself from taking out the phone and looking at her mother's name in the contact list. She couldn't bring herself to delete it. Erin knew she would, eventually. Just not yet.

The cold helped, though, and by the time she had speed-walked the three blocks to the parking garage, the pressure behind her eyes had dissipated. She took a deep breath. God, she missed her mother.

The traffic was light heading out of the city, and no more than ten minutes later Erin pulled into the modest parking lot of the three-story red-brick Georgian-style building where her grandmother lived. The building, easily the largest structure on its residential street, was nestled between magnolia trees and willow oaks, which provided blessed shade in the summer and an unhealthy dose of pollen at least six months out of the year. With its symmetrical arrangement of black-shuttered windows and an impressive front door framed by four white columns and a matching arch overtop, the house had always reminded Erin of the Old South, or at least her vision of the Old South based on the numerous period-pieces she had watched over the years. Her grandmother claimed the building used to be the home of one of the more prominent families in Charlotte in the 1800s but that, decades back, it had been converted into apartments. The grand entrance now opened into a common hall that led to the different units.

Her grandmother's apartment was on the first floor, near the entryway, and the old woman's door opened before Erin could raise her hand to knock. Erin stepped inside and shrugged off her coat.

"Hi, Grandma," she said, bending down over a foot to kiss her grandmother on the cheek. "Sometimes I think you're psychic with how quick you are to open the door."

Her grandmother chuckled. "That would solve a lot of my problems and create a whole host of new ones. No, I was just watching for you at the window. It's too cold out there today, and there's not much heat in the hallway."

The old woman, who stood no more than 4 feet tall, pushed her walker back toward the chair she sat in most of the day in the living room. She eased herself down into the seat, her joints audibly creaking as she did so.

The naturally dark hair her grandmother was so proud of did little to disguise the old woman's eighty-seven years, thanks to the arthritis she had endured since as far back as Erin could remember. But as old and broken down as her body was, her mind was sharp, and she had the sense of humor of a mischievous twelve-year-old boy. It was that same playful twinkle in her eyes that caused Erin to smile now, and she quickly put her work bag down by the door and took a seat on the couch, close to where her grandmother was sitting.

"So, what have you been up to, Grandma? Anyone

come to visit you today?"

Her grandmother shook her head. "Too cold for visitors, apparently. Even your father didn't come to eat lunch with me today. Maybe he had an appointment or something, although he usually tells me when he's not coming. You should probably call him tonight and just make sure he's okay."

Erin looked down at her hands, a familiar bitterness rising within her at the mention of her father.

"I'm sure he's fine, Grandma. Did you eat dinner yet?" Erin rose from the couch and took a few steps into the small galley kitchen to see if she could make herself useful.

"Yes, dear, I ate some leftovers that your father brought over for me earlier in the week. What about you, are you hungry?"

Erin looked up from the dishes she had started to scrub before she answered. Her grandmother couldn't hear very well, but she had a knack for reading lips. "Don't worry about me, Grandma. I'll eat when I get home."

After finishing with the dishes, Erin turned to the refrigerator to take stock of what her grandmother might need from the store for the following week.

"I made a list for you, dear. It's over there on the table. Now come sit next to me and relax for a few minutes before you rush out of here. I have some interesting news to tell you."

Erin plucked the grocery list off the dining room table and, scanning it quickly, put it in her pocket before moving back to the couch. Her grandmother's "interesting news" usually had to do with who she saw leaving Mrs. Myer's apartment that afternoon with a guilty look on his face while Mr. Myer was at work. If only half the stories her grandmother told were true, Mrs. Myer was either running a booming massage parlor from inside her apartment or was the sole proprietor of a very different type of establishment. "What gossip do you have for me today, Grandma?"

Her grandmother's eyes lit up. "Do you remember when I told you about the apartment on the third floor? The one that takes up two units? Well, on Monday I found out why no one lives there. It belongs to the landlord, the man who owns this building. I met him—a charming man named Mr. Abbott."

"I see," Erin replied dryly, already sensing where the conversation was going and having no desire to encourage her grandmother's line of thought.

"He came around and introduced himself to each tenant close to dinnertime on Monday. It was almost like an interview. I invited him in, and he sat across from me at that table over there, drinking some tea I had just made. He was very polite, but he asked a lot of questions, like whether I lived alone. That one made me laugh. I almost wanted to tell him I had a jealous live-in boyfriend who would be home any minute!"

Her grandmother chuckled. She had been a widow for nearly a third of her life, and Erin was sure she had never had a boyfriend at all, let alone a live-in one, before or after her husband.

"Anyway, he asked me where I was from, what family I had in the area, how I liked living here, whether I intended to stay for a while—I had to laugh at that one, too. I told him I intended to stay here as long as the good Lord intended to keep me among the living, which might not be too much longer!"

Erin couldn't help smiling. No matter what difficulties her grandmother faced or what losses she endured, she always maintained a sense of adventure in what the future had in store. Her indomitable spirit had kept her optimistic when Erin's aunt—her grandmother's oldest daughter, with whom she had lived for decades—passed away unexpectedly and her grandmother had been moved from New York to California to live with Erin's uncle and his family. And it was that same optimism that had helped her adjust yet again when only five months later her uncle thought it best for her grandmother to move back to the East Coast to be closer to Erin's widowed father. It had been wonderful having her grandmother nearby, and, as selfish as it was, Erin was glad things hadn't worked out for her grandmother in California.

"I haven't told you the best part," continued her grandmother. "He's young, handsome, and single." The old woman leaned forward, a sly smile playing on her lips. "Okay, handsome is an understatement—he's gorgeous. If I weren't eighty-seven years old and all bound up with arthritis, I would have propositioned him."

"Grandma!"

"It's true! I'm sure Mrs. Myer was beside herself. Luckily for Mr. Abbott, though, Mr. Myer had already come home for the evening when Mr. Abbott went knocking on that door."

They both laughed. Curious, but trying to keep her grandmother's matchmaking tendencies at bay, Erin thought twice before asking her next questions. "Did he say why he's visiting everyone? Is he selling the building or something?"

"No," answered her grandmother, "quite the opposite. He's planning to live upstairs in that apartment of his for a little while. He said he just wanted to get to know his neighbors."

"Interesting." Erin clasped her hands together in thought. "That's not exactly typical slumlord behavior."

"Slumlord! Hmmph. Wait until you meet him."

Erin snorted quietly. "Meet him? When would I ever meet your landlord?"

"Right now," replied her grandmother, as though it were obvious. "I need you to take my rent up to him."

"What?" gasped Erin. "Absolutely not. I am not going up there to check him out, Grandma. I'm sure our paths will cross eventually." She added under her breath, "And I'm sure he's not as 'handsome' as you say he is."

"Get up, Erin. My rent check is already made out. It's under the saltshaker on the table."

Erin sat up straight and crossed her arms, feeling like a petulant child. "No, Grandma, I'm not going up there."

Her grandmother rubbed her hands together, then looked up at Erin with a crinkle in her brow that was designed to elicit sympathy.

"Honey, I really need you to take it. It's almost the end of the month, and I forgot to give it to him when he came for his visit. It'll be late if I mail it. You know I would take it up there myself if it weren't for my arthritis."

"I'm sure there's a grace period," replied Erin, already feeling her resolve weaken. "Or you can have Dad do it when he comes over tomorrow."

"Please, Pumpkin." The crinkles in her forehead

deepened masterfully. "I would sleep a lot easier knowing my rent is paid."

Erin never could resist a "Pumpkin" plea from her grandmother. She knew she had no choice.

"He's probably not even up there," said Erin, pulling herself up and walking reluctantly to the table where the check lay, mocking her. She picked it up and slipped it into the back pocket of her jeans. "There's probably a mail slot or some basket for rent checks up there, now that he's here," she reasoned, walking to the door. "Your devious little scheme to have me meet this mysterious Mr. Abbott is not going to work, you know." Erin reached for the doorknob. "I'll be back in a minute, Grandma. Prepare to be sorely disappointed."

She could hear the old woman chuckling from her chair as she closed the door behind her.

Shaking her head, Erin walked up the three flights of stairs to the apartment where the allegedly gorgeous Mr. Abbott resided. Half annoyed, and half amused, she wished she could have just a fraction of her grandmother's spunk when she turned twenty-seven later that year, let alone when she was in her eighties.

As she climbed up the last few steps to the third floor, she scanned the area all around the door marked 3A for a mailbox or a slot for dropping off rent without success. *Too soon*, she thought. The poor guy hadn't even gotten himself situated yet, and her grandmother wanted her to stalk him.

Taking a breath, Erin raised a fisted hand and gave the heavy wooden door three strong knocks. She would wait about five seconds, and, if there was no answer, she would return to her grandmother's apartment victorious.

Two seconds had gone by when the door opened.

"Can I help you?"

Damn it. He was gorgeous.

Chapter Two

Standing before Erin was hands-down the most attractive man she had ever laid eyes on. His hair was a rich brown, like the color of dark chocolate, and his eyes, which were a lighter shade of brown flecked with gold, were both warm and welcoming. His nose was perfectly proportioned, as was his mouth, although Erin tried not to let her gaze linger there. His skin was flawless; his jawline was masculine, but not too square; and his lips were curved slightly, as though in anticipation of a smile. He was, in short, a work of art.

"Hi," said Erin, afraid that she had been stunned into too long a silence. Managing to find the smile she had perfected for making clients feel at ease, she continued. "I'm sorry to bother you. I'm just here to drop off a rent check."

She pulled the folded-up check out of her back pocket to prove that she wasn't just a random stalker.

"You're not a resident, are you?" he asked, his dark eyebrows pulling together inquisitively.

"Oh, no, it's not for me. It's for my grandmother, Rose Dovetree."

He smiled, and the effect was breathtaking. "Yes, of course, Mrs. Dovetree in 1A. Please come in and I'll write up a receipt for you."

The invitation took Erin by surprise. She paused for a moment, unsure what to do and lost in his gaze.

Surely, he was only waiting for some sign that she had heard his invitation, but her heart palpitated all the same.

Catching herself, she laughed brightly to cover up her unreasonable delay in responding.

"My grandmother doesn't need a receipt," she replied, putting the check forward and hoping he would just take it and close the door.

Unfortunately, he only opened the door wider and stepped out of the way. "Please," he said kindly, "it will only take a moment. I would hate to have your grandmother accuse you of pocketing her check when I maliciously charge her for February's rent again in a few days, with late fees of course."

This time Erin's laugh was genuine. "I'm sure you don't make a habit of robbing old ladies of their Social Security income," she said. Finding no reason to decline his invitation, though, she entered Mr. Abbott's apartment, and he closed the door behind them.

"My apologies," he said, turning away from the door and back toward her, "I haven't actually introduced myself. My name is Will Abbott. It's a pleasure to meet Mrs. Dovetree's granddaughter."

He extended his hand, and she shook it professionally, without the slightest tremor or swoon.

"I'm Erin. Erin Dovetree. I check in on my grandmother a couple of times a week, usually on Friday nights after work and during the day on Saturdays. I bring her groceries on Saturdays when she needs them, but she doesn't go through too much food—she eats like a bird. I've always been annoyed that I didn't get her eating genes—unlike her, I go through a lot of food."

Clamping her lips together, she silently rebuked herself for providing such a detailed visitation schedule and confessing her love of food to the gorgeous man she had just met.

"Well, Erin," he said with another dashing smile, "your grandmother has a very young soul. She is quite a pleasant person, very full of laughter and joy. I can see why you like to spend time with her when you could be spending time with friends, especially on the weekends."

"Oh, I don't mind," she replied, her lips unclamping despite her best intent. "Most of the people I know are the people I work with, and I see enough of them at work. I usually use the weekends to unwind and get stuff done around the house, like the laundry and cleaning that I neglect all week. I also like to cook. Mostly because I like to eat, as, oddly enough, I've already mentioned to you during this brief conversation."

She resisted the urge to lower her head in defeat. It seemed she had lost all control over her faculties in the presence of this man. The only thing she could do was leave as quickly as possible to avoid further embarrassment.

Flashing her another smile, Will walked across the room to an old-fashioned-looking piece of furniture. It had the appearance of a chest of drawers on little feet, but with a slanted front above the uppermost drawer. As she glanced around the rest of the living room, she noticed that all the furniture was made of the same dark wood. Was it mahogany? It all had the same feel to it, as though she had stepped into a recreation of a nineteenth-century drawing room. Perhaps the furniture had come with the building, preserved by the original owners, or maybe he just liked antique furniture. It did have a charm to it. Even if he was into antiques, though, it seemed Mr. Abbott also had an appreciation for movies, judging by the sixty-inch flat-screen television and state-of-the-art sound system on the wall.

When Erin looked back over at Will, she found that he had raised the slanted front panel on the chest of drawers to reveal a desktop. On its surface lay a large, leather-bound book and two stacks of paper that were neatly clipped together.

"It was very nice of you to go around meeting all of your tenants," Erin said, ignoring once again her edict of silence.

He removed the clip from the smaller of the two stacks, added the check Erin had given him, then re-clipped the papers. "I like knowing who I'm living with," he replied, opening the leather-bound book. "We are all neighbors, after all."

He filled out what Erin guessed was her grandmother's receipt and closed the desk, turning once more toward Erin. She realized then that she had been watching his every action while he was turned away from her, enjoying the flexing of his arms beneath the crisp white button-down shirt he wore as he had made his notes. Immediately she felt the blush rise in her cheeks.

Instead of looking down shyly, as was her first instinct, Erin forced herself to hold his gaze, returning his amused look with a smile of her own. "That's a nice desk. Is it an antique?"

Will nodded. "Yes. It's been in my family for a long time."

She couldn't help studying his face as he gave her the receipt. His wide, brown eyes were kind and gentle, but there was a sadness in them that made him seem suddenly much older. His melancholy look, although subtle, still struck her as being out of place next to the youthful arrangement of dark hair that framed his perfect face.

"Are you all right?" The words spilled out of Erin's mouth before she could stop them.

Will froze for a moment, then asked, without a hint of annoyance or offense, "What do you mean?"

Mortified, she looked down at her feet and took a small step back toward the door she wished she could run through. "I'm so sorry," she began, looking back into Will's eyes so he would see that she meant it. "I don't even know you, and it's none of my business. I'm really an idiot sometimes when it comes to saying the first thing that pops into my head. I should leave you alone and get back to my grandmother."

She turned to reach for the doorknob, but somehow Will's hand got there first, and her hand ended up on top of his. The contact sent an unwanted jolt of electricity through her, and her hand snapped back away from the door.

"Please," he said softly, almost imploringly, "please tell me what you meant. What made you ask that question?"

Erin sighed, resigned to the fact that there was no way to salvage this encounter. "You have a certain look of sadness about you. Of loss. I'm sure you're just tired after moving, and being bored to death by the endless stream-of-consciousness conversation I've subjected you to in the last few minutes doesn't help any. I'm really sorry—I'll get out of your hair and let you get back to…"

"You know what sadness looks like."

It was a statement, not a question, but she found herself nodding slowly in response. "My mother died a little over a year ago. I didn't even know a person could feel that way. It was the greatest sadness I have ever known." Her throat closed with emotion as she spoke, and she had to take a deep breath to steady herself.

Looking back into Will's eyes, she saw him nod, and again there was a hint of a smile on his lips. He seemed almost comforted by her words.

After a brief silence, he extended his hand, and she shook it. It was less formal than their first handshake and lasted a moment longer, as though whatever had passed between them just then had made them friends.

"It was a pleasure meeting you, Erin."

"Thank you, Will. The pleasure was all mine." Her tone poked fun at his formality, and he smiled, recognizing the jest.

He released her hand and opened the door for her. Reluctantly, she turned away from him to leave.

"Erin, one more question, if you don't mind."

She looked back at him, thankful for the extra time she could spend lingering on his doorstep. "Sure."

"What's the story with Mrs. Myer?"

Will's question caught Erin completely by surprise and, juxtaposed with the last few minutes of conversation, seemed completely absurd. She burst out laughing.

Her laughter was apparently contagious, and Will began laughing along with her.

Once Erin had collected herself, she replied quite

calmly, "Whatever do you mean?"

"Well," he began slowly, "I mean that when I stepped into her apartment I felt like a lamb walking into the den of a hungry lion. She has a certain gaze that, well, might make some men…"

"Fear for their clothing?" she finished his sentence, immediately feeling her face flush.

Will laughed. "I was going to say 'fear for their lives,' but I think your assessment is much more on point."

"You have very good instincts, Will," she replied, chuckling softly. "Have a good night." Erin waved at him with a smile before turning toward the stairs.

As she heard the door click shut behind her, she wondered how she was going to wait another whole month before her grandmother's rent would be due again.

****

Will stood staring at the closed door for a moment before moving back to the dining room table, where his laptop computer was waiting patiently for his return. Binders and ledger books were spread out across the mahogany surface, and suddenly the task of digitizing the last ten years of expenses and revenues from his various properties seemed very unappealing.

Erin Dovetree. He was no stranger to the exaggerated descriptions of marriageable young women by their mothers, grandmothers, and aunts, but, in the case of Ms. Dovetree, her grandmother's doting account had proven to be quite accurate. His first impression of the young woman who had knocked on his door was that she was lovely. Her caramel-colored hair was pulled back in a simple ponytail, and she had a natural and unassuming beauty in how she dressed and the light makeup she wore. In fact, the only makeup he could see was around her beautiful, twilight-colored eyes. Her darkened lashes made her wide-eyed innocence more pronounced.

But it wasn't just her beauty that intrigued him. Erin seemed to be a very genuine person. She held nothing back when she spoke, although there were a couple of moments when her loquaciousness seemed to embarrass her. And in just those few minutes they had spent together, she had seen more of him than anyone had in years. She had seen past his smile to the heart of him, and, somehow, she had understood.

Will let out the deep breath he had been holding in and shook his head, pulling his Boston ledger book closer with one hand and setting his other hand on the computer mouse. In the end, it didn't matter what his tenant's granddaughter looked like or how kind or genuine or empathetic she was. Will was not meant for such things. His curse was to exist, only to exist. And considering what he had done, he should have been thankful.

Because his fate should have been much, much worse.

Chapter Three

Much had changed about the city in the last twenty years. New skyscrapers, new restaurants, and more people. So many more people. As he walked up Church Street toward First Presbyterian Church, Will wondered where all these people had come from. Charlotte was supposed to be his home, but each time he returned, he belonged a little less. Someday, he knew, he wouldn't belong at all. But he would still come back.

It used to take half an hour in a horse-drawn carriage to get to church on Sunday. Will's clothes would be dusty, and he would be chilled to the bone in the winter months and sweating through his Sunday best the rest of the year. Now, the trip took less than six minutes by car, and he was hardly outside long enough to notice the weather. The funny thing was that Will had gone to church every Sunday with his family back then, whereas he could count on one hand the number of times he'd set foot on hallowed ground in the past year.

Looking up at the gray spire rising from the faded brown brick church, Will contemplated going inside for a few minutes. There would be no service taking place on a weekday afternoon, but he could sit for a moment and perhaps say a prayer for Bessie and the child she had carried.

Breathing deeply, he turned his head and kept

walking. He had said hundreds of prayers, confessed his sins hundreds of times, but all those words could not undo what he had done. Bessie was still dead, her child with her. God had no doubt grown weary of hearing Will's voice, if He had been listening at all.

Turning left on Fifth Street, Will walked several more blocks before cutting across to Elmwood Cemetery. A plaque near the entrance designated it as a historic site for the city. To Will, it was the resting place of the woman he had loved.

The last time he was here was almost thirty years ago, but still, his feet knew the way to Bessie's grave. The writing on the stone marker had eroded over time, and, to anyone else who passed by, the grave was unmarked. But he could still see the name that had been etched in that stone all those years ago: Elizabeth Fitzhenry Gaines.

How different would things have been if Will had stayed in Charlotte instead of leaving to seek his fortune? He had only been trying to make a name for himself. He wished to be a proper suitor, worthy of Bessie's hand, and there had been no work in the city for him. California had been the opportunity he was waiting for—a place where he could put his civil engineering degree to good use building irrigation systems for the growing population.

And Bessie had understood. She had given her blessing and told him she would wait. A year or two or three apart was nothing when compared to the rest of their lives together.

He should have never left her.

Kneeling, Will pressed his hand to the weathered stone and closed his eyes, trying to envision Bessie's youthful countenance once more. Instead, a pair of brilliant blue eyes framed by dark lashes looked back at him. Her honey-brown hair was pulled back in a ponytail, its bouncing movements punctuating her carefree laughter.

His hand flew from the stone as if he'd been scorched by it, and he leapt to his feet, his eyes wide open now. The image his mind had conjured had not been Bessie's. It had been Erin Dovetree's.

Shocked and confused, Will stood there staring at the blank stone marker, wondering what had possessed him to think of Ms. Dovetree. He had only met her once, a few days ago, and he hadn't thought of her since.

Closing his eyes, he shook his head to clear away all thoughts of his tenant's granddaughter. Will was tired; that was all. He never slept well after moving. He never slept well, ever.

Satisfied that he had regained control of himself, Will crouched down again and, kissing his fingers, transferred the kiss to Bessie's stone. He would never forget her or what he had done to deserve his punishment.

On his feet once more, he bent his head in a silent farewell, then left the cemetery. He had almost reached his parked car when he heard a man call out.

"Will? Will Abbott?"

Turning toward the voice, Will recognized an older version of the attorney he had engaged the last time he was in town.

"No," the man continued, squinting his eyes and pushing his wire-framed glasses up the bridge of his bulbous nose. "It can't possibly be you. Can it?"

His attorney had to be over sixty by now. His hair had turned mostly gray, and he had put on a few pounds, but otherwise, he seemed healthy and fit. Will wondered if the man still practiced or if he had retired.

"I think you must know my father, William Abbott Senior," Will lied, putting on a smile and extending his hand. "I'm Will Junior."

"Good Lord, you look just like him." The attorney reached out to shake Will's hand. "I'm Tom Quigley, of Ungston and Underwood. I've been managing your family's trusts for the past, oh," —the man scratched his head again— "must be going on twenty-nine, thirty years now. I had only been practicing for a few years when I started working with your father." He laughed. "Now look at me—I'm an old man. Tell me, how is your father? Is he still in Arizona?"

"Sadly, he passed suddenly about a month ago. I'm in town to see to his affairs." Will had told this story so many times, it hardly seemed like a lie anymore.

The poor man seemed flustered by the "news," and his eyes narrowed in sympathy. "I'm so sorry to hear that, young man. What a terrible loss. I always enjoyed working with him." He shook his head sadly.

"Thank you," replied Will. "We had been estranged, but I'm thankful that we reconciled before he passed."

Mr. Quigley's face brightened. "Well, that is very good to hear. It's tragic when family dies before anyone has had time to make amends."

The words struck a painful chord, and Will could only nod his agreement.

"In any case," the man continued, "I suppose I'll be seeing you in our office before too long." Reaching into his pocket, the lawyer pulled out a business card and handed it to Will. "That second number there is for my assistant, Dawn. Just give her a call and she'll set up a day and time for us to meet. She'll tell you what paperwork to bring, too, and then we can get everything transferred over to you."

Will thanked him and shook his hand again, then the man took his leave.

As he continued walking in the direction of his car, Will thought about how much he had left to do to reset his life as a Charlotte resident for the next ten years. It would not be difficult; he had done it so many times that it came as second nature to him now. He didn't even need anyone to forge his papers anymore. He had learned how to do it all himself.

Still, he needed to maintain his focus. Unlike him, technology was always advancing. He couldn't afford to make a careless mistake.

Glancing at the cardstock in his hand with Thomas Quigley's name on it, Will shoved it in his pocket. He would call Dawn tomorrow.

Chapter Four

"Hi, gorgeous."

Erin feigned a look of shock as she turned to face the man who had addressed her so boldly.

"Has no one at your firm sued you for sexual harassment yet?"

"It's not sexual harassment if it's true," the young man replied, flashing her a wickedly charming smile.

"I believe you've got sexual harassment confused with slander," she said, rolling her eyes at her friend teasingly. "But I suppose that's to be expected. After all, you work at Laurent & Kessler."

"Ouch!" He put a hand to his heart. "That was uncalled for. Need I remind you that I turned down an offer from your firm to work for Laurent & Kessler?"

She dismissed his question with a wave of her hand. "Just another indication of your poor decision-making skills."

He laughed, and she joined him.

One of the few good friends she had in Charlotte, Blake Duron always seemed to raise Erin's spirits with his carefree attitude and natural charm. They had met on their first day of law school when she was a scared first-year quietly waiting for her Criminal Law class to start. With last names that both began with "D," they had been assigned seats next to each other, and she knew she would never have survived her Crim Law professor's sadistic interpretation of the Socratic Method without him.

"Let's get in line before it gets too crowded," he said, walking to the counter of the sandwich shop they were standing in front of. "I can argue the finer points of the law with you using my top-notch decision-making skills while we eat."

Blake led the way through the seating area of the indoor food court and got in line to order. It was a convenient place to meet, close to where they both worked.

As they made small talk in line, Erin remembered being struck by Blake's easy smile and clean-cut good looks back in law school. His dirty blond hair was cut short, military style, and he had a permanent five o'clock shadow on his face that she still teased him about. Did he have a special setting on his electric razor for that look? Did he shave at midnight to get his scruff to be just the right length the next day?

Blake had been one of the only people in law school who wasn't scared off by Erin's serious expression and no-nonsense demeanor. His persistent invitations to hang out with him and his friends at football games and parties had eventually worn her down, and she developed a bit of a crush on him in the process. Of course, she had never said anything about her feelings, and he'd had a constant string of girlfriends from the moment they'd met, so nothing ever happened between them. As they spent time together, studying in the same groups and tailgating at football games, though, Erin's infatuation gradually receded into a comfortable friendship. Well, a comfortable friendship with a little bit of flirtatious banter thrown in.

When Erin found out they had landed jobs in the same city, she was thrilled at the prospect of having a friend in a new place with so many unfamiliar faces. Even with her parents relocating to the suburbs of Charlotte to live closer to her, it was nice to have someone to hang out with in the city after work. But with her mom's illness and Blake resuming his ambitious dating schedule, their outings had tapered off. They didn't see each other too often anymore, but they still did manage to get together for lunch at least once a month.

"You know, you don't always have to pay for lunch," he said as they sat down at a table by a row of potted ferns.

"I didn't—the firm paid. I always put our lunches on my PDA, you know that. After all, you might end up being my client someday."

"I have a Professional Development Account, too," he countered.

"Yes, but if I let you pay, you're liable to think we're on a date."

"What's wrong with that?" he asked, biting into his sandwich.

Erin chuckled at his flirty remark, but something seemed different. She shrugged off the feeling.

"So, how is the exciting world of mergers and acquisitions? Are you working on any big deals?"

Blake nodded, taking a sip from his soda. "Always. The next few days are going to be brutal. Everyone always wants to close at the end of the month."

"I don't know how you can pull off a twenty-hour workday," she replied, shaking her head sympathetically. "I can hardly put in a solid eight hours of billable time."

"Patent law is a little different. You scientists are so damn smart."

Erin smiled. Blake had always been complimentary of her technical background from the time he first learned she had graduated from an Ivy League school with a degree in biochemistry. It made her feel special, and it had likely contributed to her infatuation with him in law school.

They filled the next half hour with easy conversation about the goings-on at work, complaints about billable hour requirements, stories about the co-workers they both knew, and more complaints about billable hours. Blake told her how he had been selected to be on the pro bono committee at work, and Erin once again expressed her sympathy.

"Pro bono work is all well and good," she replied, locating an orphaned potato chip in the bag she was about to crumple up, "but how do they expect you to put in the hours you do and then, on top of that, do volunteer work? You have no time for yourself as it is."

"I know. I think that's part of the reason Kate just dumped me."

Erin blinked at him. "She dumped you? How long had you guys been going out, like five minutes?"

He laughed. "A little longer than that, Erin. More like five weeks. We'd just been on our first date when you and I had lunch last month. And I took her to the firm's holiday party as my plus one."

"Well, at least you didn't have time to get too attached to her."

Blake made no reply to her last comment, looking

down instead at his half-eaten sandwich. There was definitely something off.

"Hey," she said softly, "I'm sorry about Kate. But I know someone better for you will come along." She grinned at him. "Knowing you, you'll probably meet her in a day or two. You won't be single long."

"What if I've already met her?" He didn't look up as he said this.

Erin ignored the seriousness of his tone. "I told you it wouldn't take long. So, who's the lucky girl?"

When he finally did raise his eyes to her, she got a sinking feeling in her stomach.

"What would you say if I asked you to go out with me?"

"I *am* out with you," she replied, knowing full well that wasn't what he was asking. Trying to find an excuse not to look at him, she began consolidating her dirty napkins and wrappers. Although Blake was admittedly a big flirt, even with her, he had never before said anything that could have possibly been interpreted as true romantic interest. He had never tried to kiss her, never even held her hand.

"You know what I mean, Erin. We get along well, you laugh at all my jokes, you find my facial hair sexy…"

"Let's not go overboard, now," she interrupted, relaxing a little now that he was cracking jokes again.

"You know you like it," he teased, stroking his chin. His expression sobered once more as his hand fell away from his face. "Haven't you ever thought about it, Erin? What it would be like if we were, well, more than friends?"

Of course she had thought about it. Each time he

had leaned over in class when the professor's back was turned to ask her a question about the case they were discussing, and each time he had hugged her hello or goodbye at a party. She had thought about it when he told her about how he had broken up with a girlfriend, and she'd thought about it again each time he announced he had found a new one. She had thought about it a lot...until she didn't anymore.

"I care about you, Blake," she began, unsure of what to say, measuring her words carefully so as not to hurt his feelings. "I care about you a lot, and I want you to be happy. I just don't think I'm the one who's going to make you happy. We're not compatible in that way."

"This is about the sex thing, isn't it."

Erin wanted to crawl under the table. As one of her best friends for almost five years, he knew an uncomfortable amount of information about her.

When she didn't respond, he kept going. "Look, I know we don't have the same philosophy about sex. You're more of an 1800s kind of gal with your Bible-thumping parents, and you may or may not wear a chastity belt, I get that."

"My parents weren't Bible-thumping. But I guess my mother may have tapped on it occasionally."

"Whereas I'm more casual about the whole thing," he continued. "Two people want to strip down naked and get it on, no good reason why they shouldn't."

She could think of at least half a dozen reasons, like STDs, pregnancy, shame, regret...

"All I'm saying is why not give it a chance? Us, I mean, not sex. Although you could also give sex a chance. I've been told I'm pretty good at it. You might like it. And if you don't, then you can just go back to being a virgin."

"You literally cannot go back to being a virgin after you've had sex," she replied.

"Well," he ran a hand through his sand-colored hair, "I'm just saying you can go back to not having sex. I'm not entirely convinced you're a virgin, anyway, so you could at least prove it to me."

"What?" Erin laughed nervously at the absurdity of his statement. "You think I would lie to you and tell you I'm a virgin? I was half drunk when you asked me at that party at the end of our first year, and I was so embarrassed after I told you. Don't you think it would've been easier for me to tell you I wasn't?"

"I know, but I just can't get my head around it, you know? I mean, it's not even like you're average, Erin. You're hot. Like 'damn'-level hot. Any straight man would want to get in your pants, no questions asked."

Erin pushed her chair away from the table and stood up, feeling herself begin to blush and hoping no one she knew was sitting anywhere near them. "All right, then. This conversation has devolved into something we probably shouldn't be discussing in—"

"Is it because of your dad?"

Erin froze, one hand on a wad of dirty napkins, the other on her empty bag of chips. She slowly raised her eyes to look at him.

"Sex isn't just fun and games to me, Blake. There are consequences. People get hurt. Yes, it's my religious upbringing, and it's my dad. It's also the fact that I don't know if you can ever be sure. Even if you love a person and you think they love you and you're committed to each other. Even if you're married and you wear vials of each other's blood around your necks.

Even still, you don't know it's forever. You can never know."

He reached out and covered her hand with his. "I'm sorry, Erin," he said softly. "What I had wanted to say when I first brought this all up was that I know how you feel about these things, and I respect that. I just think we can be good together, even if we can't be 'together' in the Biblical sense for a while."

She let out a slow breath. "Thanks, Blake. I appreciate that."

Erin suddenly felt like crying, and she wasn't sure why.

He let go of her hand and rose to his feet, gathering his own mess and following her to the trash bin.

After throwing out their garbage, they walked in awkward silence to the escalator and rode it up to the indoor walkway that connected to the building across the street. Although the sun was shining, it was just too cold to walk outside.

It didn't take long to reach the spot where they would part ways, and they stood there at their literal crossroads. Blake still said nothing, and Erin wasn't quite sure what to say.

Finally, she smiled shyly and gave Blake a chummy punch on the arm, as she always did when she said goodbye. This time, however, he stopped her fist with the palm of his hand and held it for a minute.

"Think about it, Erin," he said, looking her in the eyes. "Think about it, and let me know if you change your mind."

She knew exactly what he was talking about, and her first instinct was to tell him that he was just hurting because he missed his girlfriend of five weeks. But then she stopped herself and simply replied, "Okay."

He squeezed her hand before letting it go.

"I'll be sure to let you know of our next big inter-firm pro bono event," he joked half-heartedly over his shoulder as he walked toward his building. "I know how you can't help yourself when it comes to pro bono."

"You do that," she called back, trying to take some comfort in the fact that he was teasing her again.

Glad to have the elevator to herself as she rode up to the thirty-seventh floor, she thought about what had just happened. It was a dream come true, wasn't it? The guy she had pined for over the course of her law school years—an attractive, witty, and intelligent guy, no less—was interested in something more. But now she didn't want it. She didn't even want to consider it.

What was wrong with her?

Could she try it, maybe? Go out with him a few times, not as friends, but as a couple? It would be nice to hold his hand, sit close to him, maybe rest her head on his shoulder. What would it be like to kiss him? He was probably a good kisser. He'd certainly had a lot of practice.

So why didn't she want to?

Erin knew exactly what her mother would say if she were listening to Erin's thoughts. *If you have to ask yourself all these questions, then he's not the one for you.* You didn't need to rationalize love. It just was. It had no reason; it took no convincing or persuasion.

But Blake hadn't said anything about love. He just said they would be good together. Erin didn't even know what that meant.

She walked into her office, without being fully

aware of how she had gotten there, then closed the door behind her. Sitting down at her computer, she pulled up the invention disclosure she had been working on before lunch.

Nothing better than carbon chains to bring a person back to reality.

Chapter Five

The day after her lunch with Blake, everyone was talking about the big storm that would hit that night. Some weather forecasters were saying it would be five or six inches of snow. In eastern Pennsylvania, where Erin had grown up, five or six inches of snow might have meant a two-hour delay for schools, depending on what time of day the snow started to fall.

In Charlotte, however, the mere mention of snow generated a feeling in the population that landed somewhere between excitement and panic, and actual snow accumulation of any kind totally incapacitated the city. After all, there were hardly any plows, and no one bothered to invest in a shovel.

The snow was expected to arrive right at rush hour, and the mayor announced early in the day that all government offices would close at two o'clock to allow employees to get home before it started coming down. He urged other businesses to do the same.

At three in the afternoon, the firm's office manager sent out a firm-wide email announcing that the Charlotte office would be closing at four. Erin looked outside the windows of her office. It was cloudy, but there was certainly no snow falling. She opened the weather app on her phone. The temperature was holding steady at thirty-four degrees. Didn't that mean that any precipitation would be in the form of rain?

Despite her skepticism, an hour later she undocked her laptop and put a couple of files in her bag along with it. On the off chance the office didn't open the following day, she didn't want to lose a whole day's worth of billable hours.

Although it was not quite freezing outside, the lack of sun and gusting wind made Erin cold to the core. She walked as fast as she could the few blocks to the parking garage and flew up the stairs to where she had parked her car.

While driving out of the garage, it occurred to her to check in on her grandmother. After all, if the "snow-pocalypse" actually hit that night, Erin wouldn't be able to get to her for a few days.

The streets were already deserted, and she pulled into her grandmother's apartment complex in record time. With everyone already home from work and hunkered down for the night, there were no parking spots out front where she usually parked, so she had to use the overflow lot behind the building.

Erin found an empty spot, parked, and got out of the car, instantly regretting wearing a dress to work that day as the wind whipped around her nylon-clad legs.

As she hurried around to the front of the building, the sound of a car drew her attention to the entrance of the lot. The sight of her father's blue sedan pulling into a spot that had just opened up sent a wave of panic through her, and her feet suddenly became blocks of lead, anchored to the ground. All Erin could do was stare at the vehicle, cursing her poor timing.

Inclined to turn around and run back to her car, Erin regained control of her legs and took a step back before stopping. Despite her cowardice, she couldn't retreat and risk having her grandmother or father catch her fleeing the scene. As much as she hated being in the same room with her father, the prospect of having to explain to her grandmother why she'd run away was even worse.

Taking in a chilled breath to settle herself, Erin turned away from the car where her father still sat with the doors closed and the engine running.

"Erin?" a voice suddenly boomed from somewhere above her.

From the tingling in her body, she knew whose voice had called her. She looked up to find Will's head and shoulders hanging out of an open window on the third floor, confirming her suspicions.

At the sight of his handsome face looking down at her in concern, she almost coughed out the cold air she had just drawn into her lungs. Somehow, though, she managed to maintain an appearance of composure and waved to him, as though she had not a care in the world.

The noise of the running engine suddenly stopped, and on reflex, Erin's focus shifted back to her father's car. Her father was still inside, no doubt gearing up to face the cold.

Will called out again, pulling her from her trance. "Would you like to come inside? I was about to make some hot tea." Erin looked back up to his window to find him smiling kindly at her, waiting for a response.

She hesitated, but only for a moment. "Sure," she replied, even though she wasn't. "That sounds great."

Without another glance at her father's car, she dashed to the front door, praying she wouldn't slip and fall under the gaze of her grandmother's attractive landlord, then practically ran up the stairs without stopping in an uncharacteristic show of athleticism. Will was holding the door to his apartment open for her by the time she had reached the top.

"Thanks," she said breathlessly, attributing the pounding in her chest to the last thirty seconds of impromptu cardio, and stepped inside. He closed the door quickly and quietly behind her.

"Can I hang up your coat for you?" he asked.

"Okay," she said, taking off the long black dress coat she typically wore to work on days like today when she had the urge to look like a lawyer. Underneath the coat, she was wearing one of her favorite work dresses—a cap-sleeve navy blue dress with cream-colored trim and an empire waist that made the most of her modest bosom and hugged her posterior in a very flattering way. Now, as Will took the coat from her, Erin felt suddenly shy and exposed. At least she hadn't taken off the button-down sweater she wore over her dress.

Will closed the closet door and moved gracefully toward her, a peaceful expression on his face, save for two tiny wrinkles of concern that interrupted his flawless brow. His eyes studied her unabashedly, and she knew he was curious about her strange display outside.

Raising her hands from where they still lingered on her sweater, Erin smoothed out her hair and smiled sheepishly at Will. His lips curved slightly as he moved past her and entered the galley kitchen, which was twice the size of her grandmother's. She turned to follow him and watched as he opened the cupboard above the stove to retrieve a teakettle, which he then filled with water.

"How do you feel about green tea?" he asked, opening another cupboard.

"I feel good about green tea," she replied, her feet steering her to the open doorway between the dining room and the kitchen.

Will was wearing a forest green collared shirt with long sleeves and dark blue jeans that, she quickly discovered when he turned away from her, fit him just right.

They were both silent as he placed the kettle on the stove and turned the knob to adjust the gas burner. She watched as he brought out tea, spoons, saucers, and cups with a delicate indigo floral pattern along the rim. In fluid movements that seemed almost like a ritual, he arranged the items on the counter near the pass-through to the kitchen to create two perfect place settings.

Erin moved from the doorway to stand on the other side of the counter, in front of the place settings and looked down at the exquisite china. She had never seen such a delicate pattern, even amongst her grandmother's serving ware. It was absolutely beautiful. The whole place setting looked like it belonged in a museum, and she was almost afraid to touch it.

Raising her eyes from the china, she observed Will as he opened the cupboard where he had found the tea and withdrew a small canister with the same indigo pattern as the teacups and saucers. The sugar bowl, Erin presumed.

"Would you mind putting this on the dining room table for us?" he asked, handing it to her.

"Sure." She held the delicate bowl carefully in her

hands and stepped over to the large oval table, which had two modern-looking blue-and-white checkered placemats already laid out. She placed the sugar bowl in between the two place settings and removed the cover.

When she walked back to the kitchen, she found Will standing near the stove where the kettle was still heating, his hands stuck casually in his pockets. He gazed at her intently, as though studying her. Still, he said nothing.

Her skin tingled again, and she lowered her eyes to her empty teacup, hoping she did not look as unsettled as she felt. Needing to occupy her hands, Erin picked up the tiny silver spoon and turned it over, tracing the lovely design on its handle with her finger. It looked like real silver.

She let out a breath, put down the spoon gently, and found the courage to look at Will again. He still stood staring at her, but now she detected a gentle smile tugging at the corners of his mouth.

"Thank you," Erin finally said, breaking the silence. "For inviting me in."

Will nodded graciously.

"Were you watching me?"

He hesitated, then nodded again. "I happened to be looking out my window to see what the weather was doing and noticed you standing there, like a deer in headlights, when that car pulled in. It looked like you needed a hand. I apologize for my intrusion. I may have misread the situation."

"You didn't," she replied quickly, her cheeks heating.

There was another moment of silence. She owed him some sort of explanation. Although she had only just met Will last week, Erin sensed he would never try to pry for information. He had a timelessness about him, a wise and patient air, like a boulder in the desert waiting for the hundred-year rains to come.

"It was my father in that car. It hadn't occurred to me that he would be coming to check on my grandmother before the storm. We're not exactly on speaking terms, my father and I. I didn't feel like being in a cramped apartment with him, trying to avoid his small talk. I guess I froze. I didn't know what to do."

She looked at Will to gauge his reaction, but he was unreadable. Then his mouth curled up at the corners, just slightly. "Are you saying my apartments are too small?"

A very unladylike chortle escaped Erin's lips as the joke caught her by surprise, and she quickly covered her mouth with her hand, mortified. Will smiled unabashedly, victorious.

He took a few steps forward until he was directly opposite the counter where she stood, with only the prim and proper teacups between them. Even when he smiled, his gaze was intense, and the air around her thickened somehow, damping her surprised laughter.

She withdrew her hand from her mouth, feeling brave. "Do you think there are just certain things people do that can't be forgiven?"

"Yes," he quickly answered, almost as though he had spent a lot of time thinking about the answer to that exact question.

"I mean, the person can say he's sorry," she went on, "and he might actually mean it, but you just can't do it. You can't let it go. You can't understand in the first place how this person could have done this thing, and the idea that you can pretend it never happened—well, it's just ridiculous."

Will nodded understandingly.

"I know I should forgive him," she added in a quieter voice. "To err is human and to forgive is divine and all that. We're supposed to forgive because nobody's perfect. But I just can't do it. I look at his face and I get so angry. I want nothing to do with him. I could manage to stay away from him just fine if it wasn't for my grandmother. She's his mother, and it happens from time to time that I run into him, without intending to. And every time it happens, it just messes me up."

Erin knew it was awful of her to dump all her issues on this poor man she'd barely just met, but once she had started talking, she couldn't stop. And now, looking into his kind eyes and seeing that compassionate crease between his beautiful eyebrows, she wanted nothing more than to have him wrap his arms around her as she cried into his shoulder.

She had clearly lost her mind.

Erin looked down at the empty teacups as she tried to collect her thoughts, and this time, it was Will who spoke up.

"You don't have to answer this, but what exactly did he do? Did he…hurt you?"

"Oh no. He's never hurt me or done anything to me. He was actually a pretty good father. I mean, he tried to be. It's…it's what he did to my mom."

A low whistle sounded and grew louder and more insistent. Will removed the teakettle from the stove and began pouring hot water over each of the teabags waiting patiently in their teacups. Putting the kettle back on the stove, he picked up his teacup and saucer and inclined his head toward the large dining room table.

"Shall we sit down?"

"Sure," she replied, following him with her cup. He indicated the seat at the head of the table for her to sit in, then took his place beside her.

"Some sugar?" he asked, extending the sugar bowl in her direction.

"Yes, thank you." The spoon made a pleasant sound against the sides of the teacup as Erin stirred sugar into hers. She watched as Will put three times the amount of sugar into his teacup.

"You like your tea sweet, I see," she said, teasingly. "I suppose that's a southern thing."

"It's the only way I can get this stuff down," he replied, looking over at her with an easy smile.

"If you don't like tea, why do you drink it?"

Will shrugged. "It's something to do."

"What else do you do that you may or may not enjoy?" she asked, before proceeding to burn her upper lip testing the temperature of the still scalding-hot beverage.

"I didn't say I don't enjoy drinking tea," he corrected her. "In fact, this particular cup of tea is the most enjoyable cup I've had in years."

At the realization that he had just paid her a compliment, Erin proceeded to administer third-degree burns to the rest of her mouth by taking another sip.

They drank their tea in comfortable silence for a few minutes before Erin asked another question.

"Where are you from, Will? From your accent, it doesn't sound like you're a native Southerner."

"I am, actually," he replied. "One of the few born and raised here in Charlotte. But I've lived in New York and Boston for many years, so I think all of my accents have canceled each other out."

"New York and Boston? Do you own other rental property there? I mean is that what you do, manage property?"

"I suppose you could say that. I have a couple of low-rise condominiums in White Plains, New York, and four clusters of townhomes scattered around the residential neighborhoods in Boston proper. I split my time among the three cities, living in one of the unrented units I keep for myself in each community for a few years before moving to the next, and so on. But Charlotte is my home. I love coming back here."

Will picked up his cup and drained the last bit of tea from it.

"A few years in each city?" she asked, puzzled. "You can't have been doing this for too long. I mean, you're not that old." He certainly didn't look a day older than thirty.

Though Will smiled with his lips at her comment, his eyes were distant, and Erin wondered if she had offended him. "I've been doing this for a long time," he finally replied. "I'm older than I look."

He put his teacup down, returning his eyes to her. "What about you? Where are you from? You sound like you've spent some time up north yourself. New York? Connecticut?"

"Pennsylvania," she said, happy to change the subject. "I grew up near Allentown. My dad was a chemical engineer, and he worked at an industrial gas and chemicals company there. My mom was a lab technician at that same company. That's how they met. After they got married and had me, he kept working there while she stayed home to raise me."

"A stay-at-home mother," he remarked. "I had one of those, too."

Erin swallowed the emerging lump in her throat, willing herself to talk about her mother without getting emotional. "I feel very fortunate to have had that time with her. A lot of moms go back to work when their kids are in school full-time, but she never did. She saw being a housewife and a stay-at-home mom as her calling. And you know what, she was really good at it. She was my counselor, my cheerleader, my teacher. She was my best friend. And she was good to my dad. She kept the house spotless for him and had dinner on the table when he came home at night. She was an excellent cook. She was good at everything."

Her voice dropped off, and she swallowed again, forcing a smile. The last thing Erin wanted to do was to get all teary-eyed in front of her grandmother's hot landlord.

Will's lips parted as though he was about to say something, then pressed together again. After a moment, he asked, "So what brought you to Charlotte?"

Erin shook off her melancholy as she recalled the circumstances of her relocation. "I thought it was near the beach."

"You're kidding," he replied, chuckling. He had a low, rumbling laughter that was warm and inviting, and the sound of it brightened her mood from just moments ago.

"Sadly, it's true. I was looking through the list of law firms that were interviewing at this big job fair they have near Chicago every year for intellectual property attorneys, and I saw a posting by a law firm in Charlotte, North Carolina. We used to drive through North Carolina every year when I was younger to go to Florida for a couple of weeks in the summer, and I automatically assumed Charlotte was near the beach. So, I marked the little check box to request an interview slot, I got the interview, landed the job, and here I am, three hours away from the Atlantic Ocean."

Will folded his arms and placed them on the table. "So you're a lawyer, then." From the way he raised his eyebrows as he said this, Erin could tell he'd had dealings with attorneys.

"Yes," she admitted, holding up her hands, "I'm a lawyer. Don't hold it against me, please."

He laughed, and she found herself smiling again. "I don't have anything against lawyers," he explained. "In fact, I need lawyers for my business and for my personal life. And I like the firm I use. It's the same firm my father used, and his before him. They're honest, and they've always done a good job."

"People have a bad impression of lawyers. Mostly for good reason."

He shook his head. "I don't think lawyers are bad. Lawyers are people. Some are bad and some are good. Some do bad, and some do good. I have a feeling you're one of the ones that do good."

"I just do patents," Erin replied, shrugging. "And I love it. I get to learn about new inventions, I get to write and be creative, and most days I feel like I've helped someone. It's not like I'm finding a cure for cancer or anything like that, but it's still working toward building something. I can be proud of that."

Their teacups had been empty for a while, and Erin suddenly noticed that the room had grown dark over the time they had been talking. As though he were thinking the same thing, Will got up and walked over to the light switch on the wall. The room was suddenly bright with the light of an old-fashioned crystal chandelier hanging above the table.

"I'm sorry," she said, pushing her chair back from the table and standing up. "I've stayed too long. It's dark outside already. I'm so sorry."

As she fumbled with her empty teacup, saucer, and spoon, Will came around the table to her and placed his hand on her left shoulder, bringing every nerve ending in her arm to attention. "Please, Erin, there's no need to apologize, and there's certainly no need to rush out."

"Thank you," she replied, taking her hands off the china to avoid breaking it. She turned to look at him, hoping the pleasure she felt at his touch and the sound of his voice saying her name wasn't reflected in her eyes. "That's very nice of you," she continued, "but I should get home. I'm not even going to stop in at my grandmother's. If my dad was here, I know she's okay. It's probably already snowing outside, according to the forecast."

"Let's take a look, shall we?" Letting go of her shoulder, he took a few steps to the set of bay windows that overlooked the front parking lot of the building and pushed aside the royal purple brocade fabric. "Indeed, it's quite a display of nature out there. That prediction I heard this morning of zero to six inches was accurate."

Intrigued, Erin went to stand beside Will and looked out at the parking lot. He let the curtains fall behind them to block the light from the room so she could see outside. Nothing. No snow, no ice, no rain. Just falling darkness. And the unnatural thumping of her heart.

Ignoring her heart palpitations, she chuckled softly. "Anything for a story. Snowstorms in Charlotte are big ticket news items, I guess, regardless of whether they actually happen."

Will shifted his weight from one foot to the other, unwittingly heightening her already sharp awareness of how close he was standing to her. In contrast with the cold seeping in through the window glass, Erin could feel the warmth emanating from Will's body. Her breath caught in her lungs, and she closed her eyes for a moment, secretly reveling in his nearness.

They stayed that way for several moments before she somehow regained the capacity for rational thought and opened her eyes. As Erin turned to part the curtains, their shoulders brushed against each other, making her want to drop the curtains back into place around them so she could enjoy his nearness for just a few more seconds.

"I'll grab my coat and get out of your way," she managed to say.

"You're not in my way."

Will's voice was low, the tone almost seductive, and her gaze shifted from the front door back to his eyes. He held her gaze, and an intense warmth spread through her. Did he mean to make her feel this way?

As she stood there, transfixed, silently hoping the heavens would let loose in the next thirty seconds so they could be snowed in together, he moved to the closet to get her coat. With his usual purposeful grace, Will took the coat off the hanger and held it open for

Erin to step into. She turned her back to him as she placed one arm into the coat, then the other, again enjoying his proximity.

"Thank you for rescuing me," she said softly.

"You're very welcome, Erin." She loved the way her name rolled off his tongue.

"I wonder if my grandmother will see me sneaking past her apartment," she said with a small laugh, trying to distract herself from Will's magnetism as she turned around to face him once more.

"She's a sharp lady. I'm guessing she already knows you're up here."

"You know, the poor woman can only hear out of one ear, and not very well, yet she knows exactly what's going on around her at all times."

He slipped his hands into the pockets of his jeans again as he watched her button her coat. His movements were all so fluid, so easy. It was as if he'd done everything a thousand times over and it was all muscle memory, a well-practiced exercise that required no thought at all. And it made his every motion that much more seductive. "Just tell her you were here to have some tea with her very nice landlord."

"Yeah," she almost snorted, turning her attention to the belt on her coat to avoid staring at him. "That would really get her imagination going. She's a big fan of yours, you know. If she were fifty years younger, she would really give Mrs. Myer a run for her money."

Erin cringed inwardly as soon as the words escaped her lips. She looked back up at him, trying to keep her expression neutral. Did he realize she had just told him that her grandmother thought he was hot?

If he did, he didn't seem at all discomfited by the

revelation, and his lips curled in response. "She doesn't need to be fifty years younger. You can tell her that I prefer her company, and that of her charming granddaughter, over Mrs. Myer's any day of the week."

He opened the door, and thankfully the cooler air from the hallway counteracted the heat currently consuming her face.

"Thanks again for inviting me up," she said, walking toward the door.

"Thank you for coming."

Erin nodded, smiling, and stepped past him through the open doorway. She could see out of the corner of her eye that he continued to stand there as she started going down the stairs. At the third step, she turned around to look at him, sensing another rush of courage within herself that she was unable to stop.

"Will?"

"Yes?"

"That was the most enjoyable cup of tea I've had in years, too. Thank you."

The line of his lips curved slowly into a smile. "Just imagine if you'd had more sugar with it."

****

What. Was. He. Thinking.

Closing the door, Will bent his head until it rested on the rough wooden surface. He squeezed his eyes shut, willing his heart to slow down its frantic pace, and balled his hands into fists to stop them from trembling.

Will didn't fault himself for inviting Erin upstairs for tea. He had been watching as her father pulled into the lot. He had seen her body freeze. She had panicked, and he was right to call down to her.

But there hadn't been a need to comment on how

much he was enjoying her visit or to put his hand on her shoulder. And there certainly was no excuse for enclosing the two of them in the curtains to gaze out the window at the clear, darkening skies. The smell of apples from her hair had compelled him to shift his body closer to hers, and she had noticed. He had wanted her closer, and he had almost reached for her. He had wanted to touch her.

Why was this happening to him now? What was she doing to him?

He relaxed his hands and stepped away from the door, turning to glance at the closed curtains where they had been standing together minutes ago.

Being with Erin made him feel…happy. She made him laugh. She made him think. She made him aware of sights and scents and sounds and movements—subtle things that were always around him but that he had stopped noticing a long time ago. He enjoyed being with her. And it had been so long since he had enjoyed anything.

It had been so long since he had *felt* anything.

Will crossed the living room to his desk. He pulled open the bottom drawer, which was two drawers deep, and reached behind the various folders and papers to the back. He found the wooden box he sought with his fingertips and carefully lifted it out of the drawer.

Taking the box to the dining room table, he sat down and opened the lid to reveal a stack of neatly folded papers that were held together with a thin white ribbon. The papers were yellow with age and brittle. The corners were already well-worn, the edges uneven.

With the careful hands of a museum curator, Will removed the bundled stack of papers from the box and placed it on the tabletop. Closing his eyes for a moment, he breathed in their musty scent, trying to displace the smell of apples that seemed to surround him still.

Underneath the bundle were two envelopes that were just as old. Those were from his sister. He knew the contents of one of the letters by heart. The other—a thicker one he suspected held more than just a letter—he had never opened. It was not addressed to him, and he could never disrespect his beloved sister's wishes.

Setting aside his sister's letters, he turned to the bundled stack. Carefully, Will pulled off the white ribbon and slid the paper that was sitting on top closer to him. Turning it over, he let his eyes take in the small, girlish strokes.

He had committed Bessie's letters to heart, as well. He knew every word of every letter she had written to him while he was in California. But he would read them again now.

Because it seemed he was starting to forget.

Chapter Six

Charlotte, North Carolina
September 1879

"William! Sweet boy, you're home!"

William placed his two traveling bags on the floor of his mother's foyer to free his arms for her embrace.

"It's good to be home, Mother. I've missed this place, I've missed you."

"What about us?" Two of his sisters, Abigail and Sarah, emerged from the sitting room and stood at the threshold, hands on their hips, as though they had rehearsed.

"Abby! Sarah! Come here and give your brother a hug."

At their mother's command, the two girls giggled and threw themselves on William in synchronized fashion, nearly knocking him back out the door that had been left open behind him. William laughed, holding his ground. "You girls aren't as light as you were three years ago, you know. Don't you two have husbands you can wrestle with by now?"

"William!" his mother reprimanded. "Mind your manners. This isn't the wild frontier you've grown accustomed to in your time away. You are back in a civilized, God-fearing society now. Your sisters are but fourteen and seventeen. No husbands for them quite yet."

"Oh, Mother," whined Sarah, the older of the two. "Anna was married last month and she's only a year older than me."

"Yes, but Anna's family is not as well off as we are. We were lucky not to lose your father in the war as Anna did, and your father worked hard until the day he died to give us this life. Anna's family needs someone to take her off their hands. You should thank God for the life you have, rather than wishing for hers."

Sarah sulked back toward the sitting room without another word, but not before throwing William a despondent look.

"Mother, you're too hard on her," said William, his heart going out to his sister.

"You've been home for less than a minute and you presume to tell me how to rear my daughters?" His mother's tone softened when she spoke again. "Abigail, where are your other silly sisters?"

Abigail stood close to William, holding his hand in both of hers. "I don't know why you think I should know where Mary is. She hardly talks to me now that she's married, and I expect it will be even worse when she has her baby. Jane is likely at the Porter house, pretending to get along with Alice and Eleanor so that she can catch a glimpse of that handsome brother of theirs." Turning her eyes to her own brother, her curly brown hair bouncing, she continued, "You wouldn't recognize Thomas if you saw him, William. He's grown quite a bit in the last couple of years, and now all the girls are mad for him. I think he's taken a fancy to Jane, though, because she was always nice to him, even before, when he was so awkward-looking. If I know

Martha, she's probably with Jane, following her around like a little puppy. Martha can't do anything on her own, you know."

"That's enough, Abigail. Why don't you run along to the Porters and see if you can't find at least some of your sisters? I'll send Radka to go fetch Mary and her husband. Everyone can dine with us tonight."

Husband. Baby. Beau. William had missed much in the last three years. His oldest little sister was now a wife, and she would soon be a mother. He would be an uncle. Mary had written to tell him of Peter's proposal, and William, as the man of the house, had written back to give his permission. He had wanted to be present for the ceremony, to give his congratulations in person to his little sister and her husband, but the trip across the country simply couldn't be undertaken for such a brief visit. So, he had missed his little Mary's growing up. He prayed that was all he had missed during his long absence.

From the sound of it, Jane's day was just around the corner. It was appropriate—Jane had just turned twenty-two. Martha was only nineteen, but he didn't figure she would last too long as a young maiden. Of his five sisters, she had always been the most beautiful, as well as the gentlest and most kind. He only hoped that Tommy Porter's affections were truly for Jane, and not the younger sister who accompanied Jane wherever she went.

"I trust you remember where your room is, William dear?"

"Yes, Mother, of course I do."

"Well, go get yourself cleaned up from your travels and settle in. Dinner will be on the table in a little over an hour."

The stern but handsome woman moved toward William and took him in her arms once more. "Part of me never thought I would see you again, dear boy," she said softly as she held him. "You look so much like your father. It's almost like having him back with me. Almost."

She released him and took a step back. Then, regaining her Southern propriety, she went off to oversee the preparations that were underway in the kitchen, leaving William standing alone in the foyer.

William closed the front door, picked up his two bags, and walked to the staircase that spiraled dramatically upward to the sleeping quarters. At the top of the stairs, he went to the end of the hallway, passing each of his sisters' rooms. Mary's room was still there, although some of the furniture had been taken out.

He entered his own room and closed the door gently. He was tired. The urgency coursing through William's body during the entire journey back and several weeks prior was now replaced with a subtle feeling of dread. He had not seen Bessie at the train station. He had not seen her on the road from the train station to his family home. It had been months since she had written to him, although he had kept his promise and written to her every single day.

The feeling of dread grew for no apparent reason all through dinner, but William's face and manner gave no sign of it. He told stories about the things he had seen in the "wild frontier" to entertain Abby and Sarah, teased Martha and Jane about their "impending nuptials" to Tommy Porter, which each vehemently denied, and joked with Mary's husband about what the baby's birth would do to his status in the household. William lingered at the table, listening to all the gossip his sisters had been waiting three years to tell him, and he was somewhat dismayed when his mother told the four girls who still lived under her roof to retire for the evening and Mary and Peter returned to their own home.

Perhaps he truly was sad to leave the gay scene, he thought as he ascended the stairs slowly behind his loud and boisterous sisters. What would he have to occupy him in his own chambers other than thoughts of Bessie?

Once in his room, he removed his trousers and shirt, scrubbed his hands and face with some soap and water, and put on the nightshirt that had been laid out on the bed for him by Radka, their old nursemaid who still treated them as though they were five.

As he lay in bed, William thought about what the following day would bring. The next day was a Sunday, which meant that he, his mother, and his sisters would spend much of the morning occupied with church activities and socializing. Bessie would no doubt be at services with her family, too. He would finally see her, and all the fears and doubts he had been harboring the last few months would dissipate at the sight of her sweet smile. He was almost sure of it.

William rose in the morning feeling less than rested. He hadn't slept well, waking up several times during the night. He blamed his restless sleep on the excitement of being home and the anticipation of seeing Bessie, or at least he tried to.

Outside, however, the bright sun and the clear blue sky lifted his spirits considerably. It was a good omen, he thought as the carriage he, his mother, and four of his five sisters rode in bumped uncomfortably down the road to church.

The sermon was uplifting, as well, and for the first time since he had stepped off the train the day before, he was truly happy to be home.

William and his family were seated toward the front of the church, and Bessie's family typically sat in the back on the left-hand side. He fought the urge to turn around and look for her several times during the service. He would see her soon enough, he reminded himself each time, and the last three years apart would be erased.

Finally, the service ended. As the masses made their way to the large doors in the back of the church, he caught a glimpse of her.

Somehow, Bessie was even more beautiful than he remembered. She was wearing a rust-colored dress with three-quarter sleeves, her dress bustled in a way that made her waist look even tinier than it was. Her golden hair, pulled up under a smart hat with a white daisy sewn on the side of it, framed her face. As she turned, William caught a glimpse of the curls that had escaped and now fell around her soft cheeks.

She leaned over to kiss an elderly man who William recognized as her grandfather from Atlanta. He had met her grandfather once, a year or so before leaving for California. The old man said something, and Bessie tossed her head back carelessly and laughed.

Then, as though she could feel the heat of William's gaze, she turned slowly and looked at him.

At first, her face was expressionless, as though she were trying to understand what had happened, how he had appeared before her. Then, much to William's relief, she smiled from cheek to delicate cheek.

William felt as though the weight of the last three years had been lifted off his shoulders.

Bessie whispered something to her mother, who was standing near her, and then, holding her skirts in both hands, she began making her way toward William. It was through sheer force of will that William refrained from running to her and taking her in his arms.

"Mother," said William, still looking at Bessie, "I'm going to say hello to Miss Gaines. I'll be back in a moment."

William took only a few steps before he found himself standing before Bessie.

"Miss Gaines," he said, taking the hand she offered him.

"Mr. Abbott." She addressed him with coy formality. "I had heard from your sisters that your return was imminent, though I did not believe it. How nice that you are finally home after such a long time away."

"It is, very nice," he replied, trying to discern the message in her tone. "I trust you've been well? You look—well."

"Thank you, Mr. Abbott, as do you. Life has carried on for us here in Charlotte over the last three years, as you can see."

William's mouth suddenly went dry, and he swallowed before responding. "I see you."

They were the only words he could put together to articulate how he felt. Bessie gently withdrew the hand he still held.

"Let us walk together," she said, taking a few steps away from him, toward the open church doors. "It is a shame to be inside on such a lovely day."

William gestured to his sister Sarah, and she nodded in understanding. Then he followed Bessie out of the church and into the bright sunlight.

They walked along a path that led to the gardens behind the church in silence until William could no longer hold his tongue.

"Miss Gaines," he began, "Bessie. I've missed you. Very much."

"Did you?" She spoke softly, as though from a distance. "You were gone a long time. A very long time. I am twenty-three now, you know."

"Yes, I know," he answered, the sense of urgency that he had held at bay during the church service returning now with more force. "It has been very hard, for both of us. But I am home now. I'm here. And I intend to speak with your father. This afternoon, if you will permit it."

She stopped walking and looked directly into his eyes.

"You wish for us to be married?"

"You know that I do," he replied, shocked at the question. "It has always been my wish. It is the sole thought that I've had over the past three years. And now it is finally the right time. I am back, and I have made a name for myself. I have the means to take care of you, and I wish for nothing more than—"

"There will be no need for you to take care of me, Mr. Abbott."

It was as though all the blood in William's body had suddenly evaporated. He was disembodied, watching the scene from afar.

"But," he began slowly, "that is what a husband

does. He provides for his family."

"Indeed, that is what a husband does," she agreed. "And I am certain my husband shall do no less."

Part of him could not understand what Bessie could possibly be telling him. Part of him had known all along.

"What are you saying, Bessie? Am I speaking with a married woman?"

Bessie shook her head. "Not yet. But I am to be married. Next month." She paused. "I'm twenty-three, Mr. Abbott."

"I know full well how old you are, Bessie," said William, unable to keep the anger from slipping into his speech. "You and I, we are to be married. We told each other we would be before I left. Do you not recall our conversation?"

"I do recall our conversation," she said sharply. "Every word. I remember you saying you would come home as soon as possible to claim your bride. I remember your letters, too, each one, by heart. Two years. You said you would be gone for two years. Why did you delay? My friends all married and had children while I sat at home reading your letters."

"But I'm home now! We can start our life together!"

Bessie shook her head. "It's too late, William. I'm to marry Mr. Cox in three weeks." Her tone softened somewhat. "I'm sorry."

William felt as though he had been hit by the train that had carried him across the country to that God-forsaken place where he had spent the last three years of his life.

"No, Bessie, no!" he pleaded, desperate to change

her mind.

"I'm sorry, I must go. I truly am sorry, William."

She picked up her skirts and ran to her mother, who was waving happily at William from the end of the path they had started upon a few minutes earlier.

William waved back, trying hard to keep his legs from falling out from under him.

Chapter Seven

William found it increasingly hard to breathe as he walked over to where his mother stood conversing with one of her friends. Even in his pitiable state, he somehow managed to draw in enough air to smile and make a few witty remarks about how much Charlotte had changed while he was away.

Despite the general numbness that began at the top of his head and was spreading swiftly downward throughout his body, William maintained a pleasant demeanor on the drive back home with his mother and, this time, two of his five sisters. He thought he remembered Jane announcing that she and Martha would be spending the afternoon with Alice and Eleanor Porter and his mother permitting it, but he wasn't sure and didn't care.

Throughout the rest of the day, he valiantly kept his outward appearance free from any signs of the anguish that was ripping apart his insides, even as members of his extended family and close acquaintances of his mother and late father came to their house to welcome William back home after such a long time away. Several just happened to bring their lovely young daughters with them and, with a practiced ease, also just happened to remark on how mature and marriageable those young daughters had become over the past three years. Even still, William's smile did not falter.

William was silent through supper, but not noticeably so, as his mother's commentary on her daughters and the various people she had gossiped with that day seemed to leave little room for anyone else to speak anyway.

After eating enough of his dessert as was required to not appear ill or impolite, William excused himself and retired to his bedroom. He stripped off his clothes and bathed vigorously, as though he were trying to wash Bessie's words off his skin.

As he stepped out of the bathtub, he wrapped a towel around his waist and walked with damp feet to his bed, leaving wet footprints on the wood floors. He pulled on the nightshirt that had been neatly laid on the bed, then walked over to his dresser, leaving his towel hanging on the post of his bed.

He looked at himself in the gilded mirror that hung above his dresser, and disgust rose in his throat. *How could you let her get away from you?* he asked his reflection. *You had her, you fool. She was yours, and you lost her. And for what? A few months—a couple hundred dollars?*

Disgust quickly turned to rage, and he picked up the closest breakable object—the empty vase sitting at the corner of his dresser—and hurled it against the wall. Chards of blue and white flew in all directions, some landing on the bed.

Immediately there was a knock on the door. "William, are you all right?"

It was his sister Martha. He didn't respond.

"William," she began again, in a more hushed tone. "William, may I enter?"

William put on the slippers that were by the foot of his bed and walked carefully to the door, trying not to step on the glass.

He opened the door and looked at Martha's feet to make sure she was not barefoot.

"Be careful," he warned, allowing her to enter. "There is glass everywhere."

"How did this happen?" asked Martha, looking down at some of the larger, recognizable pieces on the ground.

"It was an accident," he replied. "No—more accurately, a mistake."

"I'll go call Radka to help clean it up," Martha said. Then she looked at William's face and, instead of leaving, entered further into the room.

"Oh, William," she sighed, as though she knew everything after that one look. "What did she say to you?"

"What do you mean? Who?" asked William. As much as he loved his sister, he hated that she always knew his heart.

Martha pinched his arm, surprising him. "You know of whom I speak, Brother. Bessie. What did Bessie say to you outside after services? Has she…"— William knew she was trying to find a delicate way to put it—"…forgotten how fond she is of you?"

He smiled wryly. "Yes, Martha. She has forgotten. In fact, she appears to have so forgotten how fond she is of me that she believes herself to be fond of another man. Imagine that."

Martha shook her head slowly from side to side. Then, placing her hands gently on William's shoulders, she looked into his eyes. "William, you must remind her."

William was silent for a moment, and Martha pulled her brother into her arms. He let her embrace him, allowing himself to be comforted, just a little. He had never met anyone kinder than his sister, and he doubted he ever would.

She released him and walked toward the door. "I'll go call Radka," she said, turning back to look at him. "Before she retires for the evening."

A glint of gold caught William's eye, and he raised his head in time to see that it came from a chain that hung around Martha's neck and disappeared into her bodice.

"Wait," he said, halting her retreat.

Avoiding the broken fragments on the floor, he stepped closer to get a better look. She dropped her head to follow his gaze and laughed as she understood what had captured his attention.

Coming back into the room, she pulled the end of the necklace up to reveal a ring hanging on the chain. Three rectangular stones, the same color blue as the sky, were embedded one above the other in the gold. The ring was too large for a woman's finger, and it suddenly occurred to William that the jewelry might have been a gift to Martha from an admirer.

"Did a young man give that to you?" he couldn't help asking. "Is that why you keep it hidden from Mother?"

She laughed again as she put the ring loosely about her finger, though it was still connected to the chain.

"It was given to me," she replied, her eyes looking shyly down, "but not by a man. It was a gift from Radka on my birthday a few months ago."

"Radka?" His family had employed the kind Bulgarian woman for as long as he could remember, and she had always been well-paid, but he couldn't imagine her amassing enough money to purchase such a luxurious gift for his sister. "How could she afford to give you such a present?"

"Radka did not purchase this ring. It was handed down to her by her father, and he had received it from his father upon his twin sister's marriage. At least that's what she told me. It's a special ring. You wouldn't believe the stories that go with it."

"If that is so, and it is indeed a family heirloom, then why would she give it to you?" Even as he asked the question, he knew the answer.

"She has no one, William. Her parents have died, her only sister died as a child, and she herself has never married. She has known us all since we were born. I suppose she thinks of us as her children."

William smiled. "And you are her favorite, sweet Martha, are you not?"

"She loves us equally," Martha corrected, "but she said she felt the stone would be useful to me someday, so she wanted me to have it."

It didn't surprise him that the old woman cared for Martha as she would have her own daughter. Martha was the best of them. She was special, and anyone with a soul could see her goodness.

"Don't despair, William. Think on what I said. There is still time for you and Bessie. Make her remember what you are to each other."

He nodded and tried to smile, if only to allay his sister's concern. Was there a way to make Bessie remember how it was between them? Was there a way to make her love him again?

"I'll send Radka to help you clean up this mess. Goodnight, dear brother. Everything will work out in the end. You'll see."

Several hours later—it must have been past midnight—William tossed and turned under the covers, Martha's words echoing in his head. His mind would not rest, and, as a consequence, neither would his body. Finally, a thought caused him to sit straight up in bed. He would go to Bessie. He would do as Martha told him to do. He would remind her. At the very least, he could try.

William moved quickly and quietly to the armoire on the other side of the room and, opening it, fumbled for a pair of trousers and a shirt. He pulled them on hastily in the darkness and left the room without a sound.

The household was still. Everyone was asleep.

His feet glided noiselessly down the stairs, and he opened the front door, careful not to make a sound.

Bessie's house was normally a ten-minute walk from his. William was at Bessie's window in less than five.

Crouching in the grass beneath Bessie's window, his hands searched for something hard he could throw. He quickly found a rock and aimed it at the wooden shutters outside her bedroom. The rock found its mark effortlessly.

He waited, watching and listening for any sign of movement above him.

Nothing.

William found another rock and tried again. Once more, his aim was perfect.

This time, he saw the faint glow of an oil lamp appear. The light grew brighter as its bearer approached the window. The window opened and the shutters were pushed aside.

"Is someone down there?" she whispered.

The sweet sound of her voice made William want to scale the brick wall and be at her side at once.

He called up to her as quietly as he could. "Bessie, come down, please. I need to talk to you."

"Who's there?" Bessie paused, spotting him in the darkness below. "Is that you, William?"

"Yes," he replied, urgently. "Please, Bessie, come down and talk to me. Just for a moment."

She hesitated. "I can't, William. I can't. Come by in the morning, and we shall talk."

"No, Bessie, it can't wait until morning. Please, have pity on me. Come down and let us talk. I beg of you."

Again, Bessie hesitated. Then, shaking her head, she relented. "All right, William. But just for a moment. I'll meet you by the cherry trees."

"Thank you, Bessie! Thank you!"

William knew the grounds at the Gaines house as well as he knew his own, but he was grateful for the light of the almost full moon nonetheless. Unable to stand still, William paced from one end of the grove of cherry trees to the other until he heard a rustling sound.

He looked up and saw Bessie approaching. Despite the plain dressing gown she wore overtop her nightgown for the sake of modesty, William's breath caught at the sight of her.

He quickly closed the gap between them and took her two hands in his.

"Bessie, my sweet Bessie. Tell me you were simply playing a joke on me today. Tell me I'm the only man you love."

"Oh, William," she sighed, sounding almost defeated. "I could say that, and it may be the truth, but it would not change the fact that I will be marrying Robert Cox in less than a month's time."

"Why, Bessie, why? I don't understand it! You've all but admitted you still love me. How can you marry another?"

She pulled away from him and started to walk back toward the house. He caught her in his arms and turned her body so that she faced him.

"William, it is not that simple! Would that it were…"

"It's as simple as you make it, dear Bessie. You promised you would marry him, and you do not want to break that promise. I understand that. But why live a lifetime less than happy, all due to a promise? You promised me first, after all. Do you remember that?"

"Yes, William! Yes, I remember! How could I forget? I've held on to that memory for the past three years, and I will hold it until the day I die. But that does not change the way things *are*."

"What do you mean? Bessie, what things? Tell me plainly, what is going on?"

Bessie shook her head, refusing to speak. So, William did the only thing he felt he could do in that moment. He pulled her to him and kissed her.

It was a passionate kiss, full of memories and longing, full of anger and desperation and love. She melted into him, her arms encircling his neck.

When he released her mouth, he no longer had to

hold her close to him. She was there freely and willingly.

Then, most unexpectedly, Bessie placed her head against his shoulder and began to cry, her little body shaking against him with each sob.

William gently moved her chin from his shoulder and tilted her head up so he could look into her beautiful brown eyes. "Tell me now, Bessie," he said softly, his fingers wiping away the tears that fell onto her cheeks. "What strange madness is behind all of this?"

"I'm so sorry, William," she began, still sobbing. "I had lost hope that you were coming back to me, despite your letters. My mother, my friends, they all urged me to find a suitable husband, one who was here. Robert Cox had always been kind to me. More so after you left. He asked me to marry him, and I accepted."

Her sobs grew stronger, and William wrapped his arms around her tightly.

"It's all right, Bessie, I understand. But I am here now. I can help you."

She took a breath between sobs and said, "William, I have to marry him. I must be his wife, for I have already been as a wife to him."

William froze, his whole body going numb.

"What do you mean, Bessie?" he asked, his words a harsh whisper. "What have you done?"

"Oh, William! His child grows inside me as we speak!"

William released Bessie and stepped back from her, repulsed by her admission.

"William! William!" Bessie reached for his arms, but he moved deftly from her grasp.

"How could you do such a thing, Bessie? Outside the bonds of marriage? With Robert Cox?"

Somehow he managed to keep his voice low and calm, despite the storm that raged within him. Bessie—his Bessie—had lain with Robert Cox. Even as her words echoed in his ears, he could not decide what offended him more—the fact of her indiscretion or the object of it.

"He came to my window one night."

He shut his eyes and shook his head. He could not bear to hear more, and yet she continued to speak. "We went for a walk. He said it was all right, that we were almost married in the eyes of the law, and likely already married in the eyes of God. Things aren't the way they were in the time of our parents and grandparents. I'm not the first to do such a thing."

His eyes snapped open, and he stared at the woman he barely recognized anymore.

"Don't look at me with such judgment in your eyes," she hissed at him. "You loved me a moment ago!"

William could not tear his gaze away from her, and yet he could think of nothing to say. He was powerless to change the past and powerless to achieve the future he wanted. He realized in that instant that nothing mattered. His words did not matter, nor did it matter that he had loved her—that he loved her still.

She reached for him, but he shook her off again and turned his back to her. He could not stay there. He could not look at her again; he could not touch her or tell her how he felt. It would accomplish nothing, just as Bessie had said. It would not change the way things were.

As William walked away, the sound of Bessie's sobs as she dropped to the ground, pierced his heart.

He walked until he knew he was out of her sight. Then he ran the rest of the way home.

Chapter Eight

Charlotte, North Carolina
Modern Day

It had been several weeks since Erin's tea party with Will, and the short-lived freeze of the southern winter was already beginning to thaw. The days were getting longer and warmer, and the trees were beginning to bud. Even the scent of the air held the early promise of springtime.

Easter was drawing nearer, and Erin knew it was inevitable that she would be spending it in her grandmother's apartment, with her father. She had managed to avoid seeing him since Christmas, thanks to Will's intervention, but she just couldn't find it in her heart to be away from her grandmother during a holiday.

Erin had hoped she would run into Will the Friday following their tea party, when she went to visit her grandmother. She told herself she had enjoyed talking to him, but "enjoyed" was not a strong enough word to capture how spending time with him had made her feel. Thoughts of Will—holding her coat open for her, putting his hand on her shoulder, smiling at her, standing so close that she could feel him there with her eyes closed—filled her waking moments and made her eager to fall asleep each night. Because he was there, in her dreams, too. And in her dreams, he was bolder, and so was she.

But that Friday came and went, as did the next and the one after that, and still, there was no sign of Will.

Erin didn't know what kind of car Will drove, so she couldn't tell if he was upstairs in his apartment or away. When her grandmother asked her to take up another rent check at the end of February, Erin hopped to her feet and grabbed the check from her grandmother's arthritic hand, heading out the door before her mind could register her grandmother's knowing smirk. But this time there was a drop box labeled "Rent," so after knocking and waiting a few seconds more than was required, Erin was forced to make use of it.

On a particularly beautiful Monday in March, with Easter two weeks away, Erin sat in her office watching the clock creep toward lunchtime, her stomach growling in discontent. Though she typically packed herself a lunch, she had been invited to a lunch meeting that was set to start at noon, so she had no choice but to wait.

Relief came in the form of an email at eleven-thirty, which announced that the meeting had to be postponed to the following week. Without a second thought, Erin grabbed her wallet and headed downstairs to get something to eat.

When the elevator reached the lobby level, she walked briskly past the adjacent bay of elevators, which serviced the lower half of the building. As Erin pondered what to eat, she noticed the back of a handsomely familiar head of hair a few steps in front of her, walking away from the elevators, and away from her.

Her heart leapt up into her throat.

"Will?" she nearly shouted, surprising herself.

Will stopped mid-step and turned toward her. She waved at him, and, seeing her, he smiled. She had caught up to him at this point, and he reached out to shake her hand.

"Hi, Erin. I didn't know you worked in this building."

Her stomach fluttered at the feel of his hand in hers, but she managed not to cling to it for too long. "Hi," she said, trying to keep her nerves at bay by forcing herself into professional attorney mode. "Yes, I'm on the thirty-seventh floor. My home away from home."

"I'm sure the view is nice up there," he replied.

"It is, especially on the side of the building where my office is. But there's only so much time you can spend looking down on the city. Sometimes you just have to come down and walk the streets."

She realized a moment after the words left her lips that she probably could have chosen a different phrase that did not immediately call to mind prostitutes plying their trade.

Trying to move on to another topic as quickly as possible, she asked, "What about you? I wouldn't have expected to see you in uptown during the day."

The corner of his mouth quirked up, and he tilted his head to one side. "As it happens, there are some very talented lawyers in uptown, patent and otherwise. And unfortunately, I find myself constantly in need of my tax attorney. Although it is a chore to come visit him, for some reason he is always very happy to see me."

"Perhaps it's because he sees dollar signs when you walk through his door," she quipped.

"Perhaps," he laughed, and Erin warmed all over.

Realizing that they were standing in the middle of a growing stream of foot traffic, and not yet wanting their conversation to end, Erin gestured to a pillar off to the right. "We should probably move to the side so we're not in the way."

He nodded, then motioned for Erin to continue walking with him. She hoped she wasn't grinning like an idiot as she nodded in agreement.

"People on their lunch hour are a force to be reckoned with," she commented nervously as they began walking again.

"Is that where you are going? To lunch?" asked Will.

"Yes. I had a lunch meeting that was canceled unexpectedly, so I am now left to my own devices. Have you had lunch yet?"

Will shook his head. "Not yet."

She could not believe she was about to say the next words that were on her lips to her grandmother's landlord, even as she said them. "Well, you're welcome to join me, if you'd like. I was just going to grab something quick and take it back to my desk, but it looks like such a gorgeous day, it might be nice to eat outside in the sun." It seemed that she was channeling Mrs. Myer every time she saw poor Will.

Thankfully, her offer did not seem to make Will uncomfortable. "That sounds like an excellent plan. Beautiful days like these can't be wasted. Where did you have in mind? I haven't been uptown for lunch in a very long while. A lot has changed."

Erin breathed a quiet sigh of relief. She just needed to relax. She was a lawyer, for crying out loud. She could handle this.

"Yes, I feel the same way," she replied, slowly regaining her composure."I don't go out for lunch very often. I usually bring in leftovers from home and eat at my desk. But it's nice to have a change of pace. And it's especially nice to have some company."

Who knew she could be so bold?

****

As Erin chattered away beside him, Will couldn't help smiling. She had a way about her that made a person feel at ease. At ease and valued. Perhaps it had something to do with her self-deprecating confidence, which really made no sense whatsoever but was genuine and relatable. And it made him feel more alive and curious than he had felt in a very long time.

"There's a new Greek place down the street and around the corner, if that sounds appealing," she offered as they surveyed their options.

"Yes, that sounds great." Despite his best efforts, Will had thought about the afternoon she'd had tea with him every day, wondering when their next chance encounter might take place, and at the same time counseling himself to avoid seeing her. He had been careful to be away from the apartment building on Fridays between five and seven, when he knew Erin might come around to visit her grandmother. But now, seeing her again, he couldn't muster the good sense to walk away.

They descended a long set of stairs to street level, and Erin led him around the corner to the Greek restaurant. They got their food to go, and again Will found himself following her as they walked out of the restaurant.

"There are some tables in the shade by the fountains, just a block away. Do you want to give that a try?"

"Sure," he replied, ignoring once more the voice in his head that told him he should make an excuse and get himself away from her.

They took a few steps in silence before Erin spoke. "They have the air conditioning up so high inside the buildings, you come out here and you actually have a chance to thaw out a little. I really need to get out more often."

He loved that she felt compelled to fill the silence.

"You're inside most of the day," he replied as they found an empty table and sat down.

"Yeah. My own fault. I just want to bill my hours and get out of there. Not that I don't enjoy what I do. And not that I have a lot going on outside of work, either. I'm not married, I don't have any kids like some of the other people I work with." She laughed. "I'm the perfect associate—I have nothing better to do than to earn money for the partners."

"Maybe that's why you don't want to spend more time there than you need to. So you can prove they don't own you."

She looked at him and smiled. "Maybe you're exactly right. But I should still probably take the time to take a walk or something during the day. Just so I don't die of a blood clot sitting at my desk for ten hours straight. After all, sitting is the new smoking, or so they say."

They were both quiet again, but Will didn't mind. He watched her take a plastic fork out of its wrapper and spear a cube of chicken off her salad with it.

Taking a long sip of water, she looked at him and smiled, almost shyly. "It's hard to believe that the last time I saw you was when we *didn't* have the storm of the century. And now, only a few weeks later, it almost feels like summer out here."

Will nodded as he finished chewing. "Yes," he replied. "It doesn't take long for the warmer days to return."

"So, have you been busy since you moved back to Charlotte?" asked Erin, her blue eyes sparkling. "I'm sure with all the properties you manage there's always some problem to fix."

"Yes, it's non-stop. Which is good. I need constant distraction to pass the time."

"I know you said you were from Charlotte originally. Do you have family here?" Erin pushed some stray hairs away from her face and looked at him expectantly.

"No, not really." Will's momentary pleasure in being with her was quickly overtaken by dread. He hoped she wouldn't ask him to elaborate on his family situation.

"Do you have brothers and sisters?" Erin asked.

He supposed that was a question he could answer. "I'm one of six children, the only boy."

"Wow!" exclaimed Erin. "Six kids. I can't imagine what that must be like. I'm an only child. I was a pretty good kid, but still, I think I drove my mom insane sometimes. Your mom must be a saint."

"She was a good mother, very kind, very loving.

Her children always came first. But she was also very stern at times, and very proper." He couldn't remember the last time he'd thought, let alone talked about, his mother. It was a strange feeling.

"I'm sorry. I take it you've lost your mother too?"

Will nodded. "It was a long time ago." He paused a moment, remembering the pain he had felt when he'd heard of his mother's passing. It had been sudden, and he hadn't been able to get home in time to see her before she was gone. That had probably been for the best. It had been several years since he had seen any of his sisters, by design, and his condition had become noticeable.

Will's gaze lifted to see Erin's somber expression, and in that moment, his own anguish vanished. All he wanted to do was to comfort her.

"It will get better for you, you know," he said, clearing his throat. "The pain will fade, and then what you will have left will be the memories. Which is why it's so important to have good ones. Good memories. Because they play over and over again in your mind. They are the backdrop to the rest of your life."

"I know," she replied, a melancholy smile on her face, "you're right. I can feel it getting better for me, each day a little more. But it will never be the same again. I know that, too. My mother was my best friend. Really, my best friend. I told her everything, and she was just perfect. She always listened to my stories, however mundane or silly, and she was always interested in what I did and what I thought and what I felt. Genuinely interested. She was such a big part of my life. She made my dad move here to Charlotte when I got the job at the firm, even though they had a nice house in Arizona that my dad loved. They had moved there while I was in law school. It was their retirement destination. But she and my dad came here so they could be closer to me."

Hearing how Erin described her mother, Will felt she must have inherited her mother's care and concern for others. When she spoke, she looked directly at him, into his eyes. And when it was his turn to speak, she still didn't take her eyes off him. It was as though she wanted to hear and understand every word he said.

"You're a good listener, too," he said, without thinking. "And kind, smart, and successful. I'm sure you made your mother very proud."

Erin gave a little shrug and looked down. "I don't know about that. But I hope so."

Realizing that he was staring at her lips as she took another bite of salad, Will looked down at his food. He was letting his guard down. He wasn't being careful. Did he think that just because they were not standing behind a curtain in the dark he could resist her charm?

"So, none of your five sisters are in Charlotte? You're the only one left here?"

At least Erin was unaware of his internal struggles.

Will took his time chewing before replying. "I'm the only one left here."

"Do you all get together during the holidays? I imagine it must be so hard with everyone having families and living in different parts of the country."

Will hesitated, his fork hovering over the last few bites of lettuce in his container. He didn't want to lie to her. But he couldn't tell her the truth.

"Each person's life takes them down a different path. It can never be the way it was when we were all children growing up together. Time heals, but it also separates us from each other. Everyone ends up alone in the end."

"I'm not sure I agree with that," said Erin.

Her quick and contrary response surprised Will, and he was reminded how very different they are. "That's only because you haven't lived that long yet."

"You know," she began, a hint of teasing in her tone, "you're not that much older than I am."

"How old are you?" he asked, knowing that whatever answer she gave, she was an infant compared to him.

She laughed. "I thought men were taught never to ask a woman that question."

He couldn't help chuckling—she was right, after all. "Well, how else will we find out who's right?"

Erin tilted her head coyly. "I'm not saying I won't tell you my age—I'm almost twenty-seven. I'm just saying it's probably not a good idea to go around asking women how old they are."

Even though Will had guessed she was in her mid-twenties, he almost gasped when he heard her say the number out loud. "Almost twenty-seven," he repeated, shaking his head. "Wow. You're not even thirty yet. You're a child."

"I am not a child!" said Erin, feigning indignation. "I'm on the cusp of thirty, I'm unmarried, and I have no kids. Most would say I'm on the verge of being an old maid, if not one already."

"You're worried about getting married and having kids?" Marriage and motherhood were not modern aspirations for women in their twenties, or so he had deduced over the years.

Erin wiped her mouth with a napkin, then tossed it into the bag her food had come in. "Well," she replied, "it's not like I'm getting any younger. Most women my age are either married, engaged, living with someone, or have decided against all of that. I've done none of those things."

Will couldn't help smiling again. "I wouldn't worry if I were you. You will get married, and you will have kids. Nature doesn't allow good things to go to waste. I think it's one of Newton's laws, like gravity."

Although he knew it was foolish to be so free with his compliments, watching a reddish hue creep into Erin's pale cheeks made it worth the risk.

"I'm sorry, I've embarrassed you," Will said, suddenly feeling contrite.

"Oh no, I'm fine. I just have this condition where I blush at the drop of a hat. My capillaries are just too close to my skin."

"I see," he replied, trying not to grin.

"Besides," Erin added, quickly regaining her composure, "I can tell that you are just trying to distract me from pursuing our original conversation regarding exactly how much older than me you are so that we can find out who is right."

"I can assure you, I'm older, and I'm right."

Erin laughed. "I will need some proof, Mr. Abbott. I am, after all, a lawyer. I deal with facts, not conclusions."

"I thought you were a patent attorney." Will knew he was enjoying their banter more than he should, but he couldn't stop himself. And the more she smiled at him, the less Will seemed to care about all his rules.

"I am, but that makes no difference in our present

situation. So, how old are you?"

Will gazed into her wide eyes as she looked at him expectantly, her lips curved in a sweet smile. She was mesmerizing.

"Your age, Mr. Abbott?"

And persistent.

"How old do you think I am, Counselor?"

"You are not supposed to answer with a question. But, since I'm guessing you are not going to tell me how old you are, I'll tell you what I think. I think you're thirty-two. Give or take a year. Am I right?"

And there it was, the familiar chill of despair sneaking back into his heart at knowing the truth Erin would never find out and acknowledging the utter hopelessness of their situation. Will forced a half-smile for her benefit.

"Close enough."

Chapter Nine

He never did tell her how old he was, Erin thought to herself a couple of days later as she brushed her teeth and got ready for bed. Why would he be so mysterious about his age? Could it be that he was in his forties? He didn't look that old, but it was certainly possible. So, what if he was? Why not just tell her how old he was? The only reason she could think of was that he didn't want her to know the age difference between them. And the only reason he wouldn't want her to know would be because he didn't want to scare her off. Did that mean he *wanted* her to be interested in him?

He didn't have to worry about that. She was interested in him—*very* interested, regardless of his age.

Just being near Will made every cell in Erin's body come to life. But it was more than that. He was just so easy to talk to. She couldn't help spilling her guts to him about her mother, work, how often she ate—anything and everything that popped into her head. It was a stream-of-consciousness nightmare, but he didn't seem to mind.

There was no way he didn't think she was at least a little crazy. But at the same time, he was never in too much of a hurry to leave. They had sat outside talking for at least half an hour after they had finished eating. Although they hadn't returned to the heavy topics that had come up during the first part of the meal, it was just as nice telling him about what she did at work. It was even nicer hearing about how he kept track of all his properties and some of the stranger problems he'd had to deal with over the years. Just regular old boring stuff, but it was wonderful.

In the end, it had been Erin who had reluctantly ended their visit to get back to the office in time for a phone call. Otherwise, who knew how long they would have sat there in the sun chatting?

As they said their goodbyes, Erin had experienced yet another surge of boldness and had basically asked Will for a second date, offering to reacquaint him with the city. She cringed as she relived the scene in her mind and how forward she must have seemed. Like a teenager with a crush, no doubt.

Will had been polite, saying he would like that, of course, because he was a nice guy. Had he really meant it? Did he want to see her again? They hadn't set a specific day or time for their meeting, so perhaps that was her answer right there.

Still, Erin couldn't help smiling at the possibilities as she pulled back her down comforter and slipped under the sheets. Propping two pillows behind her head, she picked up the novel on her nightstand, hoping she could keep her mind off Will long enough to follow the increasingly complicated plot.

An hour later, Erin found it difficult to keep her eyes open, even though it wasn't even ten o'clock yet. Giving up the struggle, she set the book aside, reached over to turn off the lamp, then rolled onto her stomach, hugging a pillow to her chest and closing her eyes. Her mind went immediately to Will. His gold and brown eyes, his dark hair, his kind smile. Will was a good guy, she could tell. He was caring and sensitive. He was confident and mature. She wanted to know more about him. She wanted to see him again.

Erin was just beginning to drift off to sleep when she heard the muffled sound of her cell phone ringing. She sat straight up in bed and heard it again.

In a half-dazed state, she remembered that she'd left her phone in her work bag and stumbled out to the living room in the dark to get it. She managed to reach her bag on the fourth ring, stubbing her toe on a kitchen barstool in the process. Ignoring the pain, her hand quickly found the phone, and she answered the call before the phone was even out of the bag.

"Hello?" she said a couple of seconds later, her voice a loud whisper.

"Hi, Erin. It's Will."

For a moment, Erin thought she was still in bed having a dream. A really good dream. But her throbbing toe was evidence that she was most likely awake.

"Will? Hi—Are you okay? Is everything okay?" Her blood suddenly ran cold. "Is my grandmother—"

"No, no, she's fine," he interrupted her, and she breathed a sigh of relief. "I'm so sorry, Erin," he continued. "I guess I didn't realize how late it was. I'm really sorry."

"Oh, no, don't worry about it," said Erin. "It's totally fine. I'm usually still awake at ten o'clock. I was just reading a book in bed, and I guess it made me sleepy. I have that problem at work, too."

She heard Will laugh and smiled. She liked making him laugh. He didn't strike her as someone who'd had much laughter in his life.

"Still, it was very thoughtless of me. I usually stay up late, and I forget what time it is." He paused. "I was just thinking of our lunch the other day. It was very nice."

A sudden rush of adrenaline dulled the pain in her foot, and at the same time brought her to the point of hyperventilating. She took in a slow breath, then let it out. "How did you get my number?" she asked, walking carefully back to her bedroom, grinning like an idiot.

"How do you think I got it?"

Erin chuckled. "Always answering a question with another question. I, on the other hand, can't leave a question unanswered, so I'm going to guess my grandmother gave it to you."

"You would be correct." She could hear the amusement in his voice. "I ran into your charming grandmother on the way back to my apartment after having lunch with you. I may have mentioned our chance meeting in the city, and she was, well, very encouraging."

"I'm sure she was," Erin laughed. "I've told you, she thinks you're quite a catch."

"No," he replied, his tone suddenly serious. "She knows you are."

Erin swallowed hard. Fainting suddenly became a more imminent threat than hyperventilation.

"Well," said Erin, quietly, "she is my grandmother, after all."

"Yes, and a smart woman. Like her granddaughter."

"Thank you," mumbled Erin. She lay down in her bed and covered herself back up, taking several deep breaths.

Don't be weird, she told herself. "I enjoyed our lunch, too. Although I'm sure that was quite apparent. I tend to say what's in my head. I don't have much of a filter, I guess, especially with you."

"I like that," he said, making her stomach flutter violently. "Now that I know your weakness, I'll be sure to take full advantage of it."

"First it was taking Social Security money from old ladies, now it's exploiting the weaknesses of unsuspecting young attorneys."

He laughed. "You are not so unsuspecting, but yes, I am guilty as charged. And I do have a question for you."

"What's your question," she asked softly, warmth flooding every inch of her body.

"What do you think of me?"

The question caught her off guard. Erin didn't know quite how to answer. Should she tell Will that she was wildly attracted to him, enjoyed every moment in his company, thought about him to the point of malpractice at work, and dreamt about him every time she closed her eyes? Of course not, unless she wanted him to run for the hills.

Erin laughed nervously. "Man, the ability to answer a question with a question would be pretty useful for me right now, wouldn't it?"

"Well," he said, "I believe you just answered with a question. You see, it's not so hard."

"But you know I can't help but follow up with a real answer."

"I'm counting on that."

Erin took another deep breath. She could be honest

without scaring him, couldn't she?

"I like talking to you, Will," she began. "Very much. And I think you're a good man. Not just nice, which you are, but good. Your heart, your essence, is good. It sounds weird, but that's the phrase that goes through my mind every time I see you or talk to you. Your heart is good. And I like that very much, too."

"You are a good person, Erin. That's why you see good in others."

"Maybe. But that doesn't mean I see good where there is none."

He paused. "You also don't know me very well yet."

They were both quiet for a moment. Will was right, they hadn't spent much time together, but Erin felt as though she did know him. There was a connection between them. She may not have known the details of his childhood, or even how old he was, but she knew the essence of him, somehow.

"What do you usually do about dinner on Friday nights, after you check in on your grandmother?"

Was Will asking her out on a date? Erin could feel her grin take over her whole face at the realization, and she was glad Will couldn't see her.

"I come home, heat up some leftovers, and watch really bad TV."

"How about this Friday you come up a few flights of stairs and have dinner with me?"

In addition to losing control of her facial muscles, Erin now couldn't seem to keep her legs from bouncing in bed. She had to get a hold of herself.

Instead of saying "yes" or "sure, that sounds great," as a normal person would, Erin asked a question. "Why?"

Then she buried her face in the pillow next to her.

To her surprise, Will answered readily. "Because I like talking to you, and I usually eat alone on Fridays, too. Not to mention every other day of the week."

Stepping back from the brink of humiliation, Erin chuckled at his response. "I like it when you actually answer my questions," she replied. "Perhaps I'm rubbing off on you."

"Perhaps."

"I think dinner with you on Friday would be great," she said, realizing she hadn't given him a response.

Erin thought she heard Will let out a slow breath, and it made her smile again. Maybe Will was just as nervous as she was.

"Great," he replied. "Make sure you come hungry. I'm a pretty good cook."

She laughed. "You know me. I love to eat. I'm sure it will be wonderful."

There was another quiet moment between them. Erin didn't want to get off the phone, although she knew she should.

"I'll let you get some sleep now," said Will, as though he had read her mind. "I imagine you have a lot of patent lawyering waiting for you tomorrow morning."

"Yes, I usually do," she replied softly. "But can I ask you another question, first?"

"Sure."

Somehow, she could tell he was smiling. "How old are you, really? Are you forty? I can't imagine that you are. Are you?"

"Does it make a difference?"

Erin chuckled. "There it is. The famous question-answer. All right, I'll leave you alone. Or maybe I'll just keep asking until you tell me." She paused just long enough to take a breath. "And no, it doesn't make a difference. Which is why you should tell me."

"Maybe I will," he replied. "Eventually."

"I'm glad you called, Will. I'll see you on Friday night."

"I'm glad you answered, Erin. Sleep well."

"You too. Good night."

Erin hung up and put the phone on the nightstand next to her. Still beaming, she pulled the covers up to her shoulders and enjoyed the warm, cozy feeling, which she knew had nothing to do with the heavy down comforter. Something important was beginning for her, she could feel it.

She turned over onto her side, eyes wide open.

There was no way she was going to be able to fall asleep.

****

Will lowered the phone slowly, his hand shaking and his heart pounding in his chest. What had he just done?

He stared at the slip of paper with Erin's name and phone number. He had carried that piece of paper in his pocket for the last two days, taking it out and looking at it, then folding it up and putting it away again. He'd even thrown it out at one point, only to rescue it from the garbage ten seconds later.

Finally, he had given in to the overwhelming desire to hear Erin's voice and had dialed her number, not even thinking about how late it was. Choosing not to think about what his actions would set into motion.

Will closed his eyes for a moment, breathing deeply, and his heart rate slowed. It was only dinner. There was nothing wrong with sharing a meal with someone whose company he enjoyed.

But he knew it was more than that. Erin was doing something to him. He couldn't think about her—her infectious smile, her awkward openness, her optimism—without smiling. It made him feel good. For the first time in a long time, Will was looking forward to something. He had hope for what was to come.

And that sense of hope frightened him to the core.

Chapter Ten

Charlotte, North Carolina
September 1879

The day after his evening visit with Bessie,
William made every effort to keep to himself. He took
his breakfast in his father's study, as well as his lunch,
and busied himself by poring over the last three years of
the family's finances to see how much damage his
sisters' spending had done. It seemed, though, that his
mother had kept their spending in check, and so far
William hadn't seen anything too disturbing in the
numerous ledger books he had stacked high on the
desk, surrounding him like a fortress.

He was still in his father's study, taking his
afternoon tea with three ledger books spread open
before him, when Radka knocked quietly at the door.

William raised his head and saw her small frame
through the slightly ajar door. He beckoned her to enter
with a wave of his hand.

"Mister Abbott," she began, "Mister Cox is here to
see you. Shall I bring him in here or would you like me
to have him wait in the front room for you?"

William felt the blood drain from his face when he
heard the caller's name. He quickly cleared his throat
and stood up from his chair, as though those actions
would help him regain control of the situation. "Please

show him in here, Radka, if you would."

Radka nodded respectfully and hurried out, leaving the door partially open behind her.

When he could no longer hear the servant's footsteps, William began pacing, taking long strides from his desk to the window overlooking his mother's rose garden and back again. Robert had been one of his closest friends when they were children. They had spent less time together in the years leading up to his leaving for university, but that was not the result of any great falling out. They had simply grown into different circles of friends.

Had Bessie told her fiancé of William's visit the night before? Had Robert come to warn William to stay away from his intended? Did the man mean to threaten William, or worse?

William had no desire to fight with Robert, despite the fact that Robert had stolen away the only woman he loved. He did not blame Robert for recent events, but rather considered the matter to be a result of Bessie's poor judgment and inconstancy. At the same time, should Robert raise a hand against him, William would not turn the other cheek.

"William?"

William looked up from the hardwood floors he had engaged in silent conversation and saw Robert in the doorway where Radka had stood a minute ago.

"Robert," William greeted, coolly but cordially. "Please, come in."

William motioned to the chairs by the window closest to the door as he walked toward them himself.

Robert smiled and, closing the distance between them, embraced William like a long-lost brother.

The man clearly had no idea where William had been the night before, and William breathed a slightly audible sigh of relief.

"Apologies, William," said Robert, loosening his grip. "I didn't mean to squeeze the wind out of you. It's just that it's been so long. It really is good to see you!"

"It's good to see you, too, Robert," replied William, taking a seat in one of the chairs as Robert lowered himself into the other. "It has been too long. I should not have stayed away all this time."

William's statement rang true for several reasons, all of which involved the woman Robert was about to marry.

"Yes, well, you were off seeing the world and making your fortune, weren't you, William? Those are good things to do. Very good things. I, on the other hand, have stayed in our lovely little town listening to the same idle prattle uttered by the same lips, year after year. Unlike you, the only growing I've done is in the vicinity of my waistline."

William forced a laugh. "Three years in a hovel in the desert is hardly a trip around the world, Robert. In any case, it is good to be home."

"Your sisters and your mother, they are well I hope?"

William nodded. "All is well, thank God. And with one of them married and another halfway there, things are only getting better. For my mother, at least."

Robert laughed, "Yes, yes indeed. It's a shame you missed Mary's wedding. It was a splendid affair. And I hear she is very happy with her new husband and a baby on the way." Robert paused. "That is the way of things, isn't it William? One marries, has children, raises those children and watches the cycle repeat itself?"

"Indeed," replied William, a bit stiffly.

For a moment, Robert looked as though he were struggling with himself as to whether to speak or hold his tongue.

"William, we have known each other for quite some time. We are, in many ways, like brothers. Wouldn't you agree?"

William was unsure of the turn the conversation had taken, but he sensed no trap being laid. Still, he answered with a wary "yes."

"Might I confide in you, then, William? As a brother?"

Trap or no trap, the familiar sense of dread that had been residing in his gut for far too long rose into William's throat once more, threatening to strangle him.

"Of course," William reluctantly responded. "Speak your peace."

"You may have heard that Miss Gaines and I are to be married. Two weeks from Friday."

"Yes, yes, I have heard. Although it does not appear to be public knowledge, as my sisters knew nothing of it."

"Miss Gaines wishes it to be a very small affair," replied Robert. "And perhaps it is better that few know of it, as I am now having doubts."

"Doubts?" William was taken aback. Placing his hands on his thighs and turning his elbows out, he leaned forward, toward Robert. "What do you mean, doubts?"

"William, promise me you will say not a word of

this to anyone. This is the sort of thing that ruins a young woman's reputation, and even if I don't marry Miss Gaines, I should hope someone will."

"Yes, yes," replied William, almost too quickly. "Of course, I understand. Please, do explain what you mean. Why are you having doubts?"

Robert took in a deep breath. "I saw her last night. With a man."

William froze. Was it possible Robert had seen him with Bessie under the cherry trees? Robert had given no indication of ill will toward him, so it seemed unlikely. Still, what purpose did Robert have to come and tell William what he had seen, if not to call William out?

Bracing himself, William asked, "What man did you see?"

Robert pushed his chair back, away from the table, and stood up abruptly. He rubbed the back of his head with his hand and walked over to the window. "I don't know, William, I don't know. All I know is that I was walking down the street late last night, just getting some air, you know, and of course I looked over toward Miss Gaines' window as I passed by her house. I was thinking of her, after all, and so naturally I looked over in her direction."

William doubted his friend had been out for air and had merely happened to walk past the Gaines' house. He clasped his hands together in his lap to keep them from forming into fists as the reality of what had passed between Robert and Bessie struck him once more.

Robert turned to look at William and continued. "My eyes never made it to her window, because I saw movement under the cherry trees—you know the ones I'm talking about."

"Yes," said William, with a calmness he did not feel.

"Well, I feared for her safety and the safety of her family, of course, so I crossed onto the property to get a closer look. It was easy to see Bessie's face, so beautiful in the moonlight. And she was with a man. Unfortunately, his back was toward me, so I never got a good look at the fellow. But he was clearly not threatening her."

An anguished groan passed out of Robert's lips as he now raised both his hands to his head.

William knew the feeling.

"They were in each other's arms, William! They were having an amorous encounter! My bride and another man!"

Relieved that Robert had not seen his face, and feeling foolish he had come so close to getting caught, William was at a loss for what to say. It was a delicate situation, after all. He did not wish to cause Robert or Bessie any pain. At the same time, though, William wondered if, perhaps, with the right words, a favorable outcome might be achieved—if he could set things right, as they should have been all along.

"Did you ask Miss Gaines about what she was doing last night?"

His friend nodded. "I did. I left the grounds as soon as I saw Miss Gaines was not in any danger. I didn't know who the man was or how he would react to my watching them do whatever it was they were doing, so I did not think interjecting myself into their little party would be prudent. But this morning I confronted Miss Gaines about the whole thing."

With another groan, Robert came to stand before

him, his chin trembling. "Do you know what she did when I asked her?"

William shook his head, slowly. "What did she do?"

"She started crying and kissing my hands. She was begging me to marry her, William. Begging me! Does that not indicate to you that she was doing something sordid with that man?"

William paused as the path forward became clear. And for a moment, the despair to which he had grown so accustomed started to feel a little like hope.

"Do you think she was doing something sordid, Robert?"

"She must have been!" exclaimed Robert, beginning to pace again. "She all but confessed to it. She didn't deny that it was her there under the trees with the man, and at the same time she refused to tell me who the man was or what they were doing."

William said nothing.

"There is more, William," Robert continued. "And this, also, you must keep in strict confidence."

William nodded, curious as to what more the man had to tell.

"Miss Gaines is not a maiden. She has known the pleasures of being with a man, and so I fear that, having tasted the wine, she was unable to resist taking a sip from another glass."

"You have taken her to your bed?" William knew full well the answer to his question, but he wanted Robert to account for his actions.

"I have," said Robert, plainly and with no apparent remorse. "We are—were—to be married. It is not uncommon these days, and she made no protest."

His hands balling into fists once more, William took a few deep breaths to stave off the growing desire to punch Robert in the face.

"Have you decided on your course of action, then?" William asked.

Robert walked back over to William, rubbing the back of his head again. William was beginning to find the gesture quite irritating.

"I don't know what to do, William. I don't know what to do. I want to marry her, to be married to her. She is beautiful. I would be the envy of every man in this city."

What a bastard, thought William. Bessie was no more than a prize to him. He did not love her, not as a husband should love a wife. Not as William loved her.

"But at the same time," continued Robert, "how can a man marry a woman he believes has been unfaithful to him? It cannot be done! If she is lying to me now, if she is unfaithful to me on the eve of our wedding, then she is a wanton woman, not worthy of bearing the Cox name."

"Have you told her of your decision not to marry her?" asked William, pleased with how calm he sounded, despite the rapid beating of his heart.

"Not yet," replied Robert. "I couldn't tell her this morning, when she was in such a state. And I wanted to think about it, to talk it over with someone."

Robert sighed. Then, putting a hand on William's shoulder, he looked into his eyes, nodding assent to some unasked question. "You are a good friend, William. You have helped me in this decision. You've brought me clarity and peace. I cannot marry Miss Gaines. She is a liar and no better than a harlot. She is not who I thought she was. I will tell her tonight. It is over between us."

Robert embraced William again and took his leave. As he was about to exit the room, he paused abruptly and turned around once more. "Thank you, William. You are a good man."

With that, Bessie's fiancé left the room. It was done.

William walked over to his father's desk and sat back down. He ran his fingers absently along the leather-bound spine of one of the ledger books closest to him.

He had done the right thing. More accurately, he had done nothing. He had let Robert come to his own conclusions, based on the evidence before him. If Robert thought Bessie had cheated on him, it was through no fault of William's. It was simply the natural course of events.

Once Robert gave her the news that their nuptials would no longer be taking place, Bessie would come to William for comfort. It was William who truly loved Bessie, after all. Whatever Robert felt for her was not love—not the kind of love that William could give her, in any case. And William knew that Bessie loved him, more than she could ever love Robert. She was meant for William. She had been all along.

But what of the babe? William knew Bessie would be giving birth to Robert's child in seven months or so. It was Bessie's child, too, and for that reason, and that reason alone, William knew he could and would love the child and raise it as his own.

No one need ever know the things he and Bessie knew. William would take care of Bessie, as he had

always said he would.
All would be well.

Chapter Eleven

Charlotte, North Carolina
Modern Day

"Hi, Grandma," Erin said as she stepped through her grandmother's doorway.

Giving her grandmother an extra kiss on the cheek, Erin put down her work bag and closed the door, eager to step back through it again as soon as possible. She couldn't remember the last time she had looked forward to Friday this much.

The day had been interminably long, almost as long as the day before. Erin had tried to immerse herself in work and managed to bill an amazing eleven hours on Thursday, but it still didn't make the day go by any faster.

But Friday night had finally come, and Erin was only three flights of stairs away from having dinner with Will. Each time she had caught herself grinning, she told herself not to expect too much so that she wouldn't be disappointed, but she couldn't help it. Just seeing Will's smile, even for a moment, would make the evening everything she'd hoped for.

"You're here a little earlier than usual, sweetie. Any particular reason for that?"

Erin could tell by her grandmother's coy tone and sparkling eyes that the old woman knew exactly where

Erin would be heading after her visit on the first floor, but there was no harm in playing along.

"I left work a little early, I guess," Erin replied innocently, sitting down on the couch. "And traffic wasn't bad at all. It might be Spring Break for some of the schools, I'm not sure."

"I see." Her grandmother set herself down slowly in her armchair.

"So, what's Mrs. Myer been up to lately?" asked Erin, trying to keep from smiling. "Any repeat customers?"

"Oh, I've hardly had time to watch what's going on across the hall. It's Mr. Abbott that I've been keeping an eye on this week. You won't believe what he's been up to."

A wave of apprehension washed over Erin, but then she caught a mischievous grin tugging at her grandmother's lips.

"Is that so?" she replied, looking her grandmother squarely in the eyes in an unspoken game of chicken. "Do tell."

The old woman rubbed her lower lip with the tips of her fingers, making Erin think victory was imminent. "Well, it seems that our Mr. Abbott has been courting a young woman recently."

Erin gasped dramatically. "You're kidding! Do you know who she is? Is she simply awful?"

"I do know her," replied her grandmother, admirably stoic. "Some hotshot lawyer who works in uptown. She's very self-absorbed, or so I've heard. People say she doesn't even love her grandmother."

At this, Erin burst out laughing, followed seconds later by her grandmother.

As they both recovered, her grandmother reached for her hand. "You like him, Erin?"

Like was putting it mildly.

"Yes, I do," she replied. "He's a good guy. I really like talking to him."

"I like looking at him," her grandmother interjected with a smirk.

Erin chuckled. "I like looking at him too, but there's this feeling I get when I spend time with him. Like he's really listening to what I'm saying, and he cares. It's hard to explain. It just feels good and right. It's easy to be with him, in the best way. Even when I say something stupid that I should have kept inside my head, he turns it into something good. Like it was something he wouldn't have wanted to miss." Erin shook her head and laughed. "I sound so crazy. I've only seen the guy a few times."

"There's nothing wrong with crazy," said her grandmother, smiling kindly at her. "No one ever achieved anything worthwhile being completely logical."

Erin squeezed her grandmother's hand before letting go. "I don't know. I guess we'll take it one step at a time and see what happens. It's just dinner, after all. He's still new to town and doesn't know too many people. Nothing more than a friendly get-together, an alternative to sitting at home eating leftovers on a Friday night."

"Yes, I'm sure you're right." Her grandmother's tone had become playful again, and Erin smiled as she waited for the punchline. "I suppose that's why he came down here earlier in the day to ask me if you like chocolate."

Erin couldn't help grinning. "He did?"

"Yes, ma'am. I said you were allergic."

Erin squeezed her grandmother's arm gently as she laughed again. "I'll never forgive you if you told him that!"

"Don't worry, hon. I told him you love chocolate more than your grandmother."

Erin leaned over and hugged the old woman. "You know that's not true, but it's better than telling him I'm allergic."

As Erin leaned back into the couch cushions once more, her grandmother picked up the wristwatch she always kept on the little coffee table next to her. "Are you planning on staying here all night? Go on upstairs! Don't keep the poor guy waiting!"

"I've only been here five minutes!"

"Five minutes is a lifetime to a man waiting for his date to arrive. Go on, now. And try to remember all the details, so you can tell me everything tomorrow."

Erin gave her grandmother a quick peck on the cheek before getting up.

"Have fun, Erin," said her grandmother from her chair as Erin walked out the door. "Don't do anything Mrs. Myer wouldn't do."

"Grandma!" Erin shouted in a whisper, looking behind her to make sure Mrs. Myer didn't have her door open. Turning back to her grandmother, Erin waved and smiled one more time. "I'll see you tomorrow. Love you."

Closing the door, Erin chuckled softly under her breath as she began climbing up the stairs. Her grandmother was so full of spunk, it was almost exhausting. But their playful exchange was exactly what she needed to get her relaxed and in the right mindset to enjoy her evening with Will.

Despite her grandmother's antics, though, butterflies burst out of invisible cocoons in Erin's stomach as she approached Will's door.

Taking a deep breath to rally her internal troops, she raised a hand to knock on the door. Before she could make contact with the wood, the door opened. And Erin forgot how to speak.

****

Each time he saw her, Will was struck by the simplicity of Erin's beauty. Her caramel-colored locks were held back in a loose ponytail; her black sweater dipped down toward her enticing curves; and her light blue jeans hugged her hips and legs in a most flattering manner. She stared at him with wide blue eyes framed by thick, dark lashes, her parted lips hinting at surprise.

He had clearly caught her off-guard opening the door before she'd had a chance to knock. He should offer an explanation.

"I thought I heard footsteps on the landing."

Erin smiled. "I've been told I walk around like I have bricks for feet."

Will could already feel his heart start to beat faster in his chest at hearing her voice. This did not bode well for the evening.

"It's a good thing you don't live above me, then."

She laughed. It occurred to him that she was still standing in the hallway.

"Come on in, Erin," he finally said, stepping aside to let her enter.

"Thanks."

She carried her coat on her arm, along with a

leather workbag. "I can put those in the closet for you, if you'd like."

"Sure, thank you." Erin handed him her belongings, careful not to brush his hands. "I could have left them downstairs in my grandmother's apartment, but I didn't want to have to wake her up to get them later."

Her eyes grew even wider as she realized how her statement had sounded, and Will tried very hard not to grin.

"I mean, she goes to sleep early," she backtracked. "Really, very early."

Will finally let his lips curl into a smile. "Old people."

That made her laugh again, and pleasure coursed through him at the sound.

"Have a seat and make yourself comfortable." Will gestured to the couches in the living room. "Can I get you something to drink?" he asked, moving into the kitchen. "I have a variety of wines, red and white, and cranberry juice. I have some tequila around here somewhere, too. A housewarming present from Mrs. Myer."

"Are you sure *she* wasn't the housewarming present?"

He found himself chuckling as he glanced up at her suggestive smirk. He couldn't remember a time in his life when he had laughed so often or so effortlessly.

"That might explain the pout she gave me when I didn't invite her in."

Instead of going into the living room, Erin came over to stand at the entrance to the kitchen. "I'll just have some water for now, if that's okay. I'm not really much of a drinker."

"No problem. Ice?"

"Okay, thanks."

Will got out a tall glass and filled it with some ice and water from the fridge, then poured some red wine into a glass for himself.

"Thanks," said Erin as he handed her the glass of water.

Will couldn't help noticing once more how lovely Erin looked as he stood back and took a fortifying sip of wine. Her soft pink lips seemed permanently curled in a smile, and her eyes were large and innocent.

Again, he reprimanded himself for inviting her. Why was he doing this to himself?

"Something smells good," she said, looking over his shoulder into the kitchen.

"Chicken piccata. With pasta and asparagus. I should have asked you about ingredients before I came up with the menu, but I have this notion that you are pretty easygoing when it comes to food."

"Yes, I suppose my love of food has come up once or twice." Her expression was playful, and he longed to stand closer to her.

He took another swallow of wine.

"The menu sounds fantastic," she continued, "and your customer is starving, which works in your favor."

"That's exactly how I like my customers— easygoing and hungry."

Will watched her take a sip of water, then forced himself to unglue his eyes from her lips.

"So, how is the crazy world of patent law? Did you hear about any particularly amazing inventions today?"

Erin laughed. "I don't think I've heard of a

particularly amazing invention since the day I started. What about you? Any harrowing encounters with your tenants today?"

"Only one this morning with Mrs. Myer. It's become our daily routine."

His guest raised her delicate eyebrows in disbelief. "Really? That's hilarious. What does she say to you?"

"Well, it seems she's figured out my schedule because she always just happens to be outside watering the plants on her patio when I go out for a walk in the morning—in her pajamas. And I'm not talking about fleece or cotton pajamas. I'm talking about the silky, lacy kind that people don't actually sleep in. She turns to look at me as I come walking past her, as though I've caught her by surprise. She bats her mascara eyes at me and asks me how I'm doing. I say I'm fine, and I just keep on walking."

"You know," began Erin, teasingly, "if you ever succumb to her mascara and lacy pajamas, my grandmother will see you go in there."

"Believe me, that's way down on the list of things that go through my mind when I'm running away from her, although you can rest assured it is on that list somewhere."

Erin giggled and pushed some stray hairs that had slipped out of her ponytail away from her face. He wondered if her hair felt as soft as it looked.

The timer on the oven sounded, and Will was grateful for the interruption. Silencing the annoying beeping, he grabbed a couple of hot pads from a drawer and pulled out the two covered glassware dishes he was keeping warm in the oven.

"Do you like to cook?" asked Erin as he turned

back toward her.

"'Like' is a pretty strong word. I would say I don't mind cooking. It gives me something to do."

She nodded agreeably. "Can I help with anything?"

"Well," he replied, "since you refuse to sit down and relax, I suppose you could bring me those two plates on the table behind you. There's a bowl of salad in the fridge, too, if you want to get that out."

Erin brought him the two empty dinner plates, then opened the refrigerator to search for the salad. It was only when Erin looked over at him with a grin, still holding the refrigerator door open, that he remembered what else he had put in there.

"Wow," she remarked, pulling out the salad. "Is that chocolate mousse what we're having for dessert?"

Why did it please him to see her excited about chocolate mousse?

"I forgot those were in there. Now it won't be a surprise."

She moved past him to place the bowl of salad on the dining room table. "I'm surprised right now, and looking forward to it. I might even be drooling a little. It looks delicious. You made it from scratch?"

He focused on arranging the chicken, pasta, and asparagus on the plates. She had a way of inflating his ego that he knew he should not be getting used to. "It's not too hard. Just takes a little time and patience."

"You are an impressive man, Will," said Erin.

He didn't feel impressive. He just had the inexplicable need to make her happy. It was why he had knocked on her grandmother's door to ask the old woman what her granddaughter liked to eat, like some lovesick teenager.

Erin was standing near the table as he set down their plates, and he motioned to the chair at the head of the table. "Please, have a seat."

He sat adjacent to her in the same arrangement as the last time they were at the table together, for tea. She had brought the bottle of wine to the table at some point, and Will reached to pour himself another glass, offering her some in the process. Again, she declined.

They began eating in silence, and Will wondered if she could sense how difficult it was for him to be near her. Even with his eyes focused on the colorful arrangement of food on his plate, all he could think about was reaching over and touching her cheek, tracing an eyebrow with his finger, tasting the sauce on her lips.

He had to stop this foolishness. He could have no future with her. He could have no future at all. All he had was existence—interminable existence—and he could not expose her to such a fate.

He should never have succumbed to this untenable desire to be with her. He had to stop whatever this was he was doing, and he had to stop it now before he lost all logic and reason. Before he was too far gone to recognize that all he was doing was perpetuating a fantasy that could never be.

Looking up from his food, Will turned his eyes to her, only to see her surprised expression at what must have been a sudden change in his formerly composed expression. He waited a moment before speaking.

"I hope you know that I'm not trying to be impressive or anything like that."

Her surprise faded to a warm regard, and she smiled. It would have broken Will's heart, had his heart been whole to begin with.

"Of course, I know that. If you were trying to be impressive, you'd just come off as annoying. And you are far from annoying."

"You have a way of interpreting everything in the best light. I admire this about you, among other things. But sometimes a person isn't worth your best interpretation."

Will could tell she was about to say something about how good or kind or worthy he was, and he just couldn't bear it. It was time for him to be direct.

It was time for him to lie.

"What I'm trying to say is that I have no…" he searched for the right word "…intentions toward you. I'm not trying to charm you or make you care for me in a way that is anything more than a person would care for their grandmother's landlord."

Erin laughed, but it rang hollow. He hated himself in that moment, more so than usual.

"Are you trying to tell me this is not a date, Mr. Abbott?"

She must have sensed that he didn't know how to respond because she continued. "Look, Will, it's obvious that I hold you in high regard, and I do have somewhat of a soft spot for you. I mean, you made chocolate mousse for me for dessert—if you didn't want me to like you, you should have gone with stewed fruit or something."

Will couldn't help smiling at her joke. How could she make him smile when he had no joy left in him?

"But I didn't come over here thinking this was a date or anything like that. You're new in town, you're alone, and sometimes it's nice to talk to someone.

Sometimes you *need* to talk to someone, even when you don't think you want to. I think that's why you called me two nights ago, and I think that's why I'm here. So, this doesn't have to be a 'date,' Will. It's just two people who enjoy talking to each other and spending some time together. That's all. Don't worry about me thinking it's anything else."

Erin's speech sounded very logical, and in many ways it was true. He did enjoy talking to her, so much so that he could hardly admit it to himself. And he was alone. When Will was with her, though, he didn't feel it as much. He forgot about who he was and why he was here. He hung on her every word, watched her every movement. He enjoyed the time he spent with her, just as she had said.

But although he would never say it out loud, Will knew it was more than that.

It made no difference. He had told Erin their relationship was strictly platonic, and she seemed to accept it. She made no move to leave. She said she understood. And part of him—a large part—was relieved that she could be so practical, so kind, after everything he had just said to her. Because Will really didn't want her to leave. At least now, though, he had said the words. Even if Erin stayed to finish out the meal with him, he had said what his conscience dictated he should. Perhaps, in return, his conscience would allow him to enjoy the short time he had left in her company.

Realizing he had been quiet for an uncomfortably long amount of time, Will broke the silence with a feeble laugh, then took another sip of wine. "Well," he said, putting the glass down, "I'm glad we got all that out of the way. Otherwise, you might have tried to throw yourself at me after eating some of my chocolate mousse, and that would have been very awkward."

Erin laughed sweetly, making him look at her beautiful smile again. Making him smile in return.

"I might still throw myself at you after the chocolate mousse," she replied, raising her eyebrows, "depending on how good it is."

The conversation moved on to lighter topics, and as they told each other stories and laughed together, Will found himself losing his resolve once more.

And he wondered how he was going to get through the evening without kissing her.

Chapter Twelve

"That was the best chocolate mousse I have ever had."

Erin was sitting on Will's couch with her legs tucked under her, trying to scrape just a little more of the chocolaty goodness out of her glass. It was almost a fitting consolation prize for having been told that Will had absolutely no romantic interest in her whatsoever.

She'd handled it well, though—she had to give herself credit. She had laughed it off quite convincingly, then proceeded to tell the most handsome, most charming man she had ever known that she had *not* come to his apartment looking for romance.

Apparently, lawyers were good liars, after all.

"I think you're exaggerating," said Will, and Erin reminded herself that he was referring to how much she loved his chocolate mousse.

"Will, if you haven't noticed, I'm doing everything I can here not to lick this thing clean. I have to put it down."

She placed the empty stemware onto the coffee table and gave it a gentle nudge to send it just out of reach.

"If you've got other desserts like that in your repertoire, I'm going to be over here every Friday night."

"The Internet is full of recipes, and I'm a quick

study," he replied, smiling.

"Dinner was delicious, too. Thank you for going to all that trouble."

"It was no trouble."

Will was seated on the other side of the couch with his arm on the backrest and his legs stretched out toward the coffee table. He seemed invitingly at ease in his dark blue, short-sleeved polo shirt. The top two buttons of his shirt were undone, and he exuded an easy confidence and irresistible masculinity. As her gaze wandered from his shirt to his toned arms and broad chest, she wondered what it would feel like to be pressed against that chest with those strong arms wrapped around her.

"So," began Erin, trying to rein in her thoughts, "tell me something about yourself that you don't want me to know."

Will laughed. "Why would I tell you something I don't want you to know?"

"Because you actually *do* want me to know, even though you don't think you do."

"Is that so?"

Erin nodded confidently. "It is. So, here's how it's going to work. I'm going to ask you questions, and you're going to answer them. The only rule is that you must refrain from answering my questions with questions for the remainder of my visit. Do we have an agreement, sir?"

"I suppose I can try." He sounded reluctant.

"Okay, great," she replied, enthusiastically ignoring his dubious tone. "So, maybe we can start with something easy. What's your full name?"

"William Henry Abbott."

"Excellent! I knew you could do it."

"Gee, thanks," he replied sarcastically.

"What year were you born?"

"I know you can do math, Erin."

She grinned, even though she'd been foiled. "Oh, right, you don't want me to know how old you are for some reason. Okay, we'll pass on that one then. But you're passing on an easy question. Now they get harder."

"I'm ready," he replied, the hint of a smile on his lips.

"Have you ever been in love?"

The smile that was just about to form vanished as soon as she'd spoke the question. Erin's first instinct was to apologize for obviously bringing up a sensitive subject, but she stopped herself. He wanted to talk to her, right? That was the whole reason—the sole reason—he had invited her over. Well, now was his chance.

So, she leaned back into the soft cushions and waited.

After a minute passed that felt like ten, he spoke. "Yes, once. A very long time ago."

She watched him as he looked down at his hands and wondered if she had gotten close to the reason for the cloud of sadness that so often seemed to hang over him. Perhaps it was time to break through that cloud. "What was her name?"

Again, Will hesitated before replying, "Bessie." He looked away from her again. "That's what I called her, anyway."

"I gather it didn't end well," she said softly.

"It hardly had a chance to begin."

She paused, then ventured to ask, "What happened?"

He sighed as he looked back up at her. His pain was so obvious in his eyes that it was all Erin could do to keep from reaching out and touching his arm.

"She died. That's all. She died. People die. You know that better than most."

The emotionless tone of the answer stirred within Erin an overwhelming desire to console him, but she didn't know how to go about it, at least not without contradicting her award-winning "this is not a date" act from earlier in the evening.

"It's terrible losing someone we love," she said finally. "But it does get better. You told me so yourself. The pain goes away and the good memories remain."

"What if you don't have any good memories? What if you never had the chance to make them? What if all you made were mistakes, and you never had the chance to make things right?"

Will looked at her intently, expectantly. Then he looked away as he answered his own questions. "In that case there is nothing. There is only emptiness and regret. You lose a piece of yourself with that person that you can never get back, and you become something less. You remember the pain—you want to remember the pain—because the pain is all you have."

"Don't you want the pain to fade?" Looking into his eyes, the answer was obvious.

"No, I don't, because I don't want her to fade. I don't want to forget her."

Erin was quiet for a moment. "The pain is not the person we lost. The pain is our self-pity." She paused again, considering if she should say more. She didn't want to upset Will or make him regret revealing this part of himself. But at the same time, how could she let him continue to carry the pain of his loss on his own when she could, perhaps, lighten it just a little?

"When my mother died, I remember noticing every person walking or talking or sitting with an older woman who looked like she could be that person's mother. Women, older than me, laughing with their silver-haired mothers. She still had her mother, I would think, feeling sorry for myself. My mother had only a handful of grays when she died. It wasn't fair, to my mother or to me. She didn't deserve to die so young, and I didn't deserve to lose her so soon. Then I heard the story of a twenty-five-year-old mother dying in a car crash with her two-year-old surviving in his car seat. Was that fair? Does that little child deserve to grow up without a mother? Or the sixteen-year-old girl whose mother dies of breast cancer? Is that fair? None of it is fair. Dying is not fair. The only thing fair about it is that it will happen to all of us, eventually."

Will picked up his glass of wine and took a slow drink, then put it back down on the coffee table. It was his third glass, and Erin had found him growing more talkative, and less guarded, with each sip.

Crossing his legs, he leaned back, studying her. "You don't hold anything back, do you?"

She laughed. "I tend to say what I'm thinking, if that's what you mean."

He shook his head. "That's not all of it. You're not just genuine in what you say. You're also genuine in what you think, in what you feel. You're honest about what's in your heart, to yourself and to others, and you feel with your whole self. I'll bet you've been in love, haven't you?"

Erin shifted her knees to one side and sat up straighter, wondering how she should respond. "I've had amorous feelings for certain young men, but I'm not sure it qualified as love."

"Why not?" he asked, sounding surprised.

"Well," she began, unsure how much she should tell him, "I may have thought it was love at the time, but then I wasn't all that devastated when it went away, you know? I mean, I was sad, I felt sorry for myself, but it was more due to vanity than loss of love, and it really wasn't that hard to get over. I know I keep coming back to my mother, but when she died, that was overwhelming. I loved her, really loved her. And I haven't ever felt that way about a man. Not yet."

"Love between a man and a woman is different than love between a mother and a daughter."

"I know that," she replied, trying not to roll her eyes at him. "But some elements are the same. And the extent, the depth of that love, the fact that it reaches into you and becomes a part of you and changes you, I think that part's the same."

Seeing the thoughtful look on Will's face, Erin sighed. "But what do I know? You're the one who's been in love, not me. Maybe it's different for different people. Maybe I'm expecting too much."

"If you don't expect much, then you won't get much," he said. Then he looked at her again, in a way that made her stomach flutter. "I'll bet men have been in love with you."

Erin's gaze drifted down from his eyes to his mouth as he spoke the words, and immediately her cheeks grew warm.

Will smiled, teasingly. "There I go again, making you blush."

"I told you it's a medical condition," she countered, trying to will the blood to drain away from her skin. "In any case, I think the answer is the same. There've been a few guys, only one or two really, who have expressed those kinds of feelings for me at one point or another. But in the end, it came down to a physical attraction and not much more. When they couldn't achieve their ends, they lost their patience with me and sought their goals elsewhere."

"I see," said Will, his head slowly nodding as though he was all-knowing. "That is the curse of beauty, isn't it? It brings out the best and the worst in the men who encounter it."

"I'm under no delusions that I'm the prettiest girl on the block," she scoffed. "I hardly do my hair most days. I barely wear any make-up, and I'm too cheap to buy myself fancy clothes."

"That's the proof of beauty, isn't it? You don't even have to try."

Erin laughed nervously. "You know, for someone who started the evening telling me he's not trying to romance me, you're wasting an awful lot of time inflating my ego."

Feeling the need to get up and do something before she started blushing again, or worse, Erin reached for her empty dessert glass and Will's and headed to the kitchen sink. She kept her head down as she turned on the water and started washing the two glasses. Despite his speech earlier about how platonic this evening was supposed to be, Will had caused all sorts of romantic notions to start floating around in her head. She tried discreetly to take a deep breath. She had to get a grip on herself before she did something that would make Mrs. Myer proud.

"You didn't have to wash my dishes," he said when she returned to the couch.

"I know," replied Erin, pushing the hair away from her face and tucking it behind her ears. "But nothing cures blushing like doing some dishes."

"Well," began Will, "since you're done blushing, perhaps I could ask you another question."

"You know me, I feel compelled to answer any question I'm asked."

Will grinned before folding his arms across his chest, making Erin worry about exactly what question he meant to ask.

"So," he began, his face taking on a more serious expression, "these men who have been in love with you, what were the 'ends' they couldn't achieve, and why couldn't they achieve them?"

It took only a moment before Erin laughed out loud. "I think you know full well what 'ends' I'm talking about, Will."

"All right," said Will, laughing himself and reaching again for his glass of wine. "I'll admit that I can deduce that part. But what is not as clear is what happened to make these poor souls give up on winning your affections."

Erin hesitated, staring down at her clasped hands for a moment. She should have expected this would come up. After all, she was the one who had suggested this game of answering each other's questions. How could she expect him to open up to her if she wasn't willing to do the same?

"I don't have the same views on sex as most people," said Erin, getting the words out quickly before she could change her mind.

She looked up at Will to gauge his reaction, but he was unreadable. Aside from the kindness in his warm, brown eyes, she had no idea what he was thinking.

"So," he replied slowly, "what exactly does that mean?"

He was going to make her spell it out for him. She almost laughed again.

"It means," she replied, imitating his slow speech, "I think sex is a pretty big deal. I don't think it's just something fun that two people who met ten minutes ago at a bar should do. I don't think it's for a first date or a tenth date or a hundredth date. It's the closest, physically, that two people can ever be. How can that be shared with just anyone? How can it be shared with someone you're not just as close to on an emotional and spiritual level?"

"I see," said Will. "So, no premarital sex. You could have just said that, you know."

He was teasing her again, and it made her smile.

"Don't you think," he went on, "that maybe sometimes two people who aren't married might share that connection you're talking about?"

No one had ever presented that scenario to her, and she had certainly not experienced that kind of connection with anyone. Well, present company excluded.

The thought had come at her from nowhere, and for a moment she panicked that she had spoken the words aloud. Glancing up at Will, she saw that he still wore the same un-telling expression, and she relaxed.

He was waiting for her answer.

"I suppose that, yes, it is possible. And in the same way, some people who are married may not have that connection."

The corner of Will's mouth turned up. "So, to clarify, your position is not against pre-marital sex, but against all sex?"

She let herself laugh, and the tension eased out of her slowly. "I wouldn't go that far," she replied. "I mean, I guess we have to draw the line somewhere."

"Thank goodness for reason."

She laughed again, and the other side of his mouth raised to join his grin.

"You're very rare, Erin Dovetree. In more ways than one."

Erin shrugged. "I'm naïve and inexperienced. That makes it easier to have ideals."

"There's nothing wrong with ideals, as long as you can find someone to share them with."

Her heart pinched at his words, and she had to look away. She couldn't let him see how much she longed for that person to be him.

Without meaning to, Erin looked down at her watch and realized that it was a little after nine o'clock.

"Oh my goodness," she exclaimed, jumping to her feet. "I'm so sorry—I didn't realize it was so late!"

"Do you have another appointment to get to?"

"No," she said, chuckling, "but I'm sure you don't want me passing out on your couch."

Will said nothing, but stood up.

Erin followed him to the front door and waited as he retrieved her coat and bag from the closet.

"I had a really great time tonight," she said, trying

not to sound enamored of him, which was difficult. "The food was fantastic, and the conversation was, well, both thought-provoking and entertaining."

"I think you've described the evening perfectly," he replied, smiling.

He was standing close to her, so close that she could smell the wine on his breath and the clean scent of soap on his body. And it made her want to be even closer, to breathe him in more deeply.

Fighting every instinct to wrap her arms around him, she took a step back, and he reached to open the door.

The breeze coming in through the open door was cooler than the air in the apartment, and it felt good on her skin.

"Thanks for coming, Erin." Will's voice was soft, caressing her like the breeze that had just entered the room, and she suddenly wished she hadn't seen what time it was.

He stepped closer to her again, and this time she stood her ground. "You were right," he continued. "I haven't talked like that in a very, very long time. And it was exactly what I needed."

"Me too," said Erin. "I needed it, too." She also needed him to kiss her, but, somehow, she managed not to say the words out loud.

There was a pause, and she thought about hugging him, but they had been standing there like that for so long it would have been awkward for her to throw her arms around him now. Plus, with her coat and her bag in her arms, she was liable to cause him bodily injury if she tried.

"All right, then," she said, feeling the need to break

the silence. "I'll see you around."

"Soon, I hope," he replied.

Erin walked down the three flights of stairs without looking back up at Will, though she sensed him watching her from the doorway. Stepping out into the cool night air, she filled her lungs with it, hoping it would help. But her heart didn't stop pounding until she was halfway home.

Chapter Thirteen

Charlotte, North Carolina
September 1879

Robert Cox's visit and subsequent announcement that he would no longer be marrying Miss Elizabeth Gaines brought William the most restful sleep he had experienced in years. A night of good sleep was truly a blessing, he thought as he pushed the covers off himself and swung his legs over the edge of the bed the following morning. Slivers of the morning sun broke through the gaps between the curtains on his bedroom windows, and he marveled at the brilliant pattern they made on the floor before pushing open the curtains and letting the light flood the room.

Eager to start the day, William dressed himself quickly, pausing only for a moment in front of the full-length mirror in the corner of his room. He gazed admiringly at the image smiling back at him. After a long fight, he, William Henry Abbott, would be the victor. He would have the woman he loved, the only woman that mattered to him. And Robert Cox would have to find another prize to claim for his own.

Like the sunlight coming in through the windows, William seemed to burst into the hallway, down the stairs, and through the entrance hall on his way to the dining room to have breakfast with his mother and whichever of his sisters happened to be awake. Glancing at the clock in the entrance hall, however, William suddenly realized why the sun had been so bright. It was nearly ten in the morning. William had peacefully slept through breakfast and all of the commotion his sisters usually caused as they prepared themselves for the day.

Too hungry after his long night of sleep to wait until the midday meal, William continued through the empty dining room and into the kitchen, where the servants were busying themselves preparing the meals for the rest of the day while sharing the morning gossip. He entered just as Radka, who oversaw the work of the other servants, was remarking in somber tones that something or other was "terrible, just terrible."

Despite his disdain for encouraging the idle gossip of the servants, William couldn't help but be curious.

"What's terrible?" he asked, knowing the question sounded rather ridiculous considering the unrestrained smile on his face.

Radka, whose back had been to the door, quickly turned around to face him.

"Oh, Master William, where have you been? Your mother thought that you had already gone to the Gaines residence to help them sort through this tragic mess."

So, Robert had done as he'd said. He had broken it off with Bessie. *Good boy*, thought William, trying hard to keep his smile at bay.

"What sort of mess have the Gaineses gotten themselves into now?" asked William, feigning ignorance.

"Sir, haven't you heard what happened last night?" The hint of a Bulgarian accent, Radka's childhood tongue, which only emerged when she was distressed, compelled him to look at her more closely. Her normally radiant face appeared haggard and worn, and the skin around her eyes seemed swollen. She had been crying.

His light-heartedness quickly left him.

"Radka, tell me—what has happened?"

Radka moved closer to William and placed her hands on his upper arms, as though to physically brace him for the news. Although he was a grown man now, William knew she still thought of him as a child entrusted to her care. It was still her instinct to protect him.

"Sir," she began, "it's Miss Elizabeth. They found her this morning, in the creek behind their house. She's passed from this life, sir. She's gone."

The blood drained from William's face in that instant, and if not for Radka's sturdy hands, his legs may well have folded under him.

"No, it's not true." His voice was a whisper, and he shook his head. He couldn't stop. Slowly, he backed away from Radka, and her hands released him and fell to her sides, idle and useless.

"It's not true," William repeated, this time louder as the distance between him and Radka grew. The three other servants in the kitchen stood motionless, staring at him. He looked from one to the next, then back at Radka.

Then he turned on his heels and bolted from the kitchen. He dashed through the dining room, knocking a chair over in his haste, into the entrance hall, and out the front door, which slowed him down only momentarily.

For the second time in almost as many days, William ran the distance between his own home and Bessie's. But while he thought he felt despair in the knowledge of Bessie's betrayal the first time running home, this time, running toward Bessie's house with the knowledge of her death, William knew true despair. For this time, he knew he would never hear her voice or see her smile again. And this time he would have given anything to get her back—not to have her as his wife, but merely to have the chance to see her face at church or on the street, even if only from a distance, and even if only as the wife of another man.

The sound of his pounding heart was deafening and overpowered his thoughts, and with each beat came a sharp stab of self-loathing. Why had he been so greedy? Why did he have to make her his wife? Couldn't he have accepted that she would be wed to another man and just let things be?

Knowing her death couldn't have been an accident, his anguish at that moment dwarfed the hopelessness he knew Bessie must have experienced hearing Robert say he would not marry her. She had pictured herself cloaked in shame at being unmarried and with child. And who would have taken her in that state? Who would have loved her and the spawn of another man that grew inside her?

I would have, Bessie! William screamed in his mind. *How could you not know that I love you above all else!*

And then he remembered, her voice ringing in his ears.

You loved me a moment ago! she had chastised him when he had withdrawn from her embrace.

William had said nothing in reply, arrogant as he was. He had simply turned and left Bessie there, sobbing.

She had not killed herself. It was clear to William now—*he* had killed her, by taking away any hope she may have had.

William slowed as he turned off the main street and stepped onto the Gaines' property, nearly doubling over at the exertion of his sprint and the dark realization of his deeds. With bleary eyes, he could see the owner of the funeral home, Mr. Johns, leaning over Mrs. Gaines' hunched, shaking body, offering her words of comfort, no doubt. Bessie's younger brother was standing nearby, holding his aunt's hand. And behind the aunt, standing in the shadow of the cherry trees where William had kissed Bessie just days before, was a somber-looking Robert Cox.

William quickly looked away from Robert's face before the urge to throw him to the ground and beat him senseless could overtake him.

Any thoughts of propriety and decorum seemed to depart from William as he approached the sorrowful mother and the funeral home owner.

"Where is she?" William blurted out. "I need to see her!"

Mr. Johns turned away from the sobbing Mrs. Gaines and, putting an arm around William, pulled him gently aside.

"William," he began with a well-practiced calmness, "you must think of how very difficult this ordeal has been and will continue to be for Mrs. Gaines. She has lost her only daughter, and on the eve of her wedding, no less. She is inconsolable, and you must hold your tongue when you are near her. Do you understand?"

"Yes, yes," said William, already losing patience with the man. "I understand. Please, tell me where I can find Elizabeth."

Mr. Johns looked at William, as though he knew the content of William's heart. "She has been laid in the back of the carriage," the man replied, pointing to the vehicle in the driveway. "We were getting ready to take her to the funeral home."

William raised his eyes to the carriage, where his Bessie lay. For all his urgency just moments ago, now William paused for a long moment, unprepared to face her. He turned again to Mr. Johns. "Do you know exactly what happened?"

Mr. Johns glanced back toward Mrs. Gaines, then at William again. In a hushed voice, he replied, "Two of the household servants found her in the creek in the woods behind the house this morning, just before sunrise. She was face down in only two feet of water. She was dead when they came upon her. From my estimation, she likely died a few hours before she was discovered."

William looked intently at Mr. Johns, trying to make sense of his words. "Did she drown?"

Mr. Johns heaved a low sigh. "The servants reported that Miss Gaines went out for some air last night around nine in the evening, just as everyone in the house was retiring to their rooms for the night. They say that they, too, went to their rooms and did not hear her return, although they thought nothing of it at the time. They say that they believe she must have stumbled in the dark and fallen into the creek, and that she must have gotten disoriented when this all occurred and so became unable to pull herself up and to safety, thus drowning where they found her this morning."

The kindness in the funeral home owner's eyes gave William the courage to ask his next question.

"What do you believe happened, Mr. Johns?"

Again, the man sighed. "I do not believe it is possible that Miss Gaines died as early in the evening as nine or ten o'clock, based on the condition of her body. Mr. Cox told me about a quarrel they had last night. It was a serious sort of disagreement, one that would upset any young woman on the eve of her wedding. I tell you this in confidence; he has told no one else. If she did go out for air as the servants report, I believe she returned home. But alas, the demons that live inside all of us tend to speak loudest in the hours between midnight and sunrise, and I believe she may have felt compelled by those demons to go out a second time."

"She did not drown, did she?" William knew the answer before the words had passed his lips.

"It is very difficult, if not impossible, for a person to drown themselves without some force keeping them submerged. Purposely inhaling water causes such great pain, the body will not allow it."

"If she did not drown, then how did she die?"

The man drew in a ragged breath. "Do you promise not to tell a single living soul what I am about to reveal to you?"

William nodded wordlessly.

"There was an empty bottle of laudanum only a few steps from where her body was found. It was hidden in the long grass by the creek, and only I saw it."

William's heart stopped beating, even though the man was only confirming what William had suspected all along. "You believe she took her own life?"

"What I believe is of no consequence. What good would come of my telling the heartbroken Mrs. Gaines my theories and conjectures? It would only prevent the poor girl from receiving a proper Christian burial, and I'll not have that on my conscience."

His body numb and his skin cold, William looked in the direction of the carriage once more.

"Go," said the man, "say what you need to say to the girl. She is no longer in that body, but she will hear you just the same."

With that, Mr. Johns patted William's shoulder firmly and walked back to stand with Mrs. Gaines. William was alone, the cold gradually seeping into his heart.

Feet heavy with grief, William trudged to where the carriage stood. He hesitated a moment before peering into the back. There he saw the body of his beloved Bessie, wrapped in a sheet of white linen, and new shards of pain seemed to explode within him.

Bessie's face was hidden by the sheet, and much of the sheet was damp where it clung to her wet hair and clothing.

William climbed up into the back of the carriage and knelt as best he could beside her still, wrapped body. Tears streamed down his face as he reached with unsteady hands to unveil her face. The beauty of her lifeless countenance struck him, and he could hardly breathe.

Unable to stop his trembling, William stroked

Bessie's cheek with his fingers and was shocked at how cold her skin was to the touch, despite the warmth of that late summer morning.

"Oh, Bessie," he sighed, his voice rough with emotion. "What have I done to you? I was selfish. Proud. I wanted you for myself, and I thought only of how to get you back. I blamed you for your indiscretion with Robert Cox when I should have blamed myself for staying away for far too long. What did I think would happen?"

He shook his head, the tears continuing to fall. "It was not your fault, my love. You were so beautiful, so kind and trusting. Beauty attracts all manner of attention, good and bad. It was not your fault."

His voice faltering, William drew in a stilted breath before continuing his confession.

"I took away your hope that night when I led you to believe I didn't love you. Then I proceeded to encourage the man you were to marry to think that it was in his best interest to leave you. I never thought of how my words and actions—my silence and inaction— might harm you. And now, look what I've done."

His words became sobs as his head fell under the weight of his grief.

A few minutes passed, and William collected himself once more. Passing his eyes slowly over Bessie's pale, yet peaceful face, it was as though he were looking at an angel.

"This is not your sin, Bessie," he said, his voice calm and steady this time. "Your blood and the blood of your unborn child are on my hands, my soul. I am the one to blame, and I shall carry that burden on my shoulders for the rest of my life. Any peace that I would have had in this life, I give to you that you shall rest in it. You are as innocent as the child that grew inside you. May the Lord have mercy on your soul and the soul of your child. I accept whatever punishment He deems commensurate with the gravity of my sins."

William bent down and touched Bessie's cold, damp forehead with his lips. Then, taking one last look at her, he covered her once more with the sheet.

He said a prayer under his breath for Bessie and her child, then whispered a promise, like the wedding vows he never had the chance to make. "For as long as I would have loved you, sweet Bessie, I shall now mourn you. Rest in peace, my love. My life."

Chapter Fourteen

Charlotte, North Carolina
Modern Day

From the moment Erin left Will's apartment on
Friday night, she longed to see him again. When she
dropped off her grandmother's groceries the next
morning, she couldn't stop herself from glancing up at
his window, hoping he would see her and call her up for
tea. She would have been happy just to get a glimpse of
him heading out to run some errands or taking a walk.
But she had no such luck.

Back at work, she found herself scanning all her
unread emails each morning to see if perhaps Will had
emailed her. It would have been easy for him to find her
email address on the firm's website, if he wanted to.

At night, Erin even started leaving her phone on
her nightstand with the ringer turned on, just on the off-
chance Will lost track of the hour and had the urge to
call her again.

Will didn't email her, though, and he didn't call,
either. She shouldn't have been surprised. He'd set the
tone early in the evening that their little get-together
was not a date. But friends still called each other, didn't
they? Then again, all that talk about her dead mother
and her medieval views on sex would have been
enough to quell anyone's interest, romantic or

otherwise. She had to learn to keep her mouth shut sometimes.

Another thought struck her. Could Will have sensed how attractive she found him? Was it written on her face that she had desperately wanted him to hold her and kiss her? Was he just trying to protect her from a pointless crush?

Suddenly, she found herself hoping Will just thought she was crazy or boring. The alternative was mortifying.

The Friday after her visit with Will was Good Friday, and Erin had already told her grandmother she wouldn't be visiting, knowing that her father would likely stop by. While she hated missing an opportunity to potentially run into Will, she had no desire to cross paths with her father. It was bad enough she would have to endure being in the same room with him on Sunday when they celebrated Easter at her grandmother's. There was no need to pile on.

Will. Just the thought of her grandmother's handsome landlord made her smile, even as she told herself to *stop* thinking of him. Aside from the fact that it was bordering on obsession, she needed all her wits about her to mentally prepare for seeing her father on Sunday.

On Saturday, Erin spent most of the afternoon trying to recreate the sugar cookies her mother always used to make for Easter. She burned the first batch and had to throw them out, but on her second try, she was cautiously optimistic. The cookies came out of the oven looking perfectly baked and smelling just as sweet and buttery as her mother's. Unfortunately, when they had cooled enough for her to try one, Erin couldn't even bite through it. It was like trying to eat a very sweet hockey puck. Grunting in frustration, she again threw the whole batch out. She didn't have the heart to try baking a third batch. The grocery store down the street would be open for a few hours on Easter morning, and some nice, soft, store-bought cookies would be better than no cookies at all.

The next morning, Erin put together the green salad she had promised her grandmother she would bring. It was the only thing she was allowed to contribute to the meal. Her father had insisted on making everything else, according to her grandmother.

Setting the salad aside, she went to her bedroom to get dressed. She had picked out a lacy turquoise skirt and simple white V-neck blouse for the occasion, and, looking at herself in the mirror, she approved of her choice. After getting dressed, Erin found her curling iron and tried to do something with her hair. It was Easter, after all. She could at least try to look a little festive.

Erin wasn't one to wear much makeup, but she was on a roll. Stowing the hairspray she had used to style her curls back under the sink, she reached for her small makeup bag. After applying beige eyeshadow, brown eyeliner, and mascara, she turned to her lips. Although simple lip gloss or subdued tones were more her style, her fingers landed on the dark mauve lipstick her aunt had sent her as a Christmas present a few months earlier. She had never been bold enough to try it at work, but she was only going to her grandmother's today. It was the perfect test run.

Pulling off the cover, Erin applied the color to her lips and examined herself in the mirror. It was definitely a different look for her, but it had a certain appeal.

With one last look at her reflection, she went to collect everything she would be bringing to her grandmother's house.

It was just before noon when Erin stepped out the door. The grocery store down the street was thankfully still open, so she made a quick stop and picked up the cookies she had failed to bake before continuing to her grandmother's place.

As she pulled into the parking lot of her grandmother's building, Erin quickly scanned the cars. Not spotting her father's blue sedan, she instinctively let out a sigh of relief. Erin knew she would be eating at the same table with him before long, but at least she wouldn't have to deal with him as soon as she stepped into the apartment. And there was always a small chance that he might not come at all, wasn't there?

Walking to the sidewalk that led to the front doors of the building, Erin couldn't help but look up at Will's window. Unfortunately, the curtains were closed, so that was that.

A few moments later she was inside, knocking on the door to her grandmother's unit.

"Come in, it's open!" she heard her grandmother's voice called out.

Balancing the canvas bag that held the salad and the cookies on one shoulder and her purse on the other, Erin turned the knob and pushed the door open to enter.

"Hi, Grandma, Happy Easter!" Erin smiled warmly at the old woman as she closed the door and stepped into the apartment. Placing the bag of food on the floor, Erin hung her purse up on the hooks by the door, trying to ignore her frayed nerves.

"What a cute skirt," said her grandmother, fondly.

Erin walked over to where the old woman was sitting at the dining room table, filling a couple of small bowls with peanuts, and hugged her. "Thanks, Grandma. I got it a few weeks ago."

She stepped back to the door to pick up the bag, then took it over to the kitchen to unpack it. Noticing the oven was on, Erin cracked the door open and snuck a peek. One pan had an aluminum-foil-covered bulge, which Erin presumed to be the ham, and another had what looked like potatoes and carrots under a glass cover.

"Your father brought those over at the break of dawn this morning and told me to start cooking!" laughed her grandmother.

Erin smiled politely. So, her father would be coming after all.

"What time are we eating?" asked Erin. They called it "Easter dinner," but they typically ate around one or two. Erin assumed it would be no different this year.

"What time is it now, dear?"

"It's getting close to twelve-thirty."

Her grandmother looked up from her peanuts. "I would start putting the cold dishes out."

Erin obeyed. She took the cookies out and placed them on the kitchen counter so she could get to the salad at the bottom of the bag.

"Do you have tongs or something we can use to serve the salad? And where do you keep your oil and vinegar, for the dressing?"

"What did you say, dear?" Without a clear view of

her face, her grandmother hadn't heard her questions.

Erin was heading to the dining room so her grandmother could read her lips as she repeated the questions when there was a knock at the door. Without a word, Erin moved back to the kitchen, deciding to search through the drawers and cabinets herself for what she needed. The door was unlocked—her dad could let himself in.

"Erin, why don't you open the door?"

"It's just Dad. He doesn't need me to open the door for him. Just tell him it's open and he'll come in."

Her grandmother let out a disapproving huff. "Your father doesn't knock, Erin. Could you please open the door for Mr. Abbott?"

Tingles ran down Erin's spine and her head popped up to look at her grandmother. "Why do you think that's Mr. Abbott? He wouldn't be knocking on your door today. It's Easter."

"Yes, I know it's Easter. That's why I invited him."

Erin's jaw dropped, and she hurried out of the kitchen to face her grandmother. "You did what?"

"It's my Easter dinner, and I invited Mr. Abbott. Now, would you please go open the door for the poor man so he doesn't give up and go back upstairs to his apartment?"

Shaking her head in disbelief, Erin took a deep breath and went to the front door to open it.

Sure enough, Will's handsome face was smiling at her from the other side.

"Everything okay in there?" he asked. Erin recognized the teasing lilt in his voice, which was reflected in his warm brown eyes.

"Yes, I'm sorry we kept you waiting," Erin replied, motioning for him to come in. "A little miscommunication with my grandmother. She's hard of hearing, you know."

"I heard that," called her grandmother from the dining room.

"Except when I'm talking about her, of course," added Erin under her breath. Will chuckled as he entered.

He presented her with a decorative bag that held a bottle of wine. "I didn't know what to bring, so I brought wine, even though I know you don't really drink."

"I think I might today," Erin replied, taking the bag from him. "Besides, this is much better than the store-bought cookies and lettuce I brought."

Will seemed different, she thought as she went back into the kitchen to get some wine glasses. His eyes were bright, almost cheerful, and his mouth hinted at a smile, even when he wasn't speaking. It was nice seeing him this way, and Erin wondered what had brought about the change. She watched out of the corner of her eye as Will helped her grandmother up from her seat at the dining room table and led her to her chair in the living room. He was good with her, and Erin's heart swelled with a pride she had no right to feel. He wasn't her boyfriend, after all.

Erin cleared her throat and turned back to the task at hand.

"I'm afraid my grandmother doesn't have any wine glasses," she announced, having looked in each cabinet twice. "We'll have to make do with regular glasses. But I did find the oil and vinegar for the salad, as well as the salad tongs, so that's a plus."

"We could just pass around the bottle, save the glasses altogether," Will replied from the living room.

Erin laughed, picturing her grandmother taking a swig. "That would be fun."

Will had seated himself on the couch where Erin usually sat during her Friday visits, closest to her grandmother's chair. He held one of her grandmother's hands in both of his as he spoke to her. She could hear Will tell the old woman how nice she had been to invite him to celebrate Easter with them. Erin's eyes lingered on his hands just before she miraculously found a corkscrew in one of the drawers and attempted to uncork the bottle of Pinot Grigio.

Struggling with the cork, Erin listened quietly as Will told her grandmother about a leak in an apartment on the other side of the building and how it took his plumber two hours to find the source. After fishing out a few pieces of floating cork from each glass, Erin delivered the drinks to the living room.

Will thanked her as he took a glass from her hand. Her grandmother, however, emphatically refused.

"Grandma, I only poured a little bit for you."

"You know it doesn't take much to get me tipsy," replied the old woman.

"A little bit of wine is good for you, Grandma. This is hardly a mouthful!"

"No, thank you."

Erin looked imploringly at Will, who was obviously amused at the exchange between grandmother and granddaughter. "Would you please tell her there's nothing wrong with a little wine?"

"Me?" He looked shocked that Erin had dragged

him into the conversation. "If she won't listen to her granddaughter, she's not going to listen to me."

"You'd be surprised. Just try."

Setting his own drink down on the coffee table, Will took the glass from Erin and offered it to her grandmother. "Go on, Mrs. Dovetree. It's hardly anything at all. And Erin's right, they say a little wine now and then is good for your heart."

The old lady looked somewhat doubtful, then accepted the glass from Will and took a sip.

"It's quite good," she remarked, taking another sip.

Erin rolled her eyes as she retreated to the kitchen. She could hear Will chuckling under his breath.

Taking a swig from her glass, Erin reached for the oil and vinegar and began dressing the salad that sat neglected on the counter near the stove. As she sprinkled some basil and oregano flakes on top, she heard the sound of Will's footsteps approaching from the living room, followed by the sound of her heart pounding in her ears.

She looked over her shoulder and smiled at him, ignoring her quickening pulse.

"Nice work, Mr. Abbott. We'll have my grandmother drunk in no time."

"Is that your goal? You naughty granddaughter."

She shrugged innocently as she began mixing the salad. "It's your fault. You brought the wine."

Will took a step closer to her, and his arm brushed her shoulder. "Why is it that your grandmother took the drink from me when she refused to take it from you?"

Erin chuckled softly, trying not to think about how near he stood. "Because you're a man, and according to my grandmother men are to be listened to and obeyed, because they are always right. And if they are ever wrong, it's probably through no fault of their own, poor dears."

Will nodded his head in agreement. "Smart lady."

Erin put down the tongs and slapped his arm.

"Ouch!" He laughed, rubbing his arm in mock pain, and Erin unsuccessfully tried to keep from giggling.

When he had recovered from his fake injury, Will reached for the salad bowl. "On the table?"

"Yes, please," she replied.

He took the bowl and moved away from her, and Erin suddenly regretted having given him a chore to do. She liked having him close to her, and his absence left her wanting.

She sighed, then tried to distract herself by finding halfway decent plates for setting the table.

"Do you need those out there, too?" Will asked when he returned to the kitchen, pointing to the four plates she was pulling out of a cabinet.

"Yes, but you don't have to do it. You're a guest. You shouldn't be in the kitchen mingling with the help."

"But the help is so charming," he replied, his expression devilishly seductive. "And I'm afraid your grandmother is only able to hear about fifty percent of my wildly amusing stories."

"You greatly overestimate her hearing."

"Damn. She's better at faking it than I thought."

Erin laughed and followed Will out of the kitchen with silverware and napkins to set out on the table by the plates he had arranged.

She knew she shouldn't be enjoying the simple act

of folding napkins in half and setting out the silverware. She was not playing house with her grandmother's adorable landlord, she reminded herself. But her fluttering stomach begged to differ.

Erin's thoughts were cut short by a quick succession of knocks on the door. Before she could register what the sound meant, the door opened.

It was her father.

Chapter Fifteen

Will watched as the smile fell from Erin's lovely face, and the muscles in his arms and shoulders tensed reflexively.

He turned to see Erin's father strut into the apartment, pushing the door shut behind him. He was a tall man with an angular face and a large, shining bald spot at the top of his head.

"Hello, Mother," he said in a booming voice. Then he looked to Erin and Will. Erin had inched closer to Will at some point, and it was all Will could do not to pull her into his arms and offer her protection.

"Erin, Happy Easter," said her father, still standing by the door.

"Happy Easter, Dad," she replied. Will had never heard such a lack of feeling in her voice, and it spoke volumes.

"You must be Mr. Abbott. Happy Easter, Mr. Abbott. And thank you for coming to spend your Easter with us."

Erin's father strode toward them and reached across the table to shake hands with him. Will had no choice but to engage in the handshake. "It's an honor and my pleasure to be included in your family's celebration. Please, call me Will, Mr. Dovetree."

"Only if you call me Paul."

Will nodded. "Agreed."

They ended the handshake, and Erin retreated into the kitchen.

"Can we take this stuff out of the oven yet?" she called, without addressing anyone in particular.

Her father answered. "Everything should be ready. No sense in waiting around."

As Mr. Dovetree turned away from Will to walk into the living room, where Erin's grandmother still sat, his eyes fell on the plastic container of cookies sitting on the edge of the counter.

"What are these?" he asked, his tone hinting at some yet unspoken derision.

Erin looked up from the pan she had removed from the oven. Her fingers were pulling at the edges of the aluminum foil, and steam billowed out of a small gap that had formed between the foil and the corner of the pan.

"Those are the cookies I brought over for dessert."

Her father grunted his disapproval. "Nobody cooks anymore, not even for Easter."

Will's body tensed as he looked from father to daughter.

Erin forced a thin laugh. "I tried, Dad, but the cookies I made turned out to be as hard as rocks, so I thought these were the safest option."

"Do you know how much shit they put in these cookies? They're filled with chemicals and artificial preservatives."

Will wondered if he should say something.

"It's not like I buy them all the time, Dad."

"Whatever makes you happy," he replied.

Erin's face took on a reddish hue, but she said nothing in response this time. Instead, she went back to carefully peeling the aluminum foil off the pan.

Having succeeded, she carried the ham over to the table and placed it in the center.

"Why don't you cut that up in the kitchen, Erin, and then bring it out? Wouldn't it be easier for everyone that way?"

Will watched as Erin bit her lip at her father's suggestion, then picked up the pan and carried the ham back into the kitchen. As she opened a drawer and pulled out a large knife, Will moved to stand beside her.

"Do you want me to do that for you?" he asked quietly.

"No, that's all right. I can take care of this." Her voice held just a trace of a tremor, and Will's heart squeezed at the sound of it.

"So, Will!" her father thundered from the living room couch. "Come over here and tell me about yourself."

Will reached up to put his hand on Erin's shoulder, and she stopped sawing at the ham for a moment, her head down. Then she looked up at him and smiled in a way that melted Will's heart.

"Go on," she said. "I'll show this ham who's boss and then we can eat."

Despite his better judgment, he slid his hand down from her shoulder to her upper arm and gave it a squeeze, then moved back out into the living room to engage her father in conversation.

Though he sat by Erin's father making small talk in the living room, Will was aware of Erin's every action as she moved around the kitchen and went back and forth to the dining room bringing out the rest of the food. As she flitted gracefully about, her skirt swayed sensually about her hips and her hair bounced happily around her face in stark contrast to the somber expression she wore. He had never seen her with her hair down—it suited her, forming the perfect frame for her high cheekbones, graceful eyebrows, and the most beautiful eyes he had ever seen. Her slender arms flexed as she carried a heavy casserole dish over to the table, and her skirt swirled around her long legs as she headed back into the kitchen for a platter piled high with rolls.

When the table was set, she took a sip of her wine, then closed her eyes for a moment, as though trying to settle herself.

"Dad, do you want some wine with dinner?" she asked, opening her eyes and picking up the half-empty bottle.

Her father stopped talking to Will only long enough to reply, "No, thank you."

Erin let her hand drop from the bottle, then reached for it again and replenished her glass.

"Well, I think everything is ready," said Erin, standing near the table and looking in the direction of the living room, trying to smile. "Shall we eat?"

Her father stood up and motioned for Will to walk in front of him to the table and select his seat.

There was a place setting at each end of the table and one on each side, so Will thought it best to leave the head of the table for Erin's father and the other end for her grandmother. He walked around to the place setting between the table and the wall, the one that was hardest to access, and sat down.

Erin's father took his place on Will's left, and Erin helped her grandmother take a seat on Will's other side.

Once her grandmother was seated, Erin took her own place in the last chair, across from Will. She glanced briefly at Will, and he nodded at her reassuringly.

"Dad, do you want to say gra—"

Erin didn't get a chance to finish her question before her father interrupted her with his own.

"What is that stuff on your mouth?"

Will could see the blood drain from Erin's face as she froze, then brushed at her cheeks with her fingers.

"Not your cheeks. Your lips. Why are you wearing such dark lipstick?"

Erin's rouged lips parted, and he could see her carefully consider her reply. "Aunt Julie sent this lipstick to me last Christmas. I thought I would give it a try."

"Well, it makes you look like a prostitute. You should wipe it off."

Will's first instinct was to punch the old man in the face, but he kept his clenched fists in his lap as he looked at Erin. Her face grew red, and she pressed her perfect lips together as her brows knotted in anger and embarrassment.

Her grandmother, with a sympathetic look, held out her napkin for Erin to take, presumably to wipe off her lipstick. For the first time, Will was disappointed in the old woman.

Not knowing what to do or say to help Erin without making matters worse, Will simply sat there, staring at each of them in turn, feeling powerless.

Erin's grandmother leaned toward Erin and extended the napkin again in her direction. "Here, Erin," she whispered. "Take it."

With a look of proud defiance, Erin turned away

from her grandmother and the napkin.

Tilting her chin up, so that she was looking somewhere above Will's head, Erin finally said, "I need some air. Please start eating without me."

Then she pushed her chair back from the table and took three quick steps to the door, opened it, and disappeared out into the hallway.

Will could hear her footsteps grow fainter. She didn't go out the front door of the building as he had expected; she was headed toward the back.

Without a word, Will rose from the table and followed her.

****

Erin ran past the stairs that led up to Will's apartment and sped down the hall to the back of the building, pushing through the fire exit as tears of humiliation rolled down her cheeks. She had no destination in mind, she just had to leave that apartment. She had to get away.

How could he embarrass her like that? And in front of a guest? In front of Will?

Her father always spoke his mind without thinking of how his words made others feel. He was completely insensitive. And completely selfish. Her mother would never have spoken to her like that. Never in a million years. She might have taken her aside and told her that the shade of lipstick wasn't the best color for her complexion or that she liked the lighter tones better. More likely, though, she would have told Erin she was beautiful wearing that lipstick, because her mother had always seen the best in Erin. Always.

At the thought of her mother, more tears washed over Erin's face. God, how she missed her mother.

"Erin?"

Erin jumped at the sound of Will's voice and turned away from the dumpster she had been staring at to look at him. "Will! You scared the crap out of me!"

She tried to surreptitiously wipe the tears that had wet both her cheeks, but she knew it was obvious she'd been crying.

She cleared her throat and straightened her back. "You didn't have to come out here. And you didn't have to listen to my grandmother if she was the one who told you to follow me. I'm fine."

Even to Erin's own ears the pain and self-pity in her voice was as clear as a bell. How pathetic she was, a grown woman—an attorney at a high-priced law firm—crying next to a dumpster over getting her feelings hurt by her thoughtless father. It was a wonder Will could even bear to look at her.

Almost in response to her thoughts, Will took a few steps closer, until he was standing just inches away.

"Nobody told me to follow you. I was worried about you."

"Well, I'm fine," she snapped. "I'm not a child. Despite how my father might speak to me. I can handle myself. I don't need you to feel sorry for me."

Her voice cracked, betraying her emotions, and she looked up into Will's eyes to gauge his reaction. All she saw was kindness and genuine compassion.

"I'm sorry." She sighed, tears welling up once again. "You were being nice, and I'm being a jerk. You should go back and eat. I'll come inside in a minute. I just needed to calm down. I'm fine now."

Will reached up with both hands to touch the hair that fell on either side of her face. Erin's breath caught in her chest as his warm fingers innocently brushed the tips of her ears.

"I like your hair down," he said in a low voice. Then he touched her lips briefly with the pad of his index finger. "And I like your lipstick. But I have to admit I like it when you wear your hair up, too, and when you're not wearing any lipstick at all."

"Maybe you're just easy to please," she whispered, feeling on the verge of passing out.

"Maybe you're just beautiful."

She could see the shadow of a thought pass across Will's face, and his brow furrowed for the briefest of moments.

His hands slid slowly from her face to rest safely at his side once more. "Shall we walk a bit, then, get some air as you suggested?"

Erin couldn't speak. She just nodded and tried to breathe, her skin still tingling where he'd touched her. He could have asked her to go get a root canal with him, and she would have happily offered to drive.

Will walked around the bay of dumpsters they had been standing in front of to the wooded area behind the rear parking lot. She followed him through a maze of scraggly trees, careful not to trip and fall. The land sloped downward, and before long they came to a clearing with a small creek running through it.

"I didn't know there was a creek back here," said Erin. "This must be Briar Creek. I pass over this creek every time I come to my grandmother's from work."

"Yes," replied Will, sounding a little distant. "This city has so many creeks. People used the creeks as their source of water for cooking, bathing, washing clothes. A long time ago, that is."

They walked alongside the water, moving in the same direction that the water flowed. Erin couldn't help noticing how well their strides matched. Or how close their hands were.

"Do you own this land along the creek?" she asked, her mouth suddenly dry.

"Some of it. My family bought much of this land from another family who owned it in the early 1900s. That other family had run across hard times, and land was the only thing they had to sell. My family paid them well for it. You could call it a charitable purchase."

Erin tried to focus on the sound of the water flowing carelessly over and around the rocks. Taking a long breath, she gazed up past the budding branches of the trees around them to the clear blue sky.

"It's beautiful," she said finally, feeling more relaxed.

Will stopped near a large, mossy rock and turned to look at the creek.

"This is where she died." He heaved a sigh, then lowered his head. Will didn't have to say who "she" was—Erin knew. His pain was palpable; he still mourned the loss, and Erin wanted nothing more than to wrap her arms around him and whisper in his ear that everything would be okay. Instead, she clasped her hands together in front of her, watching as he raised his eyes to the water once more. "They found her here, face down, in the creek. The girl I told you about. The one I loved, a long time ago."

He spoke casually, with no real emotion in his voice. It was as though he had just commented on the unseasonably warm weather they were having.

"Did she really drown? Right here, in the creek?" Erin knew it was a stupid question even as she said the words. The grief was written on Will's face.

He nodded in response.

Erin hesitated. "What happened?" she finally asked, hoping she wasn't making a mistake by asking him for more.

He didn't answer right away, his eyes still fixed on the creek bed, making Erin wonder if, in his mind, he could see his girlfriend there.

Drawing in a deep breath, Will began walking again, and Erin followed.

"Everyone said she was taking a stroll and just slipped and fell in. It was the middle of the night, and no one realized what had occurred until the next morning. But I don't think that's exactly how it happened."

"What do you think happened?" she asked, softly.

Will looked at her, almost as though he had forgotten she was there and had been talking to himself. Then he laughed quietly and shook his head.

"I've never talked to anyone about that night," he replied. "Not even my sisters. In any case, it doesn't matter. It was a long time ago."

He smiled, and Erin knew it was for her benefit. In a way, his joyless smile was more heartbreaking to see than no expression at all. "I'm sorry," he said, looking down at the path, "I've added my pain to yours. I keep forgetting how you take all these things onto yourself. Let me lighten your burden now. Tell me what the story is with your father. What happened between you?"

If Will hadn't just bared his soul to her, Erin would have found a way to change the subject with her answer. She had no desire to think about her father right now, let alone talk about him. But she couldn't deny Will an honest answer.

She shook her head, trying to figure out where to begin. "You've seen how he is." It was the best she could come up with, despite her good intentions.

Will turned them around to walk back in the direction of the apartment building.

"Yes, he's not the most agreeable man, but there's something else behind your feelings toward him. You've alluded to it yourself."

"Yes," she replied. "I have. You have a way of drawing things out of me."

"It's my disarming smile and direct line of questioning," he teased.

"It's very effective. You'd make a good litigator." She sighed, and it occurred to her that very few people knew what she was about to tell him. "He cheated on my mother. With his secretary. God, it's so cliché."

"Did your mother know?" asked Will.

"She found out about it. The crazy woman he was sleeping with had a bout of conscience or something and called my mother to tell her. My mom confronted him about it, and he confessed to everything. He said he still loved my mother. He said he just felt distant from her, like she didn't love him anymore, and he had tried to distract himself from that nagging feeling by sleeping with his secretary." Erin laughed, remembering how she had answered the phone when that woman had called, thinking it was her friend calling. She remembered the woman asking for Mrs. Dovetree. She remembered watching as her mother's face fell listening to the woman's confession. "What a bunch of crap."

Will walked with her in silence. She knew he was waiting for her to continue.

"You know what's crazier?"

Will shook his head.

"It was my mother who ended up feeling guilty about the whole thing. She forgave him, as though nothing had happened, and she poured even more of herself into doing things for him. The dinners she cooked got more elaborate. She cleaned the house more thoroughly, matched everything from the towels to the silverware. She did everything she could to make him happy, even though it was he who had hurt her. I never understood that. If I were her, I would have left him alone on the floor crying so that he could face the consequences of the decision he made to sleep with someone other than his wife."

"Did you ever ask her about it?"

"Yeah, I did. About a week after it all went down."

"What did she say?"

Erin sighed again. It had been twelve years, and yet the scene was as clear in her mind as though it had happened yesterday.

"She said that my father loved her, and that sometimes when people are hurt they do stupid things that they regret later on. She said that love was a choice, that you decide you're going to be with someone and you stay with them despite their faults, despite their mistakes."

"She sounds very wise."

Erin pushed down the anger she felt—toward her father for cheating and toward her mother for accepting it. Sometimes she didn't know whose actions angered her more.

"My father didn't deserve her," she said softly. "He didn't deserve her forgiveness."

They came to the point along the creek where they could either keep going or take the path going back up to the parking lot of Will's apartment complex, and Erin stopped.

Will looked at her with a tenderness that made her heart stop beating and brushed the hair out of her eyes. "Not all things can be forgiven, can they?"

"I wonder about that sometimes," she managed to reply, her body frozen under his gaze.

Will's hand lingered, his thumb swiping at an errant tear that still clung to her cheek.

Erin focused on breathing, hypnotized by the shimmering gold specks in Will's eyes that reflected the sunlight breaking through the trees behind them. His face came closer, and she held her breath, waiting. Hoping. But then he pulled away and she realized it had only been her imagination that had allowed her to think her grandmother's landlord was about to kiss her.

"We should probably get back and enjoy our cold ham," said Erin, torn between exhilaration and disappointment as she started walking up the path, away from the creek. She could hear him fall into step behind her.

They walked to the edge of the parking lot in silence and continued across, approaching the back door of the building.

Stopping abruptly, Erin turned to face him. "Hey, Will?"

"Yes, Erin?"

"Thank you for letting me dump all my problems

on you. I'm sure this isn't what you had in mind when you accepted by grandmother's invitation."

Will gave her a radiant smile, and her heart threatened to leap out of her chest. "Someone once told me that we all need someone to talk to. I'm glad to be that someone for you."

He was standing so close to her, she could feel his breath in her hair. Without thinking, Erin reached up and wrapped her arms around him. Almost immediately, he had pulled her closer, holding her tightly, keeping her there, against his chest.

Erin closed her eyes and turned her head to rest her cheek just below Will's shoulder, the clean smell of soap enveloping her, the warmth of his body thrilling her. It was everything she had imagined and then some. She didn't care that he had said they were only friends. She didn't care that he didn't feel for her what she felt for him. *This*—this complete and utter contentment—this was what Erin had been searching for all her life. Even as these thoughts ran through her mind, Will's hands rubbed her back slowly, moving lower and pulling her harder against him. New sensations sparked within her, hinting at the wonderful possibility that *this* was perhaps only the tip of the iceberg. That maybe there was something more.

As suddenly as it had started, the moment ended when Will's hands stopped moving, and he loosened his hold on her. Reluctantly, Erin did the same.

"Come on," he said, his voice deep and resonant. "Let's get inside and see if there's any food left for us."

He opened the door for her and she stepped into the building, still glowing from the memory of his arms around her. They walked down the hall in silence to her grandmother's apartment. Inside, her grandmother was huddled over the sink washing something and her father sat on the couch reading a newspaper. He didn't look up.

Erin could hear Will make small talk with her father as she went over to stand near her grandmother and took over washing the few items left in the sink. Whatever feelings Will had toward her father after what had transpired at the dinner table and what she had told him outside, he hid them well.

The food was all still sitting there on the table, along with her plate and Will's. She carefully arranged the ham and vegetables on each plate and popped them in the microwave for a minute. When the plates had warmed up, she added some salad and a roll, then looked over at Will to see if she could get his attention. Her heart skipped a beat when she realized he was already looking at her, even as he was speaking to her father. The thought that he had been watching her the whole time made her blush, and she quickly looked away, trying to hide her smile.

What was going on between them? Will had told her in no uncertain terms that he didn't want to romance her. But then he brushed her hair from her face, touched her lips, told her she was beautiful, and held her like he didn't want to let go. It had to mean something, didn't it?

Erin set one of the plates down on the table where Will had been sitting and took her own seat across from his as he came over to join her, still exchanging friendly words with her father.

She looked at him again and smiled, wondering how she could find her way into his arms again.

Chapter Sixteen

Monday proved to be the longest day of Erin's life, and it had nothing to do with the appeal brief she was writing. She was distracted—she couldn't focus. Instead of the computer screen in front of her, Erin's gaze kept going to the window and the perfectly blue sky and story-book white clouds beyond it, her mind, in turn, drifting to Will and how she felt in his arms.

Exhaling in frustration, Erin pushed away from her desk and stood up. How could she get anything done with these thoughts in her head?

Maybe it was because she didn't know exactly what was going on between them. Were they really just friends? Was that what Will wanted? Maybe it was the not knowing that was driving her crazy.

She had to talk to him. She had to know one way or another.

Erin was standing by the window, staring down at the street below, when her office phone rang. Immediately hoping it might be Will, she looked over at the display to see who was calling, only to be just as immediately disappointed to see Blake's number.

Not that she minded talking to Blake. It was just that Blake wasn't Will.

It had been close to two months since Erin had spoken to Blake, and with that realization came a pang of guilt for having avoided him since their lunch rendezvous.

She picked up the phone.

"Hi, Blake," she greeted, hoping he wasn't upset with her.

"Hey, Erin, how's it going?"

Blake sounded like his normal, happy-go-lucky self, and Erin took that as a good sign. "Pretty good, can't complain. What's new with you?"

"Oh, you know how it is, being single and handsome in this hopping metropolis of ours. Well, single and gorgeous in your case."

Yup, he was fine.

"Yeah, I'm just fending off the offers, left and right," Erin replied, deciding to play along.

"Well, you're a special case, my dear."

She snorted. "I'm a special case, all right. More like a head case. So, is this one of those calls where you tell me you've met someone amazing or where you tell me you're back on the market and that I should hurry up and get me some?"

"The offer for you to come get you some is a standing offer. Susan would totally understand."

Erin smiled at his revelation. "Susan? So, you *do* have a new girlfriend. And apparently, she's pretty high class." Erin had known she wasn't the right person for Blake, but she still felt bad brushing him off. After all, she knew too well what it was like to want someone who didn't want you the same way.

Blake laughed. "Yes, Susan is my girlfriend, although not all that new. We've been dating for a month."

"Wow, that must be a record for you," teased Erin.

"It may well be. But I don't keep track. You'd like

her. She is high class, and she wouldn't let me have a freebie with just anyone. Like I said, you're a special case. It would be for a good cause."

"I see." It was good to have the old Blake back. "Is she a lawyer?"

"No, a teacher. Kindergarten."

"Really?" Erin chuckled. "No wonder she knows how to handle you."

Blake laughed heartily on the other side of the line, and it was contagious. "There may be some truth to that," he agreed. "What about you? You sound different. Anything, or anyone, I should know about?"

Erin's laughter was cut short by surprise at his question. "What do you mean? I sound different?"

"So, there is something going on!" She could hear Blake clap his hands. "I had a hunch," he continued. "There's an edge to your voice. You sound a little more…mysterious than usual."

"I think you're being ridiculous, Blake."

"Look at how defensive you're being! Come on, you can tell me. I tell you about all my exploits."

"Yes, and I really never want to hear about any of them."

"Please, Erin," he pleaded. "You know how exciting it would be for me to finally hear one of your stories? You wouldn't deprive me of that, now, would you?"

Erin had to admit he had a point. The relationship conversations had been pretty much one-sided for as long as they had known each other.

"All right," she relented. "There's not much to tell, but I'll tell you. First, though, you have to give me the real reason you called."

"The real reason? What makes you think there is any reason other than for me to hear the sound of your sweet voice?"

Erin almost snorted in response. "I know you, Blake. You need something from me."

Blake laughed again. "Well, now that you mention it, I did volunteer to chair an inter-firm pro bono event to prepare wills for teachers, and I need some bodies to fill seats. The more attractive, the better."

It was good to have the old Blake back.

"I'm not that kind of attorney," she replied. "I prepare patent applications, not wills."

"It's easy, Erin. There's a software program, you ask the teachers some questions, you fill in the answers they give you, then the program spits out the will. Really, a monkey could do it. Well, a monkey with a law license."

She paused to consider.

"It's for a good cause," he added in a sing-song voice, "and it's not during the workday, so you don't have to sacrifice any billable hours. Plus, the Partners' Committee is going to want to see community involvement when they're considering you for partner, you know."

Erin didn't care about impressing anyone at her firm. If she agreed to do this, she would be doing it because her friend had asked. "How much time are we talking about?"

"Four hours, five tops. On a Saturday. Not this coming Saturday, the one after. What do you say?"

"All right," she finally replied. "But don't think I don't know why you're doing this. Trying to impress your kindergarten teacher girlfriend, no doubt."

"Nah. I've already impressed her, if you know what I mean."

Erin shook her head, grinning despite herself. "You're so predictable—and disgusting."

"You don't know the half of it. Now it's your turn. Tell me about this guy you're seeing."

"I'm not seeing anyone." Erin glanced up as someone walked by her office. "Hold on a second—let me close my door."

Erin put the receiver down for a moment and got up to quietly shut the door to her office. Sitting back down, she put the phone to her ear once more. "You still there?"

"Of course," replied Blake. "You've got me on the edge of my seat here!"

She took a deep breath. Who knew, maybe Blake would have some good advice for her. He certainly had more experience with these things than she did. "Like I said, I'm not seeing anyone really. But there's a guy I'm kind of interested in. I really enjoy talking to him and spending time with him, and I find him attractive…"

"Hold up—are you talking about me?"

"No!" She would have thrown something at him if he were in front of her.

Blake laughed freely on the other end of the line, apparently finding her vehement denial amusing. "You're being so clinical about this, Erin. You've met a guy, and your hormones are finally kicking in. Thank God! I was beginning to think there was something wrong with you."

"You see, this is why I didn't want to tell you anything."

"Okay, okay," he choked out between continued bouts of laughter, "I'm sorry. Who is this guy, anyway?"

Erin sighed. "He's my grandmother's landlord."

"And you've been out with him a few times?"

She chewed on her lower lip for a moment before answering. "Well, I don't know if you'd call it going out. I guess one of them was a date—he called me and invited me to his place for dinner."

"You slept with him! Damn, girl! Good job!"

"Blake!" she whisper-screamed at him, feeling as though everyone in the office could hear them. "I did not sleep with him! Don't you know me at all?"

Blake laughed again. He was clearly enjoying himself. "Okay, so you've spent some time with this guy, and you like him. I'm assuming he likes you, too, so what's the problem?"

"I don't know what the problem is, Blake, or if there even is a problem. Sometimes I feel like he's interested in me, you know, romantically, but then he's outright told me that he doesn't want anything like that. Almost like he doesn't want to lead me on. But then he says stuff that makes me melt, and, I don't know. It's very confusing!"

"I see," replied Blake. His tone was surprisingly thoughtful. "You haven't told him about your whole no sex before marriage thing, have you?"

"Well, yes. It kind of came up while we were talking at his place."

It sounded like Blake had dropped the phone, and there was some shuffling as he picked it back up again. Or maybe he was banging his head against the wall.

"Erin, Erin, no! Why would you do that?"

"What do you mean, why? I told you—it just came up. What did you want me to do—lie to him?"

"Erin, have I taught you nothing? The only thing a guy is thinking about when he looks at a girl he's attracted to is how to get her in bed. Hell, most guys think about that when they're looking at any girl, regardless of whether they're attracted to her or not."

"He's not like that," she protested.

"Of course he is. He's a guy, and he's got a pulse. Believe me, he's thinking about it. And now you've gone and told him you're a virgin and intend to stay that way. So, the only chance he's got to fulfill his fantasy of sleeping with you is to marry you. That kind of kills the fantasy."

"Blake, you're sick."

"Erin, I'm giving you great insight here. Guys are afraid of virgins. Not me, I love them. That's why you and I get along so well—"

"Blake..."

"—but most guys are afraid of them. Because let's face it, virgins are a little weird."

"I'm not weird!" she raised her voice, forgetting for a moment that she didn't want the whole office hearing their conversation.

"Yes, you are, Erin. In a very endearing way. But the point is that now he's afraid of you. He doesn't want to push you into getting it on with him—although I'm sure he wants to—because he doesn't want you to freak out after it happens and go all psycho on him."

Erin just sighed, tired of defending herself and Will. Blake, of course, took that as license to continue.

"What I'm saying is that you have to give him a sign. Send up a signal. He'll throw you a line."

"That's a Billy Joel song."

"And it's right on point. You have to make the next move, Erin. *You* have to come on to *him*. You have to tell him you're jonesing for a piece of your grandma's landlord. He'll get the picture."

"Well, that's fantastic, Blake. Thank you very much for your astute observations on my situation. I'm so glad I confided in you."

Blake pretended that her sarcasm was lost on him. "You're welcome. Are you trying to get me off the phone?"

"Yes," replied Erin. "I've got an appeal brief to draft and file before the end of the day today."

"Okay, good luck with that. And good luck with this guy, Erin. This'll be really good for you. You're blossoming into a woman right before my eyes."

"Remind me never to talk to you again."

Blake laughed. "All right, but I'll see you a week from Saturday at the library, down the street from our offices. Eight o'clock."

Erin cringed. "Eight in the morning? You forgot to mention that part."

"Did I? Well, it's for a good cause. It's for your good friend and confidante, me."

After their goodbyes, Erin hung up, feeling like she needed a shower.

As the day wore on, though, she thought about what Blake had said, but in a more reasonable, less skeezy light. Was Will worried about pressuring her into doing something she wasn't ready for? Not necessarily even sex, but just being in a relationship? Maybe he *was* waiting for her to make the next move.

Later that night, as she was getting ready for bed,

Erin had an epiphany. Maybe *she* could ask *him* out on a date. That was the gist of Blake's advice, after all, wasn't it?

She looked over at her cell phone sitting on the nightstand.

Why was she waiting for Will to call her? Every interaction they'd had so far had come about by chance, by him asking her, by her grandmother interfering, or by some combination of those forces.

Maybe it was time for Erin to call him.

Yes, that's exactly what she would do, but not tonight. It was only the day after their wonderfully disastrous Easter gathering. She didn't want to seem too smitten. Plus, she needed time to plan it out.

On Wednesday afternoon, as Erin continued to think about her plan, she began wondering if perhaps what she was really doing was *over*thinking. With a discouraged sigh, she got up from her desk and took a few steps to the window to stretch her legs. Her office overlooked the south side of the city, and the building complex next door was relatively new. Aptly called "the Epicentre," the perimeter of the complex was lined with stores, mostly restaurants, and in the center was an open-air courtyard. An outdoor stage formed the centerpiece for the third floor, and every Thursday during the late spring and summer months some band or another played there. The event was called "Live after Five," and the music and laughter drifted up to her on the thirty-seventh floor every week, making her want to stop working. She had heard it again for the first time last Thursday, which meant that the season had already started.

That was it! She would ask Will to go with her to

"Live after Five" and see what he'd say.

As Erin's hand reached for the phone, she stopped herself. She had just seen him three days ago. Wasn't it too soon to be asking to see him again? Besides, didn't she need some time to think about the wisdom of all this?

Driving home from work that night, Erin decided she'd had enough time to think about it, and who cared if it was too soon, anyway? She *did* want to see him, and so what if he knew it? Wasn't that the whole point of asking someone out on a date?

Annoyed at herself, Erin shook her head. She was a grown woman, not some freshman in high school. She could do this.

When she got home, she plopped herself down on the couch, cell phone in hand. It was time.

She made the call. Will picked up on the second ring.

"Hello?"

"Hi, Will, it's Erin."

"Erin, hi." He sounded happy to hear her voice.

Encouraged by his tone, she continued. "So, what are you up to on a Wednesday night, Mr. Abbott?"

"Nothing too exciting, Ms. Dovetree," he replied, imitating her formality. "Just finishing up some dinner. You?"

"I just got home and am debating what hodgepodge of leftovers I should heat up for myself."

"The possibilities are endless, I'm sure."

There was a pause. This was the point in a conversation where the person who called stated their business. Erin took a breath to steady herself.

"Are your plans just as exciting for tomorrow

night?" she began.

"Indeed, they are. Why? Are you prepared to make me an alternate proposal?"

She should have known asking Will out wouldn't be hard. Will always made things so easy and comfortable. It was one of the many things she really liked about him.

"Perhaps. I was thinking…"

"Sure, I'm in."

Erin grinned. "You haven't even heard the proposal yet."

"You're right. I should confirm a few points before I accept. First, will your grandmother be there?"

Her smile grew wider. "No."

"I'm assuming your dad's not coming?"

Erin chuckled. "Nope."

"But you'll be there?"

"Yup."

"Well then I'm in."

"Great!" said Erin, trying to sound natural. "You're easy."

"Where do you want me to be?"

"I was thinking it would probably be best if you met me uptown. There's a parking deck at the Epicentre, the building across the street from where I work. They have music starting at five on the outdoor stage there. We could grab dinner or something afterward, depending on how long we want to stay. We can just play it by ear."

"Sounds fantastic. I'll meet you in the lobby of your building. Does that work?"

Erin couldn't stop smiling. "That works perfectly."

"So, I'll see you tomorrow night?"

"Yes, tomorrow night." She paused, racking her brain for a witty remark. "Have a good night, Will." It was the best she could come up with.

"Good night, Erin."

His voice sounded low and sultry, and Erin wished she could find something to say to keep him on the phone a little while longer. But she just repeated, "Goodnight," then hung up.

The smile didn't leave her face as she sat on the couch for a few minutes, thinking about what had just happened, and what might happen when she saw Will on Thursday. Closing her eyes and letting out a dreamy sigh, she got up to choose her leftovers. "Thank you, Blake," she whispered as she opened the refrigerator.

****

Will waited to confirm that Erin had ended the call before setting the phone down. For a second, he wondered if she could have possibly heard his thoughts the last three days since they'd seen each other. It wasn't such a far-fetched theory, all things considered.

The fact was that he couldn't get Erin out of his head. Any time he heard a car pull into the lot or a door click closed downstairs, he wondered if she was in the building on an unexpected visit to see her grandmother—or maybe even him.

It was foolish; Will knew that. But apparently, he was the biggest of fools. He thought about how close he had come to kissing her on Sunday. She had looked so sad and broken after how her father had treated her. All Will had wanted to do was dry her tear-streaked cheeks and kiss the lipstick off her mouth. He chuckled as he wondered what Erin's father and grandmother would have thought if Will and Erin had come back to the apartment wearing the same offending shade.

But now Will was taking it one step further. He was encouraging Erin to pursue him. He had practically asked her out just now. How did he think this was going to end?

What was done was done, he reasoned. He wouldn't back out now, but he would be careful. He would not let Erin believe the time they spent together was anything more than just two friends enjoying each other's company.

If only Will could believe that himself.

Chapter Seventeen

Erin chose her clothes carefully the following morning. She needed something appropriate for work, yet enticing enough for a night out on the town with the handsome and pleasantly enigmatic Will Abbott. She settled on a dark brown skirt and a tan short-sleeved top with a scoop neckline.

She had a couple of phone calls scheduled for the day, and two filing deadlines to boot, so the day passed rather quickly, much to Erin's relief. She called it quits at a quarter to five, shut down her computer, and made a quick stop at the ladies' room on her way out to apply some lip gloss and check on her hair. She had tried to curl it that morning, but after running her hands through it all day it was now hopelessly flat. Unable to revive it, Erin finally got out her backup hair tie and put her hair in a low ponytail.

As soon as she stepped off the elevator downstairs, Erin saw Will sitting on one of the cushioned benches in front of the security desk in the lobby. He wasn't yet looking in her direction, which gave Erin a brief opportunity to admire what she saw. And there was much to admire—his charcoal tee-shirt stretched over his broad shoulders and complemented his skin tone and dark hair very nicely. A dark pair of jeans completed the outfit, and she was sure those fit him just as well, although she couldn't confirm quite yet.

As though sensing her evaluation, Will turned to look in her direction and flashed her an irresistible grin. A wave of giddiness washed over her as a result.

Erin raised her hand in greeting, bravely moving toward him. "Hi," she said as he rose from the bench.

"Hi, Erin."

She thought he was about to say more, but then his lips pressed together and he just smiled.

"I'm sorry I kept you waiting." It wasn't like them to have awkward pauses in their conversation. She wondered what he was thinking.

"Don't apologize," Will replied. "I didn't know what traffic would be like, and I didn't want to be late." Again, he looked at her, as though he wanted to say more.

Thankfully, the first strains of music entered the building through the double doors that people were entering and leaving through, giving her something else to say.

"I guess it's five o'clock." Erin looked briefly in the direction of the music, finding it difficult to keep her eyes off Will. "I've wanted to go to this thing ever since I moved here. Thanks for coming with me."

"I hope it's worth the wait," he replied, smiling.

"I'm sure it will be." She didn't know if he was just talking about the music. She hoped he wasn't.

"Shall we then?" He gestured toward the double doors, and she nodded as they started walking in that direction.

"Did you get any invalid patents issued today?" asked Will, teasingly.

"I only get valid patents issued, Mr. Abbott," she replied, trying not to look too obviously elated at their banter. "And you, did you evict any unsuspecting tenants today?"

"They all had fair notice."

Erin laughed, not caring that he could keep a straight face longer than she could.

Will opened the door and held it for her as she walked through it, the music louder now that they were outside.

"I think it's upstairs where they have an outdoor stage. That's what it looks like from my office window, in any case."

"So, you sit in your office every day and stare out your window at all the young people in Charlotte having fun without you?"

"No," she replied, grinning, "not every day. Only on Thursdays."

They walked up the stairs and approached the stage, and there were more and more people around them as they moved closer to the source of the music.

"You look really nice, by the way," he said after a pause. "I had wanted to tell you that when you first came off the elevator."

Butterflies fluttered in her stomach. "I'm not even wearing my hooker lipstick today."

Will burst out laughing. She was glad she had surprised him with her reply, and she couldn't help laughing with him.

When they had both recovered, Will said, "You want to get closer to the stage? It looks like there's a relatively clear spot up front, there."

"Okay," she replied, and Will started wading through the sea of people that had filled in around them while Erin did her best to stay right behind him. Feeling jostled by the dancing bodies they passed, and worried they might get separated, she reached up and grabbed hold of the fabric of his sleeve. She figured it was a platonic enough way to keep him next to her without actually touching him.

As they got to their destination, it dawned on Erin that everyone around the stage was dancing, which meant that the same would be expected of her very soon.

Will turned to face her, and she reluctantly let go of his shirt.

Suddenly, she wondered why on earth she had suggested a date that involved dancing.

"Will, I have to warn you. While I love the idea of dancing, when I actually have to do it, I'm pretty sure I look like a dying moose."

He laughed, already beginning to move his shoulders and his hips to the beat. She should have known he would be a good dancer. "Come on," he said, motioning for her to join him. "I'll admit I've never seen a moose die, but I'm quite certain it would look nothing like you dancing."

Will looked completely comfortable standing there, dancing. He looked comfortable anywhere. That was probably the sexiest thing about him.

He raised his eyebrows and nodded his head slowly, encouraging her to do something other than just stand there. She had no choice.

Letting out a resigned sigh, Erin began moving her hips and feet in her trademark dance moves—just enough so that she couldn't be accused of standing still. Will smiled approvingly, and her cheeks flamed.

Pretending she needed to focus on her dancing—if

indeed her random flailing could be called that—Erin lowered her eyes to look at the ground around their feet. Again, she questioned the wisdom of inviting Will to an activity that required them to stand close to each other with nothing to do but gyrate their hips and stare into each other's eyes. At least when they'd met for lunch or dinner, or tea even, they could talk to each other. Talking to Will was easy and natural, and it didn't make her feel like a coil of nerves about to spring out of control.

Three songs in with no noticeable change in the concrete to report, Erin decided she was being ridiculous. Not to mention rude. Slowly, she raised her eyes to his face. He was looking intently at her—had he been doing that the whole time?

"Hi," he said, though she couldn't hear his voice over the music.

"Hi," she mouthed back.

With the sun low in the sky behind her, Will's brown eyes seemed to glow brighter, the lighter flecks sparkling like gold flakes. His gaze never wavered from hers, and although they stood about a foot apart, her whole body tingled with awareness, as though his face were hovering over hers, poised for a kiss.

Suddenly, she prayed for a slow dance—a reason for him to come even closer, wrap his hands around her waist, and pull her into him. Erin thought of the hug they'd shared in the parking lot on Easter. She remembered how solid and warm he'd felt, and how tightly he'd held her. Though they weren't touching now, her body grew warm under his gaze. It was his eyes that held her, the intensity of his look wrapping itself around her and holding her close so that she couldn't move away. Not that she wanted to.

Whatever enchantment Will had cast apparently made her lose track of time, because suddenly there was no more music and everyone around them started moving in different directions, leaving the dance area. The set was over.

With ears still ringing from the loud music and her heart beating erratically in her chest, Erin took a step back from Will, trying to regain her balance. Closing the distance between them again, Will touched her arm and leaned in. "Do you want to get some dinner?"

Erin could only nod in agreement.

Still surrounded by a horde of people, Erin grasped Will's sleeve again, afraid they would be separated. Sure enough, only a few steps from where they had been standing, a particularly zealous couple bumped into her sideways and made her lose her grip. As she reached up to find his sleeve again, Will's hand intercepted hers.

It was a much more efficient way to travel together in such a large crowd, Erin told herself, trying to ignore the electric feeling of his palm rubbing against hers. His hand was so warm, so solid, and it fit with hers so perfectly. The sensation was nothing short of wonderful.

As they got farther from the stage and made their way down to the street level, the crowd thinned. Still, Will kept a firm grip on her hand. Erin, feeling lightheaded and heavy-footed as a result, concentrated her efforts on not stumbling.

The two of them came out of the building complex onto one of the two main streets that intersected at the center of uptown. Without discussion, they walked a block west then turned right on the cross street, going north. The air was warm, but there was a pleasant breeze that made it a perfect evening for a stroll. Then again, hail could have been falling from the sky, and Erin wouldn't have minded one bit.

Caught up in the pleasure of walking hand-in-hand with Will, it wasn't until they started heading north of center city that Erin thought to ask where they were going.

Will laughed in response. "I was wondering how far I could take you before you would ask. There used to be a Cuban place up here that I really liked. I'm not sure it's still in business, though—it's been a while since I was last there."

"Are you talking about Havana?"

"Yes, I think that's what it was called. Have you been there?"

"I have," replied Erin, her mouth already starting to water. "It's one of my favorite restaurants in the city. I haven't been there myself since last fall, though, so I'm not sure if it's still open. Places come and go, unfortunately. Even good places."

"Well, let's hope for the best."

They walked the next two blocks in comfortable silence, still holding hands, until they came to a crosswalk, when Will let go to press the button for the "walk" signal. Erin reluctantly allowed him to have his hand back and feigned nonchalance by redoing her ponytail.

The restaurant was still there, and Erin and Will, having beat the crowds by a few minutes, were quickly seated at a table for two.

Erin observed Will as he picked up his menu and

remarked to Erin about a couple of the menu items that he recognized from the last time he was there. She watched as he asked the waitress about the specials and, after consulting with Erin, ordered an appetizer. He was so easy to be with. He was so calm, so in control, and so exciting at the same time.

She declined his suggestion of a glass of wine with dinner, worried about driving home after consuming any alcohol, but she took a sip of her water, a little buzzed all the same. Tracing the beads of condensation that were forming on the outside of her glass, thinking about what it meant that he had come out with her tonight, that he had held her hand, Erin stole a glance at the handsome man who sat across the table. She found Will looking at her with that same intent gaze he'd had while they were dancing, his mouth turned up slightly at the corners.

"What are you thinking about, Miss Dovetree?" he asked when her eyes met his.

"A lot of things," she answered, her mouth suddenly dry.

"I know you can't help but tell me, now that I've asked. It's in your nature."

"This is true." She swallowed the lump in her throat, knowing what she was about to say would change the course of the evening, one way or another. "Well, as a preliminary matter, I'm thinking I'm really glad you came out with me tonight. I'm having a great time."

"Good. I am, too. What else?"

"Nothing, really. I'm just happy. And..." She paused, reconsidering for a moment whether to continue. He smiled at her, and she knew she couldn't stop herself now, even if she tried. "Well," she continued, "I'm just wondering what's going to happen next."

At that remark, Will was quiet. His lips were still curved in the shape of a smile, but the joy had left his face.

For some reason, his changed expression, even before she had even said anything really telling about how she felt about him, made Erin angry. It made her not care how she sounded or what Will would think. "I liked holding your hand," she said, wanting him to know, if somehow he hadn't figured it out already. Wanting to know his feelings, in return.

"Yes," he replied. His voice was flat—he had shut down, and she wanted to lash out at him for it.

"Yes to what? Yes, you liked holding my hand, too, or yes you know I liked holding your hand?"

"Yes, both."

"How about you tell me what you're thinking now, Will. What you're feeling. Because I think it's pretty clear how I feel about you, and yet I'm not really sure where you stand. Don't worry—I'm a big girl. I can handle it."

Will was visibly uncomfortable, and Erin didn't care anymore. She had to know what was going on inside his head. He said things to her that made her think he had a romantic interest in her, and she couldn't imagine that the electricity that sparked when they touched was one-sided.

"Tell me, Will," she said, softly this time. "It's okay, whatever it is."

"Erin," he began, his voice low, "I have feelings for you. I won't deny it. You are a beautiful woman.

And you're witty, and intelligent, and kind. I like being with you. I can't help it, I do."

"Okay, that's good."

"But that doesn't mean this will or should go anywhere. You and me, it's just not a good idea. It wouldn't work."

Erin tried hard to keep her breathing steady as she fixed her gaze on him. She took a slow sip of water, and a plate of calamari was placed on the table between them, their waitress having appeared out of thin air.

"Your dinner will be out in just a couple more minutes," the waitress announced pleasantly, oblivious to their conversation. Will smiled and thanked her; Erin nodded politely.

When the waitress was gone, Will motioned to Erin to help herself to some of the calamari. She picked up her fork and pushed three of them onto her plate, although she had lost her appetite. She watched as he did the same. "Why don't you think it would work?" she finally asked.

As the question left her lips, she thought of Blake and how she had, in much the same way, turned him down that last time they had eaten lunch together. Hadn't she said something like that? That it wouldn't work between them? People who had feelings for someone didn't say things like that. If you liked someone, if you cared, then you tried. You didn't shoot it down before it even began.

Which meant that she already had her answer.

"You know, I shouldn't have asked you that," she said, back-stepping. "You think what you think, and it doesn't really matter why. The result is the same. I'm sorry I brought it up. We were having a good time."

She popped a calamari in her mouth and ate it. "The calamari is good," she said, forcing a smile.

"Erin, how would you feel being with someone older than you? I mean, much older than you?"

She looked at him, incredulous. "Oh my goodness, is that what this is about, Will? I haven't even asked you how old you are since I can't remember when!"

"Just because you haven't asked doesn't mean the issue isn't still there. How would you feel being with someone younger than you? Someone much younger?"

"Will," she began, wiping her hands on the cloth napkin in her lap, "if we're talking about me being with you, then I don't care. Older, younger, I truly, honestly don't care. That's why I haven't asked you. I really don't care!"

"You say that now, but you would. I know you would."

"Do you care, Will, about whatever this age difference is that I can't fathom?"

"No, I don't care, but—"

"Then what's the big deal?"

"I'm not good for you," said Will. "You deserve someone good, someone uncomplicated."

"These are all excuses." Erin was amazed at how calm she was. "I think you're good for me. And it's my decision, after all. If you think I'm too old for you, or too young for you, or whatever, and if you think I'm not good for you, or you just don't care for me that way, then that's a different story. But don't judge yourself on my behalf. You don't see what I see, and you don't know me well enough to know what's good for me and what's not."

The food arrived and was placed in front of them.

Erin kept her eyes on her food and ate in silence. Will did the same, as far as she could tell without looking at him.

When she finally did look up, after what seemed like a long time, he was staring at her.

"Do you have something else to say?" she asked, her voice sounding tired to her own ears.

"You make it very hard, you know."

"I make what hard? What are you talking about?"

"I've never had this problem before," he continued, apparently oblivious to the fact that he wasn't making any sense. "I've never found it so easy to be pulled in and so hard to walk away."

Erin sighed. "You're talking in riddles, Will, and I just don't understand. It's not normal. This conversation we're having, it's not normal. It's not how normal people interact. I find it so easy to talk to you, and yet at the same time, you can't seem to just be straight with me. Maybe it's me, I don't know. But it shouldn't be this difficult. And to be honest, I think you're making it more difficult than it has to be."

He gave her a melancholy smile. "How nice it would be if that were the case."

Erin looked back down at her half-eaten plate of food. She couldn't eat anymore. She couldn't say anymore. She couldn't look at him anymore. She wasn't angry with him, oddly enough. She was just sad. Regardless of what Will thought, she had this notion in her head that she was good for him and he was good for her and that together they could be something wonderful. She had never felt that way about anyone, and it made her sad that he didn't feel the same, whatever his reasons were.

Erin let out another breath and looked back up at him. He was painfully beautiful, and he was still looking at her. Her heart fluttered under his gaze, despite everything he had just said to her.

Suddenly, she was overwhelmed with pity for Will and, at the same time, she regretted subjecting him to this inquisition of his feelings for her. Whatever Will was thinking, whatever his reasons were, he didn't mean to hurt her. That much she knew.

"I'm sorry," she said, giving in to her urge to apologize.

"Erin, please don't apologize." His voice was low and infuriatingly sexy. "I've been completely unfair to you, and there's no way I can make up for it. I was selfish to want to spend time with you. You've always been honest with me despite my half-answers and cryptic comments. That's a big part of what draws me to you, that honesty."

"Okay, now, you see, statements like that can be really confusing to a person in my situation and can make a person like me think you feel a certain way when you obviously don't."

Will smiled at her in that heart-melting way of his. "What I feel and what I allow myself to do are two very different things."

It was a roller-coaster of emotions with this man. Realizing that she was starting to have hope once more, Erin shook her head and looked down, trying to remember the reality of thirty seconds ago.

She was about to tell Will that he had to stop talking like that when she heard a familiar voice call her name.

"Erin?"

"Oh no," she muttered, turning toward the door of the restaurant and confirming her suspicions.

"Erin, it is you! I can't believe you're out and about on a Thursday night with a gentleman caller. Look at you! I'm so proud!"

Blake had walked right past the hostess stand and came to a stop, uninvited, in front of the table she was sharing with Will, arm-in-arm with a pretty blond who was smiling down at them.

"Hi, Blake," said Erin, praying to God that he would not say anything in the next five minutes that she would have to kill him for later.

Blake turned to Will and put out his hand. "Hi, I'm Blake. I'm a good friend of Erin's. We went to law school together way back when, and now I work at a rival firm."

Will took his hand and shook it. "Will Abbott. Very nice to meet you."

Erin turned her eyes to the blonde. What was the name of his most recent girlfriend—Susan? She couldn't assume it was Susan, though. The girl could be anyone, for all she knew.

"Erin," Blake finally said, turning to the girl at his side, "this is Susan, the wonderful young woman I told you about. Isn't she amazing?"

The girl punched him in the arm and told him to stop, laughing approvingly at the same time. "Hi, Erin," she said, reaching to shake hands with her. "I've heard a lot about you."

"You have?" asked Erin, shaking her hand.

"Sure," replied Susan, smiling. "According to Blake, you're about the only girl in this city who's had enough sense to turn him down."

Erin laughed, surprised that Blake had been so candid with this girl. Maybe there was potential there between them.

"Anyway," continued Susan, "it's very nice to meet you, but we should leave you two to your dinner. And we should go check in with the hostess so they don't give our table away, Blake. You know, you don't have as much sway at these places as you pretend to, so we're actually going to have to wait just like everyone else to get a table."

"You underestimate the power of this smile on women in positions of power," said Blake, pointing to his own face.

"Come on, Don Juan. Let's see how well that smile's going to work for getting us a table."

"That sounds like a challenge, and you're on. Will, very nice to meet you, and good job getting this girl out of the house on a school night. Erin, try to have fun tonight, if you know what I mean."

"Blake, you're terrible!" said Susan, pulling him away. "Have a good evening, guys!"

Erin waved at them, thankful the interaction didn't last longer than that, and Will turned to look at Erin. "He seems like an interesting fellow," he said with an ironic look. "One of your many suitors, I presume."

"Something like that. I'll tell you about him sometime."

They finished their meal and Will picked up the check, refusing to let Erin pay for any of it. "You can get it next time," he said, smiling.

She thanked him, but something in his tone made her think it was highly unlikely there would be a next time.

Erin took the bag of food the waitress had wrapped up for her and started walking to the door with Will two steps behind her. As she pushed open the door to go outside, Will came up beside her and held the door open for her. Her shoulder brushed against his chest, sending tingles in every direction.

"Where are you parked?" he asked, his voice filled with tenderness.

"The parking deck on Church Street," she replied. Wanting to hold his hand again as they walked in silence, Erin tightened her grip on the bag of food she was carrying with both hands instead.

There was something about the sounds of the city at night, the warm breeze blowing through her hair, and the quiet rhythm of their steps on the sidewalk that gave Erin a sense of peace and calm, despite the tumult of their dinner conversation. And with that peace came a small spark of hope that things would work out the way they were supposed to. She had spoken her mind, she had made her feelings known, and that was all she could do. She couldn't push her way into Will's life. He had to let her in. It was up to him, and that was okay. The realization was surprising to her, and the relief that came with it was welcome.

It took only a few minutes to walk to the parking deck, and they took the elevator up to the fourth level where Erin had parked her car that morning. Erin's car was only one of three cars left on that level, and as they approached Erin turned to look at Will.

"Are you okay?" she asked him.

He stopped and looked at her in astonishment.

"You're asking me if I'm okay? After everything I said at dinner, after everything you said?"

"Yes," she replied, nodding her head slowly. "I want to make sure you're okay."

"At this very moment, looking at you, I'm okay."

Erin couldn't help smiling, even though he was doing it again, confusing her with his words. She put her bag of leftovers on the roof of the car as she fished around her purse for the keys. Then, finding them, she looked back up to see that his gaze hadn't left her face.

Will looked so fragile, standing there looking at her, and the sadness she had seen in him the first time they'd met was so obvious in his eyes. She wanted to take that sadness away, she wanted to heal him. But more than anything she wanted to believe that the confusing things he said to her were true and that, someday, she would understand what was behind his words. And neither one of them would be confused anymore.

"Thank you for coming out with me tonight," said Erin, quietly. "I really did have fun, for most of it."

"I'm sorry, Erin, for everything I've put you through. You deserve so much better. You will have better, Erin, someday."

Feeling another surge of emotion, Erin reached her arms around Will and hugged him tightly. His arms automatically wrapped around her waist and pulled her even closer. His body pressed against hers in a wonderful way, and she could feel his breath in her hair as he kissed the top of her head. His hands moved slowly up and down her back, making her forget everything except the fact that he was there, with her. And it was exactly where they were supposed to be.

They held each other for what seemed like a long time, neither one of them making any move to break the embrace. Finally, Erin took a deep breath, inadvertently causing Will to loosen his hold on her.

They pulled away from each other, slowly, and for a second Erin thought he might kiss her as his cheek brushed against hers. But despite the brushed cheeks and his hesitation as he moved, there was space between them once more, and Erin's heartbeat slowed to a more reasonable rate.

Erin unlocked her car door and slipped inside, putting the bag of leftovers on the passenger seat. Buckling her seatbelt, she started the car, then rolled down her window.

"Do you want a ride back to your car?" She hoped her efforts to hide the tremor in her voice were successful.

"No, thank you. A brisk walk will serve me well right now."

"Okay," said Erin. Putting her hand on the shifter, she turned to look at him one last time. "I'm going to leave you alone, Will. But I'll be here if you ever want to get together or just talk on the phone. You know how to find me."

Will said nothing, and Erin didn't know if that was good or bad. It didn't matter. She put the car in reverse and backed out of the parking space, waving to him as she drove away.

Whatever was supposed to happen would happen. It was out of her hands now.

Chapter Eighteen

Charlotte, North Carolina
November 1879

The weeks following Bessie's funeral were the worst of William's life. It took no time at all for him to learn that the world didn't care when someone died. Not even when that someone was Bessie. Everything simply carried on the way it had before. The sun rose every morning and set every evening. The creek where Bessie had died kept flowing, murmuring its happy tune just as it always had. Children played, parents scolded, young men courted, and young women basked in the attention. Nothing had changed.

To William, though, everything was different. He couldn't look anywhere without seeing Bessie. He saw her face in every crowd, heard her voice in every conversation, smelled her scent on every breeze. The ghost of her was everywhere, with eyes that conveyed a silent accusation. *You did this to me. You took away my only prospect. You stole my only hope.*

He couldn't escape it, no matter what he did. He tried avoiding the places he had been with Bessie, but that proved to be impossible as every stone and tree held an association with her.

The long, warm days of late summer soon became shorter and cooler as September turned into October and October turned into November. William had fallen into a somber routine, rising early each day, before his mother and sisters or even Radka had awakened, and going immediately to his father's study and shutting the door. He took no social calls, claiming to have developed headaches since coming home, and he would eat nothing until lunchtime when Radka would bring him some bread and cheese and occasionally force on him a piece of fruit.

In the afternoons, after having his tea alone in his father's study, he would take a walk in his mother's rose garden. It was only then that he allowed himself to think of Bessie. He refused to consciously think of her at any other time, although he could never remove her from the backdrop of his thoughts.

After intruding on William early on and being told tersely that he needed his privacy, his mother and sisters knew better than to approach him for any reason before dinner. At dinner, William resigned himself to being in the company of his mother and his sisters, along with anyone they had invited to dine with them for the evening. While he never pretended to enjoy himself, nor did he initiate any conversation, he was always polite and responded adequately when addressed. He would retire to his room immediately following dinner, declining to play cards or engage in any other post-dinner activities.

One evening in November, William excused himself from the dinner table as was his custom and ascended the stairs to his room. As soon as he had closed the door to shut himself in for the night, a quiet knock caused him to open it again.

It was Martha.

"William, may I enter?"

He nodded and let her come in, then closed the door behind her.

Martha walked over to the bed and sat down on its edge. She smoothed her skirts over her lap as William pulled a chair over from the other side of the room.

"Radka is leaving us," she began, though he could hear in her tone this was not the reason for her visit.

He set the chair across from her and sat down. "Yes, she told me the news this morning. I've always thought of her as a permanent part of our family. Strange to think she will no longer be here with us." He knew his voice sounded tired and lifeless, even though it was not yet eight o'clock in the evening, but he couldn't bring himself to care.

Martha's fingers played nervously with the chain she wore around her neck.

"I think she has known she would be leaving us," she said. "I think that's why she gave me her family's ring and told me all she did about it." She pulled the chain away from her neck as she said this, revealing Radka's gift hanging at the end of it.

William wondered what stories Radka had told Martha about the ring, but only for a fleeting moment. He hardly had the energy to carry on their present conversation, let alone to question her about whatever folklore the woman had passed down to Martha.

"She says she has an elderly cousin up north who has asked her to come live with her," Martha continued, tucking the ring back into her bodice. "I tried to convince her to stay with us, but she says with all of us grown or almost grown, she is no longer needed as she once was."

"Perhaps she has plans to do something new."

Martha looked up at him. "Perhaps. But I will miss her, all the same."

He nodded, hoping it was the end of their conversation, but his sister remained seated, and he knew she had more to say.

"What is truly on your mind, Sister?" he asked, wishing to get to the point of her visit so he could have his room and his misery all to himself once more.

"You, William," she replied in a firmer tone than he had expected. "You are on my mind. You are not well. I see it in your eyes, and I hear it in your voice. You are not well, and I know not what to do about it."

He should have guessed that Martha—sweet, sensitive, perceptive Martha—would be the first to raise concern over his behavior. "Martha, please, do not worry yourself about me. I am fine, as well as I can be."

"No, William, you are not. You cannot continue down this path. You will not last."

William was quiet for a moment as he considered the appropriate response to Martha's statements. Truth be told, he did not want to last. He did not deserve to. But he knew he could not say so. He could only try to ease her mind. "Sister, truly, you need not worry."

Martha took a breath, then began again. "William, I am not blind, nor am I a fool. I know you are grieving, as well you should. You loved Bessie, and I know that she loved you, too. But she has passed from this life. You have not."

"Martha, do not speak of things you do not understand." William heard the harshness in his own tone, and he closed his eyes briefly, trying to collect himself.

"William, I do not profess to understand what you and Bessie were to each other or what passed between you. But equally, I do not understand the purpose of your self-imposed isolation. You are not living, William. And that is not right."

William stood and pushed the chair away from the bed in frustration.

"Do not be cross with me, William. I speak to you from a place of love, not judgment."

William walked to the far side of the room, then back again, his hands in his pockets, his head down.

"Tell me, William. Tell me what you are thinking."

He stopped and looked again at his sister. Her thick, dark brown hair fell in waves all about her shoulders. It was a beautiful mess of hair that his other sisters all envied. Her face was innocent and kind. She was like an angel, always caring for others, never worrying about herself. In the midst of his despair, William made a silent prayer that God would grant her a most fulfilling and joyful life. She deserved nothing less.

"I am wondering when my little sister became so wise," he finally answered.

Martha smiled sweetly. "I have always been this wise. It's just that no one has ever cared to listen to me."

In that moment William wanted to tell his sister everything—about his meeting with Bessie under the cherry trees, about what Bessie had done, and about what he had led Robert Cox to do for his own purposes. He wanted to tell her that Bessie's blood was on his hands, but he couldn't bring himself to speak the words. He justified his cowardly silence by telling himself that the story implicated Bessie's transgressions as well as his own and that it was not honorable to divulge her secrets for the sake of his own peace. But he knew that, yet again, his silence was nothing more than self-serving. He was a despicable human being.

Not wanting to lie to Martha, he decided to answer with a different truth.

"I cannot escape the thoughts of her, Martha. She is there, everywhere I turn. The pain inside me grows, and nothing I do diminishes it."

"Oh, William," she said, standing up and coming toward him, "I can't even begin to imagine how you must feel. The closest pain I've known in my short life was when Father died. But he was sick for months before he passed, and his passing was in many ways a relief, for him and for us who cared for him. I loved him and miss him terribly, but I know enough to know it is not the same."

She reached over and held William's hands in hers, and he tried to take some small comfort from the gesture.

"William, if this place is full of ghosts for you, then perhaps you need to be somewhere else for a while. Somewhere new where you can find your peace once more."

"Leave home? Leave Charlotte? But I've only just returned."

"Oh, William, you know I want you here with us more than anything, but the fact is that you are not here. You are not yourself. You need to find the man you once were. Then you can come back to us—mind, body, and soul."

She released his hands and reached up to embrace

him, hugging him tightly, as though she would absorb all the hopelessness and pain from his body if she could.

After some time, Martha stepped away from him and moved to leave. Reaching for the doorknob, however, she stopped and looked back at him, her eyes wide and bright.

"Uncle James is coming, you know," she said, her voice hinting at excitement.

"Uncle James? It's only been a couple of months since he returned from California, and he was in Atlanta the last I'd heard. Is he done with his business there already?"

"It would appear so. He wrote to our mother a few days ago and said he would be here on Monday, stopping for a day or two on his way back up to Boston. He has always been fond of you, William. That's why he took you with him to California. Perhaps you can make time to speak with him when he is home."

"Yes, perhaps," William replied, understanding his sister's meaning.

"I've never been to Boston," said Martha, almost as an afterthought. "Or California. Or even Atlanta for that matter."

"You will soon be able to go wherever you please," said William gently. "Just be sure to marry a kind man, Martha. Someone as kind and as caring as you are."

Her subtle smile compelled William to pry.

"Who is it that has brought a smile to your face, Martha? Is it that Tommy Porter you have spent so much time with of late?"

Martha rushed over to him and slapped his arm, smiling more freely. "Do not say a word of this to anyone, William. I'm warning you!"

William laughed, for the first time in over a month.

"So you do have eyes for Mr. Porter. I knew it!"

"William, I'm serious! You cannot let Jane know. She has eyes for him, too, and I've asked her time and time again to go to the Porters' without me, but she insists on bringing me along."

"The question is, which Abbott does Mr. Porter have eyes for?"

Martha crossed her arms and walked back to the still-closed door.

"Martha," William called, taking a more serious tone. "If it is you he wants to be with, and you with him, then no one can fault you. He is not right for Jane if it is you who has his heart."

As Martha looked back at him, her brow furrowed. "I know, William. But that will not make Jane any less cross with me."

William smiled. "She is your sister, Martha. She will learn to live with it. Especially when she finds another fine young suitor of her own."

Martha nodded, opening the door. "Time will tell, I suppose. Perhaps you will let me accompany you on your afternoon walk in the rose garden tomorrow afternoon, and I can tell you more about Mr. Porter."

"That sounds nice," replied William, wishing he meant it.

"Oh, and Mother wanted me to remind you about the photograph that will be taken tomorrow, mid-morning."

"Ah, yes. The 'this is my family before I had grandchildren' photograph. I don't know why she won't just wait until the baby is born to have the photograph taken."

"You said it yourself. She wants to remember her children how they were, before they grew up and started to have children of their own."

"It's a little late for that," said William, walking over to her. "Mary is eight months pregnant."

"I'm sure the photographer will have special instructions from our mother to make Mary stand behind Peter so no one will notice." Martha laughed.

William kissed his sister on the cheek and bid her goodnight.

"Goodnight, William. Sleep well."

He shut the door behind her and stood there a moment, listening to the sound of her footsteps as she walked past Jane's room to her own. His conversation with Martha had brought him some comfort, but the moment was fleeting and the anguish that had become something of a friend in its familiarity was upon him again even before the sound of Martha shutting her bedroom door had reached his ears.

Perhaps if he had told Martha the truth about what had happened between him and Bessie and Cox, perhaps as his confessor, she would have been able to absolve him of the guilt that permeated his soul. No— he knew it would not have had such an effect. A confessor could not remove an unforgivable sin, and what he had done to Bessie, what he had caused her to do, was nothing if not unforgivable.

His sin was eternal; it was part of him now and always would be. The best William could hope for was to learn to live with it.

Even as he got ready for bed, he knew he would not sleep well, despite Martha's benediction. He would not sleep well tonight, nor any other night. And even that was not punishment enough for his sins.

Chapter Nineteen

Charlotte, North Carolina
Modern Day

At the blaring sound of her alarm clock, Erin quickly hit the snooze button and rolled over to get a few more minutes of sleep. She had no desire to wake up—not only because it was six-thirty in the morning on a Saturday, but also because she didn't want to face the reality that whatever she had with Will was gone.

She dozed off, only to be abruptly awakened nine minutes later by her alarm clock again. She shut it off with a groan and sat up in bed. To make matters worse, she was most likely going to see Blake at the pro bono event, and he would ask her how it was going with her grandmother's landlord, in some lewd way, no doubt. And then, without crying, she would have to tell him it wasn't going anywhere.

The last time she'd seen Will was when she'd waved goodbye to him as she left the parking deck after their "date" in uptown, and that was over a week ago. She remembered every word that had passed between them and had gone over their conversation in her mind countless times. He loves me, he loves me not—she still couldn't figure out which petal they had landed on. And to add to the confusion, she remembered her utter contentment when they had hugged, right before they'd said goodbye for the last time.

Although she hadn't wanted to let Will go, she had decided driving home that night that she was going to put him out of her mind. The next move was his, and if he didn't make it, there was nothing she could do about it.

When she had visited her grandmother the next night for her usual Friday visit, she kept her eyes focused on the path right in front of her and did not look up at Will's window. She did the same thing last night, too. What did it matter if he was standing there at the window or not? She couldn't keep looking up at his window forever, hoping he would call down to her.

Now if only she could stop thinking about him.

Heaving herself out of bed, Erin shuffled in bare feet to the bathroom. It was going to be a long day.

She arrived at the library at a quarter to eight and followed the signs around the large checkout desk to the private room where the Wills for Schools event was set up. There were ten tables distributed around the rather small room, and a laptop was set up at the end of each table. It was cramped, to say the least. A few attorneys were already sitting in front of their computers, waiting for clients. Others were coming in behind her.

"Erin, you made it!"

Blake extricated himself from a conversation with two older women and walked over to her.

"Of course I made it. I told you I would be here. Although I was seriously questioning why I agreed in the first place when my alarm clock went off this morning."

Blake grinned. "I suggested we go for a ten o'clock

start time, but nobody else seemed to think that was a good idea. So how are things going for you? How's that handsome landlord of yours?"

And there it was. She knew it wouldn't take him long.

"I'm fine. Not sure how Will is since I haven't seen him in a week and a half."

"What? Why not? I thought you guys were an item."

Erin shook her head. "We just went out that one time, Blake. Definitely not an item by any stretch of the imagination."

"That's too bad, Erin. I kind of liked him. Well, you know if I wasn't with Susan at the moment, I'd be on you like stink on…"

"A wonderful analogy, Blake. Truly appreciated." Erin's eye roll was followed by a smile. "So, you're still with Susan? Wow, that's kind of unbelievable, considering we're talking about you."

Blake gushed in a way that Erin had never seen before. "Yeah, I know," he replied. "Together and going strong. She's—I don't know, different somehow."

"I like her, Blake. I think you'd better hold on to her."

"Doin' my best." He glanced toward the door. "Hey, they're about to start letting the clients in, so we'd better get you logged in on one of the computers. You remember how this works?"

Erin had sat through a one-hour training class during her lunch hour just a few days before, and her role was pretty simple. If any tough questions came up, she was supposed to raise her hand and the actual wills and estates attorney who had volunteered to walk around the room all day fielding questions would come rescue her.

"Yes," she answered. "I'll be fine."

He walked her over to a vacant computer and gave her a folder to collect the registration forms from each client. Then he grinned at her and wished her good luck.

She sat down at the computer and entered the username and password information that was printed on a label stuck to the front of the folder.

"So far, so good," she said under her breath as the program appeared on the screen.

A few minutes later, a volunteer brought over Erin's first "clients"—a young couple who had just had a baby.

They went through the first set of questions together, and Erin collected all their personal information and entered it into the program. When they informed Erin that they wanted to set up a trust for their child if they both happened to die before the boy was 18, she had to raise her hand.

It took her about twenty minutes to get through each will, thirty if it was more complicated, like with the first couple. By the time Blake tapped her on the shoulder to let her know she could take a break and grab some of the food that had been provided for the volunteers, it was a little past noon and she had just finished up with her ninth client.

"I told you a monkey could do it," joked Blake.

"A trained monkey with a real wills and estates attorney hovering close by," corrected Erin, smiling.

She followed a group of volunteers to an adjoining

room where the food was set up and grabbed a boxed lunch and a bottle of water, then she headed outside to eat her lunch in the warm sun.

At just past two, she was one of only three attorneys left in the room, and she was wrapping up with her last client. She hit the print button, then walked over to the communal printer in the corner of the room. Picking up the copies from the printer, she handed them over to her clients to give them time to review the final product before signing.

As they thanked her and turned to leave, Erin realized no one was left in the room other than Blake, who was busy packing up documents and supplies. He acknowledged her from across the room, and she walked over to him.

"That wasn't too bad, was it?" said Blake, shoving some papers into a box.

"It was tolerable," she replied, sighing for effect. "Do you have to clean up this whole mess?"

"Oh no." He shook his head. "I just have to wait for our IT people to get here and stay until they're done. This is the only box I'm responsible for taking."

"Well, I hope they get here soon so you're not stuck here all afternoon."

Just then, two men pushing gray carts entered the room.

"And here they are. I'll see you later, Erin. And thanks again for waking up early on a Saturday to do this for me."

"I did it for the teachers," Erin teased.

Blake winked at her as he walked over to the crew starting to take apart the first computer station. "Sure you did."

Erin chuckled as she walked past him to the door, and he waved to her.

As she worked her way back to the front desk and the exit, a large sign in the area on the other side of the library caught her eye.

"May is Charlotte History Month," the sign said.

Erin paused for a moment. On a whim, instead of turning toward the doors, she continued into the other wing of the library where the non-fiction books were kept.

A corner of the room had been arranged to display books on all aspects of the city's history. One section was dedicated to the early growth of Charlotte during the textile boom, and another to the rise of the banking industry. Another displayed books on slavery and the Civil War.

Erin found herself drawn to a book that was propped up on a small table with other books on Charlotte's geography—*The Creeks of Mecklenburg County*.

She picked up the large volume and began flipping through the pages, immediately thinking of Will and the walk they had taken on Easter day along the creek behind his apartment building. Ignoring the pang of regret at how things had ended between the two of them, or more accurately had never started, she focused her attention on the beautiful pictures of the various creeks in and around Charlotte and read some of the captions.

There were over 3000 miles of creek in Mecklenburg County. Erin had never heard that before. The county's numerous creeks had played a huge role in why and how the area was settled back in the 1760s.

In fact, the creeks were the reason that the city's streets ran northeast-to-southwest, and not simply north-to-south. The streets followed the ridges between the creeks.

Erin was surprised to see a whole chapter dedicated to Briar Creek, the creek behind Will's apartment complex. Her thoughts turned to the young woman Will had once loved, the woman who had died in that same creek. She wondered when he'd lost her. He said it had happened a long time ago, but the pain had shone in his eyes so clearly when he had spoken of her, it was as though she'd died only yesterday.

Erin closed the book and put it back on its stand. She walked over to the next row of books and picked up another one that was on display—*A Pictorial History of Charlotte's First Families.* This one was almost like a photo album. Many of the prominent Charlotte families dating back to the city's settlement and up through the turn of the 19th century were included. She recognized a few of the names from the streets around the city that had been named for them, but most were names she had never heard of. She flipped through the pages, looking at the very formal poses of the men, women, and children long since dead who, regardless of how wealthy or powerful they may have been in their day, had now been mostly forgotten.

She was about to close the book when her eyes landed on a name she did recognize—Abbott. Her lips curled into a subconscious smile as she read about the history of this Charlotte family that, most likely, consisted of Will's ancestors.

The Abbotts settled in Charlotte around 1790 by way of Charleston. James Abbott was the adventurous sort, it seemed, and had dragged his young wife, who was pregnant at the time, to Charlotte in hopes of finding gold. Apparently, there were many veins of gold that were discovered in the area in the 1700s and the early 1800s, and James Abbott's attempts to strike gold were at least moderately successful.

One of his grandchildren, Charles, married the daughter of a French trader in the summer of 1852. Her name was Jacqueline. The following year, the first of their children, a son named William, was born.

Charles was a banker of sorts. He invested well, and his wealth and prominence in the community grew. In 1861, the city found itself in the midst of the Civil War, and Charles left his growing family to fight. He was one of the few to return home, and although he used his money to help those who had suffered great losses during the war, his wealth seemed only to increase. His early death in 1871 was greatly mourned by the community.

Erin found the history of the Abbotts fascinating and studied every picture in great detail. Looking at the wedding photo of Charles and Jacqueline, she could see a resemblance to the man she knew. In Charles's straight nose and proud chin, in Jacqueline's wide eyes and thick dark hair, she saw Will.

Erin turned the page to see what more she could learn about the Abbotts. As her eyes glimpsed the family picture at the top of the next page, a chill ran up her spine and her heart stopped beating for a moment. She looked again. It couldn't be!

She read the caption beneath the picture and said the names under her breath as she touched each face with her finger. An older version of the woman in the wedding photo on the previous page was standing on the left-hand side—she was identified as Jacqueline Abbott, and that made perfect sense, of course. What didn't make sense was the picture of the man on the opposite side of the photo—the man whose face was unmistakably Will's. He stood with a casual grace behind a seated adolescent girl, his hand resting on the back of her chair. The name provided in the caption only strengthened the overwhelming feeling that she was looking at Will, as it gave the man's name as "William Abbott."

Her skin tingling in disbelief, Erin read the caption over and over again, trying to understand what she was seeing. The date at the end of the caption said that the picture was taken in November of 1879 in Charlotte, North Carolina. November of *1879*? How could that be? It was as though she were looking at one of those black-and-white novelty photos you could get at a fair or a carnival, where you dress up like a cowboy or a girl working in a saloon in the Wild West.

But that wasn't what she was looking at. She was looking at a real photograph taken in 1879, and there was no question in her mind that the man on the right was Will Abbott, her grandmother's landlord. *Her Will.* She saw it in the features of the handsome face she had tried to avoid staring at so many times, the broad shoulders and strong arms that had hugged her, and the comfortable stance of humble confidence she so admired. Most importantly, she saw it in the sadness that ran like an undercurrent through his whole body and, somehow, made him even more beautiful to her.

Erin closed her eyes and shook her head. She was losing her mind. She was seeing things that weren't there, imagining resemblances that didn't exist. These were his ancestors—of course there would be some similarities. But that didn't mean the man in the picture was Will. It couldn't be. Such a thing was not possible. It would make him over a hundred years old.

I'm older than I look.

Those were his words, weren't they? Yes, but he couldn't possibly have meant that he was born in the 1800s.

She flipped back a page to the paragraph about Charles and Jacqueline. They were married in 1852. Their first child, their only son, William Henry Abbott, was born on August 6, 1853. Which would make Will...

"A hundred and sixty-nine years old," she muttered under her breath.

No human being lived to be a hundred and sixty-nine. Not even the oldest person ever to live. She had just seen something about that on television, some woman in France who lived to be a hundred and twenty-two years old. Even if it were possible to live to be a hundred and sixty-nine years old, Will certainly didn't look it. He didn't even look forty. They had shown a picture of the woman in France on her hundred and twenty-second birthday—she didn't look young.

Erin pushed the book aside, still open, and put her head in her hands, her elbows resting on the table. She sounded like a crazy person, even to herself. The man in the picture just couldn't be Will.

And yet, what if it was?

Her thoughts turned to the creek. If Will's girlfriend had died in the creek, that certainly would have made the news. There would have been an article, a news story, something describing it. And nothing made a better headline than an interview with the grieving boyfriend.

He said it happened a while ago. Maybe he was in high school or college. If she could find a picture of Will from ten or twenty years ago when his girlfriend had died, and he looked younger than he did now, then maybe she could bring herself back into the rational world. Maybe then she would accept the fact that her Will Abbott simply bore a *very* strong resemblance to his great-great-great-great-granddaddy William.

Erin dashed from her chair to the nearest computer and began searching the Internet. There were stories about the parks and greenways along the creeks, an exposé about pollution of the creeks, and one article about a group of kids in the late 1930s who had drowned in Sugar Creek, which fed into Briar Creek. But there was nothing about anyone drowning in Briar Creek.

She tried varying the terms, broadening the search, but still she got no relevant results.

Then she tried searching obituaries and found an online index for North Carolina's death records. It was organized by county, so she clicked on Mecklenburg County, where Charlotte was located. That link took her to another page, which divided the records into those dated 1991 to the present and everything before 1991. That one was called "the archive." Ignoring logic and reason, she decided to click on it.

A search engine popped up that looked like it was the first search engine ever created, but she clicked her mouse in the text box and put in a single term, "creek." She hesitated for a moment, then clicked the "search" button.

She expected the search would fail or that the website would crash, so she was more than surprised to see a single result appear. The result was for Elizabeth Fitzhenry Gaines. The dates to the right of the name indicated that she was born on April 7, 1856, and died on September 12, 1879. Erin quickly did the math in her head. The poor girl had only been twenty-three years old.

Erin moved the cursor until it was over the box to the left of the name, put a checkmark in the box, then hit the "retrieve" button at the bottom of the page. A very old-looking newspaper article appeared in a separate window. Erin expanded the window and read the brief article. She read about the girl, Miss Gaines, the only daughter of the late Edward Gaines and Mildred Gaines. The article said the girl died of accidental drowning in Briar Creek while taking a walk on her family's property. She was survived by her mother and her thirteen-year-old brother James.

Elizabeth. That wasn't the name Will had mentioned to her that night in his apartment. He had said her name was Bessie. No, she corrected herself; he had said that he *called* her Bessie.

With a trembling hand, Erin moved the cursor to run one more Internet search. She knew the answer to her question before she even saw the results.

Bessie was short for Elizabeth.

Chapter Twenty

Erin logged off the computer and closed her eyes. Her heart was beating erratically in her chest, and she had the same cold, prickly feeling on her skin that she always seemed to get when she woke up in the middle of a nightmare.

Taking a deep breath, Erin blinked her eyes open and stood up. She had to find out for sure if the man in the picture was Will or some look-alike ancestor of his. She had to know if this Elizabeth Gaines, who died in 1879, was his Bessie. And the only way she could do that was to ask him. He wouldn't lie to her.

As she turned toward the library doors, Erin glanced back at the book about the Abbotts. She decided she would check it out of the library and bring it with her when she went to see Will, so she could show it to him if she needed to.

It was almost four o'clock when she started driving out of the city. She debated going home and waiting until the next day to confront Will, but she found herself driving in the direction of the apartment complex. It was just as well—she was making herself crazy thinking about the photo and the obituary and what it all meant. The sooner she could have answers, the better.

As Erin pulled into a parking spot in the back of the lot, a terrible thought occurred to her. What if it were true—what if Will really was a hundred and sixty-nine years old? What did that make him? Was he supernatural? Was he a vampire?

She shook her head. Whatever he was, human or not, he wasn't evil. She knew that much.

Erin paused just inside the door at the bottom of the stairs that led up to Will's apartment, the large hardcover book she had borrowed from the library tucked under her arm. She breathed in the musty scent of the old building and began climbing, the wood beneath each carpeted step creaking as she ascended.

It was time to find out just who, or what, her grandmother's landlord was.

****

Will pulled his hand away from the doorknob. He could not keep going to the door each time he heard footsteps on the stairs. He could not keep hoping Erin would come to him, yet again, with her heart open. He had turned her away; he had dismissed her. And it had been the right thing to do, regardless of how his soul ached for her.

He was about to turn back to the dining room table, where he was going over the month's accounting, when there was a knock at the door.

Hope stirred within him again, and again Will beat it down. It was the second day of the month, and undoubtedly someone's rent was overdue.

He opened the door and, almost as though he had willed her into existence, there she stood, her hand still raised in a knocking posture. Erin.

She lowered her hand slowly, eyes wide and lips parted, as if she were seeing him for the first time.

"Hi," Will managed to croak, still unconvinced that

she wasn't a figment of his imagination.

She closed her mouth and swallowed, then smiled tentatively. "Hi."

They stood there, staring at each other for an inordinately long time before it occurred to Will that he should invite her in.

Moving back, he opened the door wider. "Please, come in."

She held up her hand almost immediately and shook her head. "No. I mean, I don't want to bother you."

"You never bother me." It was the truest statement he had ever uttered.

She didn't move; she didn't look away. And neither could he. "Please, Erin. You came all this way. Just for a minute."

His voice was pleading, but he couldn't help it. To have her there at his doorstep, only to watch her walk away without even talking to him—he couldn't imagine anything worse.

"I-I don't think I should," she said finally. "I just came by because, well, I have a question for you."

His gaze moved to the large, hardcover book she carried under her arm, then back to her beautiful face.

"All right," he conceded. "Ask, and I'll answer if I can."

She lowered her eyes and took a deep breath. Taking the book in both her hands, she held it in front of her, almost like a shield. He watched as her knuckles turned white.

"Were you born in eighteen fifty-three ?"

Will could feel the blood drain out of his head, and it was as though he became disconnected from his body. Had he heard her correctly? She still wouldn't look him in the eyes, and her words had come out as a whisper.

"Excuse me?" he asked. He had to be sure.

"Were you born in the year eighteen hundred and fifty-three?" she asked again, speaking louder and more slowly. There was no mistaking what she had asked this time, and relief flooded through him like sunshine breaking through the clouds after a storm.

"You should really come inside."

****

Erin was powerless to refuse. Silently, she entered and Will shut the door behind her. He gestured to his comfortable couches, and she followed him to the living room.

Not wanting to sit, she paused near the coffee table and placed the book down gently on its surface. Then she turned to face Will.

He had come to stand just inches away, and the air was electric between them. She could see his chest rise and fall with each breath in an even rhythm that was the opposite of her own fitful breathing.

His eyes were kind, as though he knew exactly what she was feeling, even though she couldn't have put it into words. His mouth curved in an understanding smile.

"Do I frighten you, Erin?" he said at last. "Please, don't be scared of me."

He reached for one of the hands that hung limp at her sides and brought it to his lips. Lowering her hand to the level of his chest, he began rubbing it slowly with his thumb, sending sparks up her arm and all through her body.

She swallowed. "I'm not, I'm not scared of you."

Ignoring the pounding in her chest, she looked down at the hand that held hers. Placing her other hand on both of theirs, she stopped his hand from moving, then turned his hand over to look at his palm. She traced the faint lines that ran from his fingers to the center of his palm, and his fingers curled reflexively.

"How is it possible?" she whispered, raising her eyes to his. "What are you?"

Carefully pulling his hand from hers, he reached up to touch her face.

"I'm just a man. A man that God has forgotten."

She closed her eyes. His hand was warm and soft across her cheek, and her heart beat faster and more violently in her chest.

"Are you sure you're not afraid?" he asked, slowly lowering his hand to place it just under her collarbone. "Your heart is racing."

"That's not fear," she breathed. Even with her eyes still closed, she knew how near he was. She could feel the heat of his body on her face. His breath mingled with hers.

"I want to kiss you," he said, almost shyly.

At that, she opened her eyes, her face already moving toward his. The hand that had lingered near her cheek tilted her chin up, and finally their lips met in the gentlest of kisses.

Her eyes fluttered shut again, and she had trouble keeping her breathing steady. As the warmth of his mouth on hers radiated through her body, she could feel her arms wrapping around him until she had her hands on his strong back.

When he pulled away, she opened her eyes to find

him looking at her. Her arms tightened around him, and he leaned in to kiss her again, his hands moving behind her neck to draw her mouth closer as he pressed his lips more boldly against hers.

When his lips left hers once more, her hands fell away from him. He caught both hands in his and held them to his chest. She could feel his heart beating through his cotton shirt, assuring her that he was real and living and present.

It was impossible, but that didn't make it any less true.

"Are you okay?" he asked.

She looked up at him, then smiled. "Of course I'm okay. Did you think I would swoon when you kissed me?"

Will laughed, and the sound made her heart lighter. She realized then that she wanted nothing more than to be the source of his joy, to see him happy.

"No, not at all. I was referring to the fact that you just found out I'm more than five times your age."

"I told you, I don't care how old you are."

He laughed again, still holding her hands against his chest. "That was when you thought I might be forty."

Will didn't look forty, she thought, studying his face. Gently pulling her right hand out of his, Erin reached up to run her finger along his brow. He closed his eyes, as though her touch was sacred, and it only made her want to be closer to him.

Gathering her thoughts once more, she focused on Will. His skin was smooth; there were only a few lines around his eyes, and none at all around his mouth. Was it because he never laughed?

Her hand brushed the hair away from his forehead, moved down over his temple, then his cheek.

"How can you be so old and look so young? So beautiful?"

He smiled at her. He was breathtaking when he smiled. "Do you have plans tonight?" he asked, his smile turning mischievous. "This might take a while."

She shook her head. "I have as much time as you need."

He bent his head to plant a quick kiss on her lips, then led her by the hand toward the kitchen. "Will you have a drink with me?"

"Sure," she replied. Perhaps a little alcohol in her blood would help her make sense of everything.

He let go of her hand as he passed through the archway and into the kitchen. She followed him and stood just inside, watching as he pulled two wine glasses out of the cupboard, uncorked a bottle of white wine, and poured the wine into their glasses.

"I was worried you might be angry with me," said Erin, taking the glass he offered.

"Angry? You don't know how relieved I am."

She smiled into her glass as she took a sip. "I figured as much when you kissed me."

"I've wanted to do that for a long time. You don't know how close I came, each time I was with you."

"Why didn't you? Before tonight, I mean?"

Will sighed. "Come, let's sit down. I'll tell you everything."

She followed him back into the living room and, as she settled herself next to him on one of the couches, she reached for the library book that was sitting on the edge of the coffee table.

"What is that?" asked Will, raising his glass to take a sip.

"It's how I found out about you."

Erin opened the book to page twenty-two and pointed to the picture at the top of the page. Her finger moved to the man on the right-hand side of the picture.

"Recognize this handsome devil?"

"I do, but I'm not sure how you did. It's quite an old picture, obviously. It's very faded. And I don't wear my hair the same way as I did back then."

"I would recognize you anywhere," she replied, and it was true. There was something about his soul that was so clearly visible to her. It didn't matter if he was right next to her, across the room, on the phone, or in a photograph. He couldn't hide from her. She could feel him.

Will looked up from the book and into Erin's eyes, sending a spark of desire right through her. "I've always thought my long life was punishment for my sins. I'm not so sure anymore."

"Tell me," she murmured, wishing she had left some space between them on the couch and at the same time hoping he would take her in his arms. "Tell me everything."

He drew in a long breath, then began recounting his story, starting at the beginning. He described his mother and his father and his five sisters. He told her about how his father had left to fight in the war and was one of the lucky few men to come home alive and intact, only to die a few years later of illness.

Then came the part about Bessie. His eyes dulled as he described their relationship—how they had met, how he had to make a name for himself before he could marry her. The whole time Will spoke of Bessie, it was as though he were speaking of something that had happened to a neighbor or a stranger, rather than to him. There was no hint of his own thoughts and feelings, and Erin wondered if that was what a lifetime of sorrow and regret did to a man. When he got to the part where he came back from California and found out that she was to be married to someone else, he paused and looked down.

"It's okay, Will," she said, reaching over to hold his hand. "It's good to talk about these things. Sadness doesn't just disappear. You have to move through it and get to the other side."

He brought her hand to his lips and kissed it, and she felt guilty at the pleasure the kiss stirred within her, knowing the depth of his despair.

"You should know, I've never told anyone what I'm about to tell you," he said finally. "Not even my sister Martha."

Erin looked down at the picture in the book that still lay open in front of them. "You may not have said it in words, but it was written on your face. Then and now."

Will poured out some more wine into both of their glasses, then continued his confession, telling Erin about his midnight rendezvous with Bessie and what he learned from her.

"She had to marry him," said Erin, starting to feel the effects of the second glass. "Even though she wanted to marry you. She believed she had no choice, and she was probably right."

"I was so angry with her. I couldn't understand how she could sleep with him, let alone the fact that she did it despite her promise to me."

"You were hurt. You felt betrayed and insulted. You had a right to feel that way." Erin looked at Will's solemn mouth and his downcast eyes, wishing she could think of a way to help him deal with all his feelings. If only she could say the right words, maybe he wouldn't be so sad anymore. In the end, though, Erin could find nothing useful to say. All she could do was urge him to keep talking.

"What happened after that, Will?"

He closed his eyes briefly and sighed. "I made her think that I didn't love her anymore—that I wanted nothing to do with her."

"That was probably not a bad thing to tell her. In a way, you were setting her free to do what she thought was right. What she had to do."

"That's not all." He paused. Erin could feel his fear and sadness building, and there was something more—something she hadn't quite seen at first. It was stronger and more destructive. It was dark and relentless, and she could almost see it wind its way around him, choking the life out of him, drowning him.

She reached for Will's hand again, and he grasped it without hesitation, accepting the lifeline she sought to give him.

Taking a breath, he began again. "A day or so later, her betrothed, Robert Cox, came to visit me. He told me he had seen her with someone under the trees."

"You!" Erin gasped.

"Yes, me. He didn't know that it was me, though, and I didn't tell him. He told me he suspected Bessie was being unfaithful to him, and he was considering revoking his offer of marriage. And do you know what

I did?" Will turned his eyes on her, his anger and self-loathing dimming the specks of gold she loved until his eyes looked almost black. "I let him go right on thinking that, encouraging him in his false conclusions. I figured if Cox didn't want to marry her, then I would. I would take care of Bessie and her child."

"You would be her hero," Erin whispered, the import of his actions sinking in. "Her rescuer."

"I would win."

Erin squeezed his hand, her heart breaking for him and for Bessie as she finally understood. That dark thing that had its grip on his heart, that wouldn't let go—it was guilt.

"You never had the chance to be her hero. She drowned in the creek before you could save her."

"She killed herself, Erin. She overdosed on laudanum and drowned in a foot of water in the creek behind her house—the same creek that runs behind this building."

After what seemed like a long silence, Erin found the courage to speak, knowing her words could never be enough to heal him. "It wasn't your fault, Will. You didn't know what would happen."

"I am guilty of the worst sin, Erin. I took away her hope. I was the cause of her utter despair."

"Will, you made a mistake. I'm not saying you didn't. But in the end the choice was hers."

"She had no choice, Erin. She was pregnant, unmarried, and alone. You don't know what it was like back then."

"You're right, Will," she said softly, still holding his hand. "It's terrible to be in that position today, and I can't even imagine how much harder it must have been back then, what she must have felt. I can't imagine the darkness a person must feel to cause them to end their own life. But what good has come of your guilt and regret for the past hundred and some years? Bessie's still dead, and you're still alive."

Will laughed wryly. "Yes, still alive, after all these years. There is no peace for me."

"Don't say that, Will," she countered, causing him to look up at her. "Everyone wishes for a long life. It's a blessing, not a curse."

"I assure you, Erin, this longevity that has been bestowed upon me, it is no blessing. It's like I'm frozen in time, unchanging, while the world around me keeps moving forward. All the people I've loved, gone. The familiar things from my past, gone. I am merely a witness, no longer a participant. I am left behind and utterly alone."

"Oh, Will," she breathed, reaching up with her other hand to touch his face. "You're not alone."

His stern expression softened into a half smile. "Erin, I may not feel alone in this very moment with you here beside me, but it is just a moment. And when the moment is over, you will be gone, too."

"All we have are moments, Will. It is what we do with those moments that is the important thing. Some people have more moments than others, but in the end we all will pass from this life. Even you, I'll bet."

He looked at her, as though considering what she had just said for the first time.

"You think I will die someday?"

She shrugged. "No one lives forever. You said it yourself, you're just a man. Maybe you've just been given a little more time than most. And if that's the case, then maybe you should stop dwelling on how you got here and start trying to figure out what to do with what you've been given."

Will's brow wrinkled slightly, almost as though she had said something he hadn't thought of before, then smoothed as he gave her a lop-sided grin. "You say the most profound things when you're drunk, Miss Dovetree."

Almost on cue, Erin's head started to spin. Letting go of his hand, she leaned back into the couch. "You know, I think you're right. Not about being profound, but about my being drunk."

"You just need a little food in you," Will replied, giving her hand a pat and standing up. "It's after six, and I know how diligent you are about not missing any meals. Would you stay and have dinner with me?"

Erin opened her eyes and looked at him, her heart warm at the thought of his tender concern for her despite all the secrets and darkness weighing down his soul. "Of course. I'd love to. Should we order a pizza?"

"That's exactly what I was thinking. And how about we rent a movie or something? You know, just something to lighten the mood." He paused as he was about to enter the kitchen and gazed at her in earnest, making the skin on her face feel like it was about to ignite. "Do you have any idea how happy I am that you're here, Erin? That you know?"

She looked down at her hands, trying not to grin. "I have an inkling."

Stepping into the kitchen, then coming back out with his cell phone in his hand, he gestured to the enormous television screen on the wall. "I've got all sorts of electronic devices hooked up to my television for procuring any movie you want."

Erin's movements seemed slow as she turned her head in the direction of the entertainment system. "I noticed you have lots of little boxes next to your TV. You like watching movies?"

"I do. It's a bad habit I have."

"There are worse habits," she replied. "Like drinking in excess, as I have done."

"You see," he said softly, his face taking on a contrite expression as he came to stand next to the couch where she still sat, "I'm a bad influence."

Erin rose to her feet slowly and reached for his arm to steady herself. It was hard with muscle and at the same time smooth and invitingly warm. She wanted to run her hands up and down his arms, wanted to kiss every exposed inch of skin. Instead of looking him in the eyes, Erin's focus shifted to Will's mouth, and she forgot what she was about to say.

Without thinking, she leaned into him, and he captured her lips with his.

The kiss was brief but potent, and she took a step back, feeling more drunk under its influence than she had before on wine alone.

Bereft of all willpower, she moved toward him again, and he cradled her face between his hands, kissing her so thoroughly that her legs almost buckled.

Out of breath, she broke contact with his mouth. With the hand that had been clutching his shirt in a death grip during their kiss, Erin reached up and ran her fingers along his warm, slightly swollen lips. He dropped a kiss on the pad of each finger as it passed over his mouth.

Sobering slightly, Erin realized she had to get her

mind off kissing him.

"So," —she pointed to the entertainment system as she sought the safety of a seated position once more— "how does all that work?"

Will grabbed two remote controls off a nearby coffee table, then sat back down beside her. Erin watched as he navigated screen after screen until he pulled up a list of new release movies.

"Here." He handed her one of the controllers. "Just use the arrows to scroll through the movies until you see the one you want. I'll watch anything—surprise me. And while you do that, I'll order the pizza."

As Erin watched him go back into the kitchen to make the call, she leaned back into the couch feeling warm and content. Will liked her, and not just as a friend. He had wanted to kiss her this whole time, and he trusted her enough to share his tragic history with her. All of the confusion of her previous interactions with her grandmother's wonderful landlord made sense, and the connection she thought she had with him had been real. He had felt it, too.

"How do you feel about everything on your pizza?" he called from the kitchen, reminding her that she was supposed to be scrolling through movie titles.

"How do you think I feel?"

She looked up and saw him smiling at her. Would she ever get tired of seeing that smile?

"What do you think about a vampire movie?" she asked, scrolling to a title that had caught her eye. "Have you seen 'Blood and Water'? It's pretty new."

Will peeked his head out the pass-through, the phone still to his ear. "Are you picking a vampire movie because I remind you of a vampire?" he teased.

"No," she replied, raising her eyebrows. "I just like vampire movies, and I haven't seen this one."

He finished ordering the pizza and came back into the living room. She suddenly became very conscious of his body as he sat down next to her on the couch.

"I've seen it, but it's good and I'd enjoy watching it again. Especially if I'm watching it with you. The pizza should be here in forty minutes, but we can start the movie."

She handed him the remote, careful not to allow her fingers to touch his hand. Her whole body was tingling with anticipation, and it would only take one small accidental touch to make her lose control of her faculties and throw caution to the wind, showering Will with endless kisses.

Will took the remote control from her and selected the movie. As the previews started, he put his feet up on the coffee table and settled back into the couch cushions. His shoulder brushed against hers in the process, and she could feel his warmth burn a hole through her sleeve.

"Are you going to relax and watch this with me, or do you always watch movies sitting straight up with your feet planted firmly on the ground?"

Erin realized that was exactly how she was sitting and chuckled.

As her rigid posture softened, Will wrapped his arm around her and pulled her closer, so that her head came to rest on his shoulder. Kissing the top of her head, he whispered into her hair, "Don't worry. I won't let you take advantage of me."

She laughed and let her body sink into his. It felt so good to be with him like this.

When the pizza came a little while later, they paused the movie and got up to get things ready for dinner. Will paid the delivery man as Erin found some plates in the kitchen cupboard and brought them over to the coffee table where Will had placed the pizza box. The pizza smelled wonderful as Erin put a slice on each of their plates.

"That's three dinners I owe you now," she called out to him. He was doing something in the kitchen.

When she heard a cork popping, she knew what that something was. "I'm just starting to sober up and you're opening another bottle of wine? What are you trying to do to me?"

"I thought we were celebrating tonight," he countered. "You figured out how old I am. You've let me share my secret for the first time in over a hundred years. I think that's worth celebrating."

Erin took the glass he gave her and they toasted. "To sharing secrets and doing higher level math," she said, raising her glass to his.

He grinned.

They ate pizza, watched the rest of the movie, and drank the second bottle of wine. By the time the credits were rolling, Erin was more than a little buzzed. Even after an extra slice of pizza, she knew there was no way she could drive home. Then again, spending more time with Will while she sobered up wasn't a bad thing.

Will turned off the television and cleared the coffee table while Erin made her way slowly to the bathroom. She caught him watching her out of the corner of her eye. "Don't worry, Will, I'm not going to fall in. I'll be back in a minute." She hardly slurred her words at all.

****

Will couldn't help staring as Erin moved down the hall. When she disappeared into the bathroom and closed the door, he let out the breath he was holding in.

He still couldn't believe what had happened. She knew. She knew *everything*. Erin knew how old he was, she knew what he'd done. And she was still there, with him. They had just watched a movie and had dinner together. Like normal people.

Not only was Erin not afraid of him and the fact that he was over a century old, she *wanted* to be with him. It was truly unbelievable, and for the first time since he could remember, Will was genuinely happy.

He was already back in position on the couch by the time Erin stumbled back from the bathroom. And as her thigh touched his innocently, Will felt something else he hadn't felt in a long time.

Desire.

Chapter Twenty-One

"You know," said Erin, lowering herself onto the couch next to him. "I feel very comfortable with you. More comfortable than I've ever been with anyone. It's a little scary."

"I know," he replied. She looked so vulnerable, the way she tried not to touch him, the way she watched him with eyes wide open and lips slightly parted. Vulnerable was perhaps not the right word. Maybe just completely open—willing to accept him with all his sins, his odd behavior, his unnatural state of existence. She would take him and all his flaws, willingly, and she would be happy doing it. And in return she would give him everything she was—good, bad, and awkward. She would hold nothing back.

He reached over and took Erin's hand. "I remember the first time you came up here with your grandmother's rent check. I could tell there was something different about you right away. You were honest, uncomplicated—you said what you thought, what you felt, without worrying about how it would sound. Even your beauty is uncomplicated. No fancy hairdos, overdone make-up, or expensive clothes. Just you. Just beautiful, kind you." He reached up with his other hand to stroke her hair. He needed to touch her— her hand, her hair, her face, her lips. He couldn't keep himself away from her any longer.

"You had a genuine concern for me," he continued, "from that very first time we met, even though you didn't know me. And then, each time I saw you after that, you made my heart feel light. I couldn't stop thinking about you, wondering when I would see you again."

She looked at him, disbelief written on her features. "Really?"

Will couldn't help chuckling. Had he kept his emotions so well hidden? "Really. You're the only person I've ever wanted to share my secret with."

"But you didn't. You never told me anything."

He shook his head, remembering all the times he had wanted to tell her who he really was. "I couldn't. I wanted to protect you from it. From me."

She crinkled her nose at him. "Protect me? Why would you need to protect me from your past or from you?"

"It's a burden, Erin, to live on and on. Everything I've ever known or loved is gone. And not just people, but technology, fashion, even the words people use to express themselves. I've been nothing more than a spectator for so many years, watching the world go by, and wanting nothing more than to pass the time. But when you knocked on my door that day, I found myself caring again, in a way I didn't think I could. I didn't just exist. I felt alive again."

A moment of silence passed between them, and she moved her hand within his, spreading her fingers until they intertwined with his own. He looked down at their interlaced hands. They fit together, just like a puzzle.

"Will," she said, almost sleepily, "most people would kill to live forever, to never worry about getting old and dying."

"I know, but most people haven't thought it through. We aren't meant to live forever. We are supposed to grow and change. We learn, and then we teach. And then we are meant to die and move on to whatever comes next."

"There must be a reason you are the way you are," she countered. "There must be something you are meant for."

Will could see her thinking things through, approaching it from every angle as though it were a chemical equation or an experimental result. She was wrong, but adorably so. "I've already told you what I think this everlasting life is—an everlasting punishment for an unforgivable sin."

"No," replied Erin, without hesitation. "That can't be it at all. Time is a gift, not a curse. If it were a punishment, then why keep you young? Why give you everything you need to live comfortably? What kind of punishment is that?"

"It is the worst kind. An eternity of uninterrupted reflection on one's failures. I am alone and forgotten. All I have are my regrets."

"But you're not alone, and you are loved."

He wouldn't be able to keep from kissing her much longer.

"Besides," she added, "maybe there's a natural explanation. Maybe your cells are just different from everyone else's in some way we haven't discovered yet. Like you have an age-resistant, super-immune system or something. Maybe it's not that you can't die, but that you just haven't yet. I mean, you've never been hit by a bus, have you? You haven't tried to kill yourself and found you couldn't die, right?"

"No, I've never tried to commit suicide," he quickly replied. "I much prefer this punishment to the eternal fires of hell."

"Oh, Will," she said, bringing his hand to her lips and kissing it. "How can you think that a good, kind, wonderful person like you could be judged so harshly?"

He pulled his hand slowly away from Erin's lips. He could see she was about to apologize, but as she opened her mouth to speak he stopped her with his own.

Her lips were soft and sweet and delicious, and he savored the taste of her, kissing her slowly and purposefully—careful not to release the fullness of desire that was building within him.

Her arms raised around his neck, and she pulled him closer. At the same time, her lips parted under his, making him forget his self-restraint. Without a second thought, Will pressed his mouth more fully onto hers, his tongue no longer constrained but exploratory, and he was met with equal fervor.

His hands found her hips and wandered to the small of her back. As she moved, her shirt lifted, and suddenly Will's fingers felt bare skin instead of cotton. Smooth, warm, inviting, he was powerless to resist the desire to touch her. Molding his hands to the curve of her back, Will pulled Erin closer, kissed her more deeply. His hands moved up her back, slowly, conscious of every muscle and every rib along the way.

She was unbelievable, the way she pressed against him and moved her mouth with his, and when her fingers slid from his neck to his hair, he felt his last ounce of willpower slip through his splayed hands.

Leaning back against the cushions, he pulled her down on top of him, and willingly she followed, not once coming up for air.

He wanted to pull her shirt off. He wanted to pass his hands over every inch of her body, and when a muffled sound of contentment escaped her lips he nearly succumbed, finding the hem of her shirt and beginning to move it upward. But then Will thought of Erin's innocent blue eyes, her unassuming smile, and he knew he had to stop. He couldn't take more from her tonight, even if she offered it to him. Even if she wanted him to.

Gently, Will broke contact with Erin's lips and withdrew his hands from under her shirt.

She opened her eyes to look at him, and surprise quickly turned to understanding, which was accompanied by a healthy dose of blushing.

"I think you were about to take advantage of me," he said, trying to catch his breath, "and I promised I wouldn't let you do that."

"I'm so sorry," she stammered, quickly pulling herself up into a sitting position and putting her hands on her still-red cheeks. "I don't know what's going on with me. I just lost control…"

He pulled her hands away from her face and held them. "Please, I was just kidding, Erin. I was the one losing control. You would be shocked and dismayed at the thoughts running through my head just a minute ago." He looked from her disheveled hair to her flushed lips, desire still coursing through his blood. "And right now, truth be told."

Erin looked at him for a long moment, and he could see she was deep in thought. He wanted to know, more than anything, what was passing through her mind.

"Would you tell me what you're contemplating?"

Her gaze lowered until she was staring at their clasped hands. "I think you would be shocked and dismayed at what I was thinking, too."

He chuckled under his breath. "I doubt that."

Tentatively, she looked up at him. "I don't know if I can even say it."

"Please," he urged.

"I…I've never wanted anyone before. You know, not like that. But now, with you…" her voice trailed off. He squeezed her hands. The things she was making him feel, it was as though he had never been alive before now.

"I would have let you do whatever you wanted," she whispered, looking away again. "I wanted you to keep going. I wanted more."

Will leaned in and kissed her lips carefully. Resting his forehead against hers, he replied, "It's not wrong to want more. But I know you have ideals, and I don't want to ruin that for you."

She smiled at him, and his chest swelled with pride.

"I told you—you're a good man."

He sat back and pulled her with him so she was resting against his chest.

"You are very tempting," he said softly into her ear, "but I promise, I will do a better job behaving myself in the future."

"You've already proven you can," Erin replied, grinning. "It's me that I'm worried about."

They lay there on the couch for several minutes,

quiet and happy. He brought his cheek down onto the top of her head as his fingers made little circles on her upper arm. He loved how she felt under his hands.

Erin closed her eyes for a minute, then opened them and looked over at him. "Tell me more about your family and what it was like to grow up here all those years ago. Do you still remember it?"

"Do you really want to hear more?" He casually stroked the hair that fell onto her shoulders with his fingers.

"I do." Her voice was low and relaxed, making him imagine how wonderful it would be to fall asleep by her side every night and wake up with her huddled against him every morning.

Taking a deep breath, Will began telling her everything he remembered about his family, starting from the time he was a little boy. He told her about how he loved following his father around the grounds and being taken on errands in town with him. He spoke of his mother and how she was very strict, especially with his sisters, but also of how she put her children before all else and loved them with all her being.

He described his sisters to Erin, one by one. He told her about Mary, who was two years younger than him, but acted as though she was his mother, and about Jane and Martha who, although they were almost three years apart, seemed to do everything together. He told her about how he always got the feeling that Martha could do things a little bit better than Jane, but that she held back just enough so that Jane, who was older, would not be offended.

"She was your favorite, your sister Martha, wasn't she?" Erin's voice was almost sleepy as she turned her face to Will's.

He smiled. "I loved all my sisters, but yes, Martha always held a special place in my heart. She knew me better than anyone, probably better than I knew myself. If there was anyone I would have told about what happened with Bessie, about my particular circumstances, it would have been her. But I didn't."

"Will," said Erin, looking intently at him. "I'm really glad you told me."

He squeezed her hand, overcome with emotion. "You'll never know how much good you've done me, by being the one with whom I could share this burden."

Erin turned her head back away from him, and he could tell she was smiling contentedly as he kissed the top of her head.

"Mary, Jane, Martha—that's three. There are two others in the picture, and a man."

"The man was Peter, Mary's husband. And the two others were my baby sisters, Sarah and Abby. Sarah was about nine years younger than me, and Abby was twelve years younger. They both adored their big brother, but I'm afraid I wasn't around much for them. I left to go to school up north when they were just little girls, then left again to work in California. By the time I came back, Sarah was probably seventeen, and Abby fourteen, I think. And it wasn't long before I left them again to go to Boston. I wasn't with them much after that."

"Tell me about Boston, about all the things you've seen and done."

Will hesitated for a moment, then the words just started coming out. He spoke for what seemed like hours, and when he finally paused, he heard a slow and rhythmic breathing that could only mean one thing—Erin had fallen asleep in his arms.

"You trust me so much that you can just fall asleep, here, with me?" he whispered softly, brushing the hair away from her face.

The room was dark by now as it was well after eleven o'clock, and they had never bothered to close the curtains or turn on any lights. But the moon was bright outside, and its light coming in through the living room windows was just enough to allow Will to see the graceful curve of Erin's neck, the soft fullness of her lips, and the warm color of her hair.

He spoke again, knowing she could not hear him as deep as she was in her sleep.

"You are too good for me," he said quietly. "Too kind, too thoughtful, too loving. You deserve so much better. But here you are, and here I am. And I don't think I can let you go, even though I know I should."

He moved to get up and let her have the couch to herself, but she shifted and put her arm across his chest possessively as she settled snugly against his side.

Will smiled and reached behind him with his free hand to the blanket he always kept on the adjacent armchair. How many times had he sat up through the night in that chair, unable to sleep, watching one movie after the next just to try and forget who he was? Alone, tortured and trapped in his own darkness. Now, as he pulled the blanket off the chair and laid it on the two of them, he marveled at how different the feeling was. To feel her warmth, the weight of her body on his, her soft stirring as she breathed deeply against him—it was exquisite and unbelievable, nothing short of a miracle. She made him feel whole, filled his soul with peace—a sensation that had long been lost in the hazy corners of his mind.

What kind of angel was this woman in his arms? She was a blessing he certainly did not deserve but was too weak to resist. All he could do was relish the feeling of her in his arms and hope that it would be this way forever. But even as Will bent his head to kiss Erin's forehead reverently, he knew it was the hope of a fool. She, too, would pass from his life. It was only a question of when.

Chapter Twenty-Two

Erin woke up to find her cheek resting on Will's chest. She had slept the whole night in his arms.

She tilted her head slightly to look up at his face. He was still asleep, his dark lashes fanned out in tranquil repose against his pale skin. He looked so serene like that—no worried creases, no sad lines around eyes, and no wry smile on his lips. Just peaceful, timeless beauty.

Will's body was solid and strong beneath her. He was real, and he was good, and he was hers to protect and care for. She loved being with him. She loved him and everything he was, no matter how damaged and imperfect he believed himself to be.

Unable to stop herself, she kissed Will's chest through his shirt.

He stirred, opening his eyes.

"Sorry, I didn't mean to wake you," she cooed, smoothing his shirt with her fingers.

He hugged her close to himself. "I've never been so happy to wake up."

"Do you know how corny that sounds?"

The corner of his mouth turned up, and she couldn't help kissing the dimple that formed in his cheek.

He tucked her tangle of hair behind her ear. "So, you're okay?"

Erin was puzzled. "Of course. Why wouldn't I be?"

"Well, because you slept with me last night."

She slapped his arm playfully in response, trying not to giggle. "Only literally, not figuratively."

Will sat up, his chest vibrating with low laughter. Then he kissed her cheek. "Are you hungry?"

Reluctantly, Erin got up and stretched her arms above her head. She was stiff, having slept curled up on a couch all night. But it felt wonderful. "I am, but I should get home and clean myself up. Do you know what time it is?"

Will looked at his watch. "It's almost eight-thirty. It's still early."

She secretly gushed that, after spending more than fifteen hours with her, he wanted her to stay a little longer.

"I should go," sighed Erin. "My dad comes to get my grandmother around eight-forty-five to go to church."

"Which is why you don't want to be here at eight-forty-five."

Erin nodded. "I know, it's stupid to live my life around his, but I can't do it any other way."

"I understand." He paused a moment. "Are you free later today? I mean, after you clean yourself up and do whatever you need to do? I was thinking maybe I could come over, later, if you think it would be—"

"Yes," she blurted out, then promptly blushed. "I mean, if you have no other plans today."

"I have no other plans."

Grinning like an idiot, Erin reached up to give Will a quick kiss, but he pulled her closer and lowered his mouth to hers. Closing her eyes, she put her hands in his hair, and he groaned softly. They moved together until her back was against the wall, and she forgot where she was. She forgot that the door was open and that her dad would be coming for her grandmother soon. She almost forgot how to breathe.

Finally, Will pulled away slightly, and Erin drew in an overdue breath. "I wish I didn't have to leave right now," she mumbled.

"I wish you didn't have to leave, ever."

Suddenly her empty stomach filled with all sorts of somersaulting butterflies, and she smiled at him. "Me too." Her lips darted to plant a kiss on his cheek, then she backed up before he could catch her in his arms again.

"I love you, Will," she said, without thinking, her hand on the door frame she was about to step through. Hearing the words spoken out loud, Erin's first instinct was to take them back or add a qualifier or laugh or something. No one said those words so soon. What would he think?

But even as she took in his stunned expression, Erin determined she would stand her ground. It was true, after all. And there was no sense in keeping the truth a secret.

Not waiting for him to emerge from his stupor, she bounced down the stairs and out the door, practically running to her car.

****

Will watched Erin from his bedroom window as she got into her car and drove away. He continued standing there after she was gone. Her father came only minutes later, and Will saw him lead Mrs. Dovetree out to his car not long after.

Erin loved him. Knowing what she knew—who Will really was, the sins he had committed, the lives he had destroyed, the punishment he had to endure—she still loved him. There was nothing forced or false about her proclamation. It was open, honest, and true, just like her.

How could this be happening to him?

He pushed all pondering aside as he showered and got ready to go to Erin's apartment. Fifteen minutes later, he found himself rushing to get out the door, even though they hadn't made plans for a specific time to meet up. As he grabbed his keys and wallet off the kitchen counter, it struck him that his sense of urgency had nothing to do with punctuality. It had everything to do with seeing Erin again.

Erin was in the middle of vacuuming when Will showed up at her doorstep, but she didn't seem to mind the interruption. When they had finished with her Sunday cleaning routine, the two went out to lunch, then spent the rest of the day together doing everyday things. It was the best day of Will's very long life.

After wandering the aisles of a nearby grocery store together that afternoon, Will and Erin headed back to her place to cook dinner. They sat on her balcony afterwards, huddled under a blanket, talking until late into the evening. Realizing that, between the soft hum of the streetlight and the occasional call of a nearby screech owl, their voices were the only sounds filling the night, Will knew it was time for him to leave. Reluctantly, he rose to his feet and dragged her up with him.

Wrapping the blanket around Erin and holding on

to the edges, he pulled her in so that her face was inches from his.

"I can't move my arms," she joked in a low voice, looking up at him.

"So, you're saying you're helpless?"

She grinned. "Pretty much. I hope you don't have something nefarious in mind."

"Nefarious?" He lowered his head, aiming for her lips. "I'm afraid I don't know what you mean."

He kissed her, tugging the blanket even closer.

"I don't want to go," he said, releasing her mouth.

"I don't want you to go either."

He considered staying, just for a little while longer, but he knew that now or ten minutes from now or an hour from now, it would still be just as difficult to tear himself away from her.

"Maybe I can see you again tomorrow?" he offered, hoping Erin would agree.

"Not maybe," she replied. "Definitely."

Will smiled, letting go of the blanket and taking hold of her hand as it emerged.

Erin walked him to the door, where he grabbed her around the waist and kissed her again.

"I love you, too, by the way," he whispered into her hair. "I didn't want to say it this morning because I didn't want you to think it was just a response. Just the thing you say when someone says it to you, you know?"

Her face lit up with a smile. "I know."

****

Over the next several weeks, Will spent almost every waking moment that Erin wasn't at work with her. As soon as she was done at the office, she would drive to his apartment for dinner. He knew he was depriving her of sleep, especially on weeknights, as they could never seem to part company before midnight. She didn't seem to mind, though, and each day she looked more radiant to him than the last.

The first time Will showed up with Erin to visit her grandmother, the old lady's eyes grew wide and her mouth grew even wider in a smile that made her look twenty years younger. "I knew you two would be good for each other," she had said. "But no one listens to their elders anymore."

Will enjoyed every minute of Erin's company. It was the happiest he could ever remember being. Whether they were driving around town, cooking together, or just sitting around watching movies, there was something about having her near that erased his pain and his doubt. He was a whole person when he was with her. She had such an easy way about her, and she cared for him so genuinely that, at times, he forgot how unworthy he was. He basked in the glow of her love, and nothing else mattered.

But when midnight came each night and he reluctantly kissed her goodbye, the darkness that Will had been fighting against would begin to permeate his soul.

Erin was too good for him, a voice would remind him as he stood at the window to watch her drive away. She deserved the best that life had to offer. Who did Will think he was to lay claim to a woman like that? How could he subject her to the curse of his perpetual existence? How could he put the weight of his unforgivable sins on her back? He was an aberration, a man destined to be alone, watching the world pass him by. How could he ask her, with all her kindness and compassion and beauty, to take part in his misery?

But then morning would come, and Will would see her again. His joy in Erin's presence would overshadow the darkness and doubt, and he would allow himself to believe once more that he could have her, even if he did not deserve her.

****

Erin smiled as she watched Will, standing at the sink scrubbing a dirty pot. His gorgeous arms flexed as he attacked a particularly stubborn spot, and he wore an expression of deep concentration that made her want to hug him.

It had been almost two months since the day she had showed up at his apartment carrying that library book, and still she had a hard time not smiling when she was with him. And an equally hard time keeping her hands off him, for that matter. She wondered if this was how love made everyone feel.

Unable to resist the urge to hold him any longer, she snuck up behind him and wrapped her arms around his chest, pressing her cheek against his back.

"You've picked a most inopportune time to express your affection for me," he bantered. "You realize I have my hands full here."

"That's all right. You can make up for it later."

"Mmmm," he purred. "Rest assured, I will."

Releasing him, she stepped to the side so she could look at his face. "Can you guess what day tomorrow is?"

Will closed his eyes briefly and put on his dramatic thinking face. "It's Thursday."

Erin laughed, crossing her arms. "Yes. But it's a

little more special than most Thursdays. For me, anyway."

Having finished rinsing out the pot, he put it aside to dry, then turned to look at her, drying his hands on a dish towel. "Why, Miss Dovetree, is it your birthday?"

She nodded, feeling like a kid. "Indeed it is, Mr. Abbott! Twenty-seven trips around the sun."

"Wow. You're certainly getting up in years, aren't you? Why, look, what is that?" He ran his fingers through her hair, sending delicious tingles up her spine. "Are those gray hairs I see?"

"Oh, you cruel man!" she gasped as she attempted to punch him in the chest. Laughing, he deflected her swing and grabbed her wrist tenderly instead.

"And these hands, look! I believe that's a wrinkle, right there. Do you see it?"

He brought her hand up to his mouth and kissed it. Was this what it was like to be courted in the 1800s?

Enjoying the touch of his lips, she studied his handsome face and thought of how she wanted nothing more than to be the object of this man's affection. She wanted to relive the last seven weeks for the rest of her days.

But as she gazed lovingly at him, she saw a shadow cross over his face, and he released her hand and looked at her.

"We should do something special tomorrow night, for your birthday," he said, his smile erasing all thoughts of the shadow from her mind.

"What kind of something?" Really, it made no difference at all what Will had in mind, as long as he would be there with her.

"Well, my lawyer, the one in your office building,

he's always telling me to let him know if I ever want to go see a show or take in the grand Charlotte opera because he has tickets at his disposal for the firm's long-standing clients. And I am, after all, one of the firm's longest-standing clients, even if he doesn't realize it. So, let me see if I can get us some tickets to see something tomorrow night. Would you like that?"

Erin wrapped her arms around him and rewarded him with a kiss before answering, "I would like that very much."

The next day after work, Will was waiting for Erin in the lobby of her office building. She saw him as soon as she stepped off the elevator, standing there with his feet a little apart, his hands clasped in front of him, looking directly at her, as though he knew she would be coming out of the elevator at that very moment. His lips curled up in a smile, and she smiled dreamily in return.

As she passed through the security gate, Will came to meet her.

"Happy birthday," he whispered into her ear as he brushed her cheek with his warm lips.

"It is now," she replied, reaching for the hand that she had gotten so accustomed to having in her own. "So, was your attorney able to get some tickets for you, or are we all dressed up with no place to go tonight?"

"He came through. It's the theater for us."

"Phantom of the Opera?"

"Indeed. Have you seen it?"

Erin nodded. "Once with my mother in high school, and once in college with a group of friends. I love it. Thank you!" She tugged on his arm, and he lowered his head to receive her kiss.

"We have time for a birthday dinner first. We

should hurry, though—our reservation was for ten minutes ago."

She followed him outside through the revolving doors and down a block to an Italian restaurant Will knew was her favorite.

They were seated right away, and Erin took the menu from the hostess. Their server came a minute later and began rattling off the evening's specials. They ordered their meals and were alone again.

Will looked at her as she took a sip of water but said nothing. Setting her glass down and ignoring the uneasy feeling in the pit of her stomach, she smiled at him. "You look like you've got something on your mind."

He shook his head slowly. "Not something, someone."

Erin nodded, knowingly. "Our waitress is very attractive in that tight black shirt."

Will chuckled, but there was something unnatural, almost forced, about his laugh. The sound was heavy with words unspoken.

Instead of pressing him to tell her what was going on in his head, Erin let the moment pass and began recounting the events of the day, trying to get his mind off whatever thoughts weighed him down. Though Will listened politely and responded at all the appropriate places, Erin couldn't shake the feeling that something was off.

When they finished the meal, they walked over to the theater a few blocks away, arriving just as the doors opened to the public. Will took her hand to lead her through the crowds of people to their very good seats in the center of the Orchestra section.

"I've never sat so close to the stage before," said Erin as they took their seats. "You must spend a lot of money on your attorney."

Will gave a forced chuckle in response to the quip, and Erin's heart sank. He'd said practically nothing through dinner, and the walk over was like a funeral march, except with less noise. Something was wrong, and Will wasn't going to tell her what.

Not knowing what else to do, Erin reached over the armrest to hold Will's hand, hoping that maybe the contact would help him in some way. Unfortunately, he didn't hold her hand so much as simply allow her to hold his, and that feeling, that Will was tolerating her presence rather than enjoying it, was more disturbing than all the brooding silence.

As the curtain rose and the show began, Erin tried to immerse herself in the music and the story she loved, hoping to distract herself from the ominous feeling that was growing inside her. She couldn't even venture a glance at the handsome man beside her, afraid of what she would see. Instead, she kept his hand firmly in her grasp, not wanting to let go.

When the lights came on at intermission, Will looked over at her and smiled politely. Erin almost cried. She could think of nothing to say, short of asking what was wrong, and she didn't feel up to hearing his answer quite yet. Instead, like a coward, she excused herself to go to the bathroom.

The second half started and ended, and Erin and Will left with the crowds to walk back to the parking garage where Erin had parked her car early that morning. Will had gotten a ride to the city so they could drive back to his place together. Though she normally jumped at every extra minute with Will, tonight he had built a wall between them, and Erin could not shake the feeling that there was something terrible on the other side. And so, she drove on in silence.

After the longest seven-minute car ride of her life, Erin pulled into a spot in the back of the apartment complex and turned off the car. She left the key in the ignition and, putting both hands on the steering wheel, simply stared out the window at the dark trees outside. The creek where they had walked on Easter day, where the girl he loved had drowned, lay just past those trees. Erin thought about the creek and about that poor, pregnant young woman and tried to draw into herself some of the sadness that must have been at the root of whatever Will was thinking and feeling now.

Finally, after sitting there with her in silence for several minutes, Will asked, "Do you want to come inside for a little while?"

His voice was devoid of feeling, and it was all Erin could do to keep her tears at bay.

"Yes," Erin replied, attempting to rally, "but I don't get the sense you really want me to."

He replied only with more silence.

Feeling defeated, Erin let out a resigned sigh and shook her head. "What's wrong, Will? What are you thinking about that you won't tell me?"

"What makes you think I'm thinking anything at all?" he replied, sounding almost annoyed.

"You're not exactly one to keep your emotions tucked away in your sleeve," she said, trying to be equally annoyed so that she wouldn't burst out crying in front of him. "Now tell me what you're thinking about so we can figure it out and move on."

"Not tonight," said Will, softening a bit. "It's your birthday, and we shouldn't waste it on my thoughts."

"Well, we're not wasting it on your words, so why not your thoughts?"

"Because they will only hurt you."

"Will," Erin pleaded, "just tell me! What's going on?"

Will slammed his hand on the panel in front of him, so hard that she thought he could have set off the air bags, then turned to look at her.

"Fine," he said with a starkly contrasting calm. "You want to know what the problem is? The problem is that you are a year older, and I am not. I never will be. Every year you will get older, and I will not. I will remain as I am, and you will move on through your life, leaving me behind, just like everyone else."

She looked at him, her mouth dropping open in disbelief. "You're upset because I'm too *old* for you? First I was too young, and now I'm too old? Are you serious?"

"No, that's not it, Erin. You're not too old—you're perfect. You're kind, intelligent, beautiful…"

"You're not making any sense!"

"Look," he replied, as though *she* were the irrational party in this conversation, "before you knew about me, about my unique situation, I told myself that it was unfair of me to be with you because you didn't know who I really was, what I had done, what I had become. So, when you came that afternoon and you knew and I could tell you everything, I convinced myself that it was okay. I could just love you, and you could love me, and it would all be okay."

He shook his head and Erin's heart plummeted to

her feet. He was going to break up with her.

"It was foolish," he continued. "It was stupid, wishful thinking. Above all, it was selfish. From the first time I saw you, Erin, I wanted you. But it can't be. I can't be with you. It's not right. It's not good for you."

Erin trembled with anger, and she was thankful for the feeling because she did not want to sink into heartbreak just yet. "Stop trying to guess what's good for me! I know what's good for me, and it's you, Will. You are good for me."

He shook his head, adamantly. "No. No, I am not. You deserve a full existence. You are meant to find someone you can go through life with, have children with, raise a family with—do all those things that normal people do."

"Why can't I do all that with you?" She knew exactly how she sounded—like a pathetic girlfriend trying everything she could to convince her boyfriend not to leave her. She hated herself for that, but she couldn't stop.

"Because I'm not supposed to have those things," he answered.

"It's you who says so," Erin quietly screamed at him, gripping the steering wheel tightly with both her hands. "Who do you think you are? God? You are not God, Will. You're just a man, you always have been. You can't control everything. You couldn't control who Bessie would choose to marry, you couldn't control her decision to end her life, and you can't control who I choose to love. I choose to love you, Will."

"If it is so easy, Erin, to choose who you will or won't love, then I must choose not to love you. Because

I do love you, and I want you to have a good and happy life. I'm sorry I allowed myself into your life at all. I take all the blame for my lack of self-control. I will remove myself, and you will find another. Someone more worthy of you."

He opened the car door and to get out, but she grabbed his arm to stop him.

"Will," she said frantically, "you have to understand—I'm not going to go chasing after you. I'm not going to show up at your doorstep and ask you again to be with me. I choose you, and you must choose me. It has to be your decision. You have to figure out this mess you've got inside your head about Bessie and why you've been wandering around aimlessly for the past hundred years." She softened her tone as she released his arm. "But when you do figure it out, Will, know that I will be waiting for you. I will wait for you to come back to me."

Will reached for her hand and brought it to his lips, and for a moment she thought she might have gotten through to him. Then, still holding her hand, he replied, "I'm afraid I've heard that one before, Miss Dovetree."

Even with the anger welling up inside her again, all she could do was shake her head as she spit out, "Not from me, Will. You never heard it from me."

He released her hand and stepped out of the car, closing the door behind him. She watched him walk to the building and disappear inside, without so much as a second glance back at her.

A flood of tears escaped from behind her closed eyes, and all Erin could do for the next few minutes was sit there in her car and cry. In the blur of sadness and tears, it occurred to her that she hadn't cried that hard since her mother had died. Her whole body shook with each sob, and she didn't care if anyone could see or hear her. She had to get it all out, right then and there, and she did.

Then, heaving one last sob, Erin found a napkin in the pocket of the car door and dried her eyes and face, wiping away mascara with the tears. She crumpled up the napkin and shoved it in the cup holder between her seat and the seat that was still warm from Will.

Finally, she turned the key that was still hanging from the ignition and drove home.

Chapter Twenty-Three

Erin couldn't bear to go to her grandmother's the next day for their usual Friday night visit. All she could think about was Will, and she knew if she went to his building she would end up at his door. Erin couldn't go back to him. She told him she wouldn't, and it would do no good. He had to figure this out for himself. Even if Will loved her, which she wanted to believe was the case, he couldn't be with her until he worked through his issues.

A small voice inside her head laughed. He'd had over a hundred years to work through his issues. Some things just weren't possible.

With her head down and a lump in her throat, Erin entered her apartment and changed into a tee shirt and leggings. There weren't even any leftovers in the fridge to speak of because they had eaten all their meals at Will's place that week, so she had to settle for making herself a cheese sandwich for dinner. She didn't even bother popping it in the toaster oven. It didn't matter. She wasn't all that hungry anyway.

Taking her cold sandwich and a glass of water to the coffee table in the living room, Erin turned on the television and started flipping through the channels. But even the simple act of sitting idle in front of the TV reminded her of the many nights she and Will had lain on the couch watching together. She had been so comfortable there, sitting close with his arm around her, her head resting on his shoulder.

"Damn it, Will," she muttered under her breath, turning off the television in frustration. "You've managed to ruin TV for me. Thanks a lot."

The following Friday Erin decided she would have to go visit her grandmother. After all, she couldn't very well go on avoiding Will's building indefinitely. There was no other way she could see her grandmother.

As she walked up the sidewalk to the building's front door, she kept her eyes low, managing to resist the temptation to look up at the window for a glimpse of his form behind the curtains in his living room.

"Come in, it's unlocked!" she heard her grandmother's voice say when she knocked loudly at the old woman's door.

Erin entered, bracing herself for the onslaught of questions she knew would come as soon as her grandmother saw that Will was not with her.

"Come in, come in, child."

Surprised that her grandmother hadn't mentioned Will, Erin went inside and kissed her grandmother on the cheek. The old woman looked up at her sympathetically, and Erin realized that her grandmother was somehow already apprised of the situation.

"Sit down, honey," said her grandmother, her brow wrinkled with tender concern. "How are you doing?"

Erin wasn't sure how to interpret that question. How was she feeling after a long week of work? How was she handling the fact that the man she loved was out of her life forever?

She sat down on the couch next to her grandmother's chair, deciding on a generic reply. "I'm fine. How are you?"

"It's going to be hard on you being away from Will while he's in Boston. Such a shame that he has to go just when you two were getting to know each other, but what's meant to be is meant to be. He'll be back before you know it."

Erin was stunned into a momentary silence. Will was in Boston?

"What do you mean, Grandma? He's not upstairs?"

Her grandmother shook her head. "No dear, he's gone. He went around visiting with everyone on Tuesday to say that he had business to attend to in Boston and that he didn't know when he would return. It's a shame. He is such a decent young man. But it will be a short absence, I'm sure." Her grandmother paused and looked at her. "Didn't he tell you he was leaving, honey?"

Erin stared blankly at her grandmother. "Yes, of course he mentioned it," she fibbed. "I just didn't realize about the dates, that's all."

Immediately, she regretted lying to her grandmother. She wasn't even sure why she had.

She got up quickly and walked over to the kitchen sink, hoping to find a pile of dirty dishes in need of washing. Turning on the water, she began vigorously scrubbing the first of only four items in the sink. In addition to providing an outlet for her nervous energy, the sound of the running water kept her from having to talk to her grandmother while she gathered her thoughts.

Will was gone. He had up and moved back to Boston, just like that, without telling her. He hadn't even said goodbye. What would he do? Wait it out the next fifty or sixty years until Erin died, then move back here? Was that his plan?

Why did he have to leave in the first place? Charlotte was Will's favorite place to live; he had told her that. Did he think Erin was so weak that she wouldn't be able to stop herself from going back to him, even though she said she would not?

Erin lay awake that night, trying to picture Will asleep in his bed in his apartment in Boston. She would have given anything to see him, just for a moment—his soft lips slightly parted, his steady breathing lending a slow and peaceful rhythm to the silence. She wished he hadn't been so closed-minded. He would have been happy with her if he had just allowed himself to be. It was his own fault he was so sad. His eternal youth could have been a blessing, but instead he had somehow turned it into a curse, poisoned by his own guilt and self-pity.

Bessie's death hadn't been Will's fault. All he had done was lie and make Bessie think he didn't love her. It was a mistake, yes, but he hadn't told Bessie to end her life. He hadn't meant for any of it to happen.

In the end, though, it didn't matter what Erin thought. Will would hold on to the truth he determined, and the result would hurt them both. They would not be together as they should have been, and there was nothing Erin could do to change that.

****

Will caught himself staring absently at the book on the side table in his home office. It was as though he had fallen under some spell. He had gotten up to get a glass of water, and, as he had turned to leave the room, he had glimpsed the book. Thoughts of Erin had immediately flooded his mind, breaking down the walls he had been trying to build each day since the day he left her as though those walls had been made of sand.

Awakening from his stupor, he went over to the book and picked it up. *A Pictorial History of Charlotte's First Families*. It was the book Erin had brought with her that afternoon in early May, when she had confronted him about the year of his birth. She'd found a copy of it at a local bookstore a few weeks later and bought it for him. When he had playfully objected to her showering him with gifts, she had told him to consider it an early birthday present.

His birthday had now come and gone. It had been a miserable day, just like every other since he had gotten out of Erin's car and vowed to remove himself from her life.

Will sank into the couch by the window and let his head fall back against the cushions, closing his eyes. He had merely existed before he had met Erin. There had been constant sadness, regret, and grief over what had happened with Bessie. He'd had remorse for what he had done, but it had been dull in comparison to what he felt now. Now there was anguish—an insufferable void, and he could feel every inch of its depth. The numbness had been replaced with searing pain. It was as though Erin had given him back his heart, only so that his heart could dole out his punishment more completely.

His personal hell had been perfected.

Sitting up, Will ran his hand lovingly across the cover of the book in his lap. He would have gone back to Erin in a heartbeat and begged her forgiveness if he thought there was any chance he could make her happy. But he knew that happiness with him was impossible.

He would not stand between her and the life she deserved.

****

Erin pulled the covers over herself as she turned onto her side and hugged an extra pillow to her body. At night, there were no deadlines or chores or errands to distract her. There was nothing to keep her mind occupied and free from thoughts of Will. And it seemed that just as her body began to rest, her imagination sprang to life. She could not keep herself from imagining that Will was with her, beside her, wrapping his arms around her and kissing her into oblivion. Six weeks had gone by, and still she could not forget.

It had been five days since Will's birthday. She wondered how well he had handled it. She wished she could have been there with him.

Perhaps tonight she would indulge in her fantasy. What would it hurt to pretend he was here, lying next to her? The dream would only last a little while, but maybe it would allow her to sleep with happy thoughts for once—thoughts of the man she once loved. Thoughts of the man she loved still.

Erin was in a transitory state between sleep and wakefulness, with warm thoughts of Will on her mind, when her cell phone rang. The ringing quickly pulled her out of the reverie, and almost instinctively she reached toward the nightstand and blindly found her phone. The hope that the person on the other end of the line would be Will sprang unsolicited from somewhere inside her.

"Hello?" she finally answered in a raspy voice. She held her breath in anticipation.

"Hi Erin. I'm sorry to wake you." It was her father.

She sat up in bed, fully awake now. "Dad, what's wrong? Is everything okay?"

"It's your grandmother. I'm at the hospital with her. She was feeling a bit under the weather earlier this week. She thought it was just a cold or something, but then tonight when I came to see her she was complaining that she couldn't breathe. We just got checked in, and she's okay. I didn't want to call and disturb you, but she said she wanted you to know."

"Which hospital are you at?" asked Erin, throwing the covers off herself and turning on the light.

"There's no need to come, Erin. You have to go to work tomorrow."

"Are you at Pineville?"

"Yes," her father relented.

"I'll be there in fifteen minutes."

Erin already had a pair of jeans on when she hung up the phone. She threw on a bra and a tee-shirt and headed for the door, her cell phone and keys in one hand and her purse in the other.

Ten minutes later, she was bursting through the front entrance of the hospital, looking for someone who could tell her where her grandmother was. Spotting a young woman behind the information desk, Erin half-walked, half-ran to her.

"Can you tell me where I can find Rose Dovetree? I'm her granddaughter. She's asked to see me."

"Spell that, please?"

Erin spelled the name out for the woman, who entered it into her computer.

"She's in the ICU, Room 5. Just take the elevators to your left up to the third floor, turn right coming off the elevators, then follow the signs."

"Thank you," Erin called out behind her as she sped to the elevators. She didn't have to wait long before the doors opened. She got on and pressed the button for the third floor.

The elevator made an excruciatingly slow ascent to the third floor, then the doors opened again. Erin jumped off the elevator, turning right, then turned right again to follow the arrows to the ICU.

There were hardly any people in the halls, only the occasional night shift nurse or orderly. Everything was peaceful, disrupted only by the squeaking of Erin's sneakers against the laminate floors.

Up ahead, above a couple of sliding glass doors, Erin saw a big sign that marked the entrance to the ICU. She slowed down as she approached and pushed a big square metal button to her right to open the doors. As she passed through, a nurse who happened to be walking by stopped her with an admonishing look. "I'm sorry, Miss, visiting hours are over."

"I'm here to see my grandmother, Rose Dovetree. She's asked for me to come."

The nurse paused to consider for a moment. "You're her granddaughter?"

Erin nodded. "Yes."

"Alright," the nurse agreed, although her tone was reluctant. "She's in the third room, that way." She gestured down the hallway to the right.

"Thank you," Erin replied, then quickly made her way to her grandmother's room. The door was closed, and she stopped just outside to look through the glass.

The room wasn't large. There was a single bed set against the wall opposite the door where her grandmother was sleeping under a pile of blankets. The old woman's head was at the far end of the room, and her feet were closer to the door, where Erin stood immobile.

Erin's father sat in one of the two chairs that were arranged on either side of the bed, turned away from her. He was leaning forward with his head resting in his hands, his elbows on his knees.

The bed, the sterile-looking white walls, and even the beeping of the equipment she could hear in the background all brought back memories of visiting her mother at Duke Medical Center.

The first time she went to Duke, her father had cut short their trip to Myrtle Beach because her mother had begun to lose the function of her right leg and could no longer walk. Erin was supposed to meet them at the beach on Friday night, but she got the call from her father that they were at the hospital, so she met them there, instead. At the hospital, it didn't take Erin long to see that her mother's condition had worsened, the growing tumor in her head pushing against the nerves that told her various limbs what to do. She remembered watching her mother trying to direct a spoonful of food to her mouth a few times, coming close but not really getting it right. Erin had made some remark about the movie they were watching together in her hospital room as she quietly took the spoon from her mother to feed her. "You're just tired," she had told her mother with a warm smile, both of them knowing full well that was not the problem.

Erin shook off the memory and moved forward, opening the door and entering the room where her grandmother lay.

Her father turned at the sound of the door opening

and, upon seeing it was Erin, stood up and came toward her. "I told you it wasn't necessary to come," he said, meeting her at the foot of her grandmother's bed. He looked tired, older, and his words didn't have much bite. Erin ignored him and moved to the side of her grandmother's bed, taking a seat in the empty chair and slinging her purse across the chair back.

Her grandmother opened her eyes and, looking over at Erin, smiled.

"Honey, you didn't have to come all this way to see me. I'm fine. They're taking good care of me."

Erin smiled back at her, taking her hand. "How do you feel?"

"I'm okay. I'm just old."

Her grandmother looked around the room after saying this, then looked past Erin to the hallway outside the room.

"Whose house is this?" she asked. "It's a big house. I wonder whose house this is…"

Her voice trailed off, and Erin looked at her father, wondering why her grandmother wasn't making any sense.

Her father simply shook his head. "Everything has been stable for the past half hour. She's just on a lot of medication, Erin, and she hasn't slept much, at home or since we got here."

Medication and lack of sleep—she had heard those excuses before. When her mother had been brought to Duke the second time—what would end up being the last time—Erin had called her mother's cell phone and her father had answered. He had given the phone to her mother, and Erin had tried to talk to her. Erin couldn't remember what exactly they had said to each other, but she remembered that her mother hadn't made any sense. That had been the last conversation she'd had with her mother. The next morning, her mother fell into a coma. Four weeks later she was taken off life support, and eight hours after that, she had died.

"You're in a hospital, Grandma," Erin finally replied to her grandmother, biting back her tears. "You're in a hospital, and you're going to be fine."

Erin's grandmother looked around the hospital room. "There." The old woman pointed to a button-down sweater that hung on a hook on the bathroom door. "Erin, dear, get me my sweater, please."

Erin didn't want to agitate her grandmother, so she got up and grabbed the sweater.

"Are you cold, Grandma?"she asked, handing it to her.

Her grandmother ignored her question and began rifling through the big pockets of the sweater. She finally pulled out an envelope and stretched out her arthritic hand to give it to Erin.

"I need to get my rent to Mr. Abbott. Would you please mail it to him, dear? The envelope is addressed to him already. He's living in Boston, you know."

Erin looked down at the envelope and took it. Her grandmother's handwriting was on the front of the envelope, and it was indeed addressed to Mr. William Abbott in Boston.

"Mother," said her father, approaching the bed from the corner of the room where he had been standing the whole time, "we already sent in your rent check for September, and it's too early to send in next month's rent."

The old lady waved Erin's father away. "Erin

needs to send in my rent. Please, Erin, take the envelope and put it in your purse."

Erin looked at her father and shook her head slightly. She walked over to the chair where she had left her purse. Subtly, she turned her back to her grandmother and flipped the envelope over as she unzipped her purse. The envelope was unsealed, and Erin slipped her hand in. As she suspected, there was no check. It was an empty, open envelope addressed to Will. She turned toward her grandmother again, so the old woman could see her put the empty envelope into her purse. She looked back up at her grandmother, and her grandmother nodded in approval.

"You'll send that envelope? You promise?"

Erin didn't know what to say. So, she nodded, a familiar sadness pushing its weight down onto her chest. "I promise, Grandma. Please don't worry about it anymore."

Erin's grandmother settled back against her pillow, satisfied with Erin's answer.

Rooted to the spot where she stood, Erin looked at her grandmother. She seemed so small, lying in that bed. Her youthful dark brown hair struck a harsh contrast with the white pillowcases and sheets, and her arms stuck out from under the blankets, I.V.s tethering her to an aluminum pole that carried bags of fluid.

As Erin sat there looking for the twinkle in her grandmother's eyes and contemplating what would happen to her, the door to the room opened, and the nurse who had begrudgingly allowed Erin to see her grandmother came in.

"I'm sorry, I need to check on Mrs. Dovetree's catheter and put some medicine on that sore on her backside."

Erin turned to her father. "She has a sore on her backside?"

Her father nodded. "It's nothing. It's getting better."

The nurse spoke again, this time in a gentler tone. "Why don't you two go downstairs to the cafeteria and get something to eat. It's open all night, and the sandwiches and snacks are discounted after midnight. I'll be done in twenty minutes, if you want to come back then."

Erin nodded and grabbed her purse, walking to the door. As she passed by her father, she glanced up at his face. He looked lost, as though he didn't know what to do with himself. Feeling a twinge of compassion, she cleared her throat. "Aren't you coming, Dad?"

Emerging from his confusion, her father nodded his head. "Sure. Right behind you."

Chapter Twenty-Four

Erin sat across from her father, eyes trained on the blueberry muffin in front of her, listening in growing irritation to her father tear through the plastic wrapper of his powdered donut. She thought about how disdainful he had been about her store-bought sugar cookies at Easter. Now look at him, biting into what was probably the most carcinogenic dessert ever synthesized. She wanted to make some sort of snide remark about the irony of it but instead chose to swallow her words with some milk.

Finally, her father broke the awkward silence. "Are you okay?"

Erin looked up from her muffin, startled, then nodded. "Are you?"

"I don't mean about your grandmother. She's going to be fine. I mean about your grandmother's landlord, Will Abbott. I heard he moved away."

Of course, her grandmother had spilled the beans about Will. Still, her father had no right to ask her about it.

Erin looked back down at her muffin. "Yeah, so what? Why should I care if he moves away?"

"Well," her father said, pausing for a second, "you two were dating, weren't you? I could tell he cared for you. He was—"

"Dad," she interrupted, trying not to yell despite

her rising temper, "I do not want to talk about Will with you."

He exhaled. "Okay." Then he went back to his donut.

A couple of minutes later he looked up at her again. "I loved her, you know. I loved her very much, your mother."

Erin could feel her face start to get hot, the anger in her rising again. Why couldn't he just sit there and eat his stupid donut without talking about Will or her mother or anything else?

She swallowed the bite of muffin that was stuck in the back of her mouth, took another sip of milk to force it down her throat, then slowly wiped her hands and mouth with a napkin.

"You want to do this here, now, Dad?" she said through gritted teeth. "You want to 'talk'? Well then fine, let's talk. You're sitting there, telling me that you loved my mother. If you loved my mother, then why did you go and screw around with someone else? Can you answer me that?"

Her question didn't seem to shock her father at all. He looked almost relieved that Erin had asked, and she couldn't decide whether she was angry that her words hadn't had the desired effect or just confused.

Her father raised his water bottle to take a drink, then set it down and focused his gaze on her, his lips pursed in an expression she couldn't figure out.

"Why has it taken you twelve years to ask me that, huh? Every day from the time it happened until now, you've made every effort to avoid me. And when you couldn't help but cross my path, I've had to endure the accusation in your eyes and the reprimand in your voice. Why have you never had the courage to just come out and ask me what happened?"

"Because!" Erin took a quick breath, her body beginning to shake with rage. "Because I already know the answer!"

"What is it then, Erin? Why did I cheat on the woman I loved, the woman I married, the mother of my child?"

"Because you could! Because some whore threw herself at you, and you weren't man enough to say no. Because you didn't care enough about us to be strong against temptation."

Erin's father leaned back in his chair, nodding his head slowly.

"That's all true, Erin. I did have the opportunity, and I could have said no. I had a choice, and I made the wrong one. But you don't know what I was feeling."

"You were feeling like you wanted to have sex." She threw the words back at him and waited for his response.

Her father's nostrils flared, his chin trembling slightly. She had made him angry, and she was glad for it.

"There was only one woman I wanted to have sex with," he replied, keeping his voice steady, "and that was your mother. But there came a point when she didn't want to anymore. She wouldn't have me. I knew she loved me, but it hurt. She wasn't attracted to me, not in that way, and it hurt my feelings."

Erin rolled her eyes. "Do you want me to feel sorry for you, Dad? Do you want me to say that it was Mom's fault you cheated on her?"

"No, Erin." Her father's voice was low and calm,

making her own tone sound hysterical in comparison. "I just want you to hear me out. I'm just saying that her refusal—well, it made me feel that she didn't love me the way I loved her. Like I repulsed her, and it hurt me. It made me wonder if she had felt that way all along. It made me think that maybe she had just been going through the motions, even before, because she thought it was her obligation as my wife."

He looked down, and the shadows from the cafeteria lights made him look older. Tired. Like he hadn't slept in years. Still, Erin could not feel any sympathy for him. He had broken his vows, and now he was trying to justify it.

"I was very sad," he continued, raising his eyes to her. "I didn't know what to do. I felt so alone."

"So you found comfort in the arms of another woman. Well, that makes it all okay, then. I'm glad we had this little chat."

Her father dropped his head and sighed. "It only happened once, you know. The woman I slept with—"

"Your secretary."

"Yes, my secretary. She got upset with me when she realized we weren't an item. I told her I loved my wife, that I had made a mistake. She was livid. She called our house to get back at me and told your mother, hoping that it would break us up. I deserved it. But it turned out to be the best thing that could have happened because I'm not sure I would have had the courage to tell your mom otherwise."

He paused, fiddling with the edge of the napkin his donut was resting on, before continuing.

"I was so afraid that I would lose her and you, and I was so disappointed with myself for letting both of you down. Until she got sick, it was the only time I'd ever cried in front of your mother."

Erin held her tongue. She remembered how her father was at the hospital. He was a mess. The first time, when her mother was conscious, Erin had to tell him several times to keep it together in front of her mother and to leave the room before he had his breakdowns. Of course, the second time they were at the hospital her mother was in a coma, and Erin didn't feel the need to bother with keeping up appearances for her mother's sake. She hardly had the strength to keep herself from crying at that point, let alone deal with her father's emotional instability.

"She forgave me, just like that," he went on. "She said she loved me and knew I loved her. She said she understood what I was feeling and that she felt bad for hurting me." He laughed ironically. "*She* felt bad for hurting *me*. Well, if I didn't feel like a pile of shit before for what I'd done, that really put me over the edge. We talked all night about us, all three of us. And we talked about sex and her thoughts about it. I'll spare you the gory details…"

"Please do."

"But in the end, I realized that if she loved me enough to forgive me for betraying her trust, then I should love her enough to be with her without needing to be with her in that way."

Erin still sat quietly, trying to quell the urge to make some snide remark about her father's sainthood, and at the same time fighting the growing feeling that perhaps she should say something reassuring instead.

He looked at her then, his eyes glimmering with a film of unshed tears. "Do you remember when your mother was in a coma—at the end, when the doctors were asking if we wanted to take her off the respirator and allow her to die? Do you know why I told them it was your decision, not mine?"

Erin frowned, puzzling over his question. "I guess I just assumed you didn't want to decide for her. I assumed you were taking the easy way out, letting someone else decide. I hated you for that, you know. For putting such a huge burden on me." Her throat closed up with emotion, but she pushed through. "How was I in any way capable of making such a terrible decision on my own? How was I in any way worthy of saying whether my mother should live or die?"

"But you were," replied her father softly, almost lovingly. "And you made the right decision. It was exactly what she wanted. She didn't want to live like a vegetable. She wanted to allow death to come, if it came to that."

"How do you know?" questioned Erin, her own tears welling up at the thought of her mother lying helpless in the hospital bed, her chest being mechanically inflated and deflated and her face and arms puffy with all the water her body was retaining. "How do you know I didn't make a mistake?" Erin repeated in a whisper.

"The first time we were in the hospital, after Myrtle Beach and before we started chemo, the doctors brought us a lot of forms to sign. One of them was a living will. It was her wish, Erin. She said so herself."

Erin couldn't believe what she was hearing. "If you knew what she wanted, then why not just do it? Why did you put all that on me?"

"Because I didn't want you to hate me any more

than you already did. I lost you when I cheated on your mother, even though I was fortunate enough that I didn't lose her. Now, when I knew I was losing your mother for good, I didn't want to lose whatever part of you might still love me as your father."

Her father's voice cracked under the weight of his emotions, but he cleared his throat and went on. "I didn't want you to think of me as the person who took your mother away from you. How could I go on with the rest of my life without either one of you?"

Erin watched as he put his head in his hands and gave in, sobbing quietly across the table from her. She took her last clean napkin and dabbed at her own cheeks and eyes, trying to buy herself some time. She didn't know how to respond. She didn't want to give up her righteous position as her mother's advocate, her father's judge. But she was beginning to question how righteous her position actually was. This twelve-year-old grudge she had been harboring against her father, when all was said and done, was a child's grudge. Everything had been black and white for her, because that was how children saw the world. There was right and there was wrong, and there was nothing in between. But in real life, everything was in between.

Erin was no longer a child, though. Perhaps it was time for her to acknowledge the gray.

She pushed her chair away from the table and stood up.

"We should go check on Grandma. The nurse is probably done in there."

Her father breathed deeply a few times, his head still in his hands, then he stood up and cleared his throat again.

"We'll grab you a napkin on the way out. Otherwise, Grandma might think she's dying or something."

Her father chuckled, wiping his cheeks with his hands.

Erin followed him back to the elevators and up to her grandmother's room. They peeked through the windows and could see that she was sleeping peacefully.

The nurse who had worked on her came over to them and smiled.

"Mrs. Dovetree seems to be doing pretty well in just the last hour. Her heartbeat is steady, her blood pressure is good, and her fever is gone. We will probably keep her for a couple more days just to monitor her due to her advanced age, but I suspect that you'll be able to take her home once the 48-hour observation period has ended."

"Is she sleeping?" Erin's father asked.

"Yes," replied the nurse. "She fell asleep just a few minutes after I left the room. She will probably sleep through the night. If I were you, I would go home, get some sleep, and come back in the morning. Visitors' hours start at nine a.m., but unlike me the dayshift nurse is a softie, so she'd probably let you get in at eight."

Erin's father turned to look at her.

"What do you think, Erin? Should we leave her be until the morning?"

Erin nodded. "I think she's in good hands. She'll be fine without us."

She and her father thanked the nurse and walked back out of the ICU, finding their way to the receptionist's desk downstairs. They walked out the sliding glass doors and onto the parking deck.

"I'm on the second floor," said Erin.

"I'm on the fourth floor. We were here before visitors' hours ended. It was a mess. I'll walk you to your car."

They walked together in silence, up one floor to where Erin's car was parked in an empty row.

"I'll meet you back here, at the receptionist's desk, at eight tomorrow morning?" Erin asked, just before she opened her car door.

Erin's father looked stunned, but it took only a moment for him to recover. "Sure. Eight a.m."

She got into the car, closed the door shut, and started the engine. She could see her father watching as she backed out of the parking spot and drove away. With one last glance, she saw him wave. She waved back.

****

Erin's grandmother was in the hospital for a total of three days before she was released. After spending most of the morning of the second day with her father at her grandmother's bedside, Erin was convinced that her grandmother would be fine. She was no longer unaware of where she was, and she was having fun-loving conversations with Erin, her father, and the hospital staff, who adored her.

Erin returned to work after lunch that day but made a point to leave a little early to visit her grandmother at the hospital before heading home. By then, her grandmother, who had been moved from the ICU, was sitting up and on solid foods again, the twinkle in her eye quickly returning.

Erin was amazed at how resilient her grandmother

was, even at eighty-seven years old. And it wasn't just her body, but her spirit—her outlook. By the following morning, the day she was to be released, she was like a child asking every ten minutes if it was time to go home yet.

As she lay on her couch on Sunday afternoon, the weekend after her grandmother had been released, Erin thought about how much time she had ended up spending with her father over the course of her grandmother's hospital stay. She had eaten several meals with him. She had even joked with him. It was more time than they had spent together since her senior year in high school.

Now that her grandmother was home and things were "back to normal," Erin wondered how she was supposed to feel about him. It still bothered her to listen to her father talk about certain things, and she still found him judgmental and narrow-minded. His mere presence, however, was perhaps slightly less offensive to her now than it had been the week before.

Still, she couldn't help thinking of her mother every time she saw him, and her mind still conjured up images of him with some faceless woman who was not her mother. Erin continued to feel the vicarious sting of betrayal when she thought of what he'd done, but, for the first time since it had happened, she allowed herself to think about how her mother had stayed with him. It wasn't weakness that had caused her mother to stay, as Erin had always believed. She was able to stay because she had forgiven him out of love and an overabundance of understanding that Erin was quite sure she herself was not capable of.

If her mother had forgiven her father and gone on

with the rest of her life, who was Erin not to do the same?

And with that realization, another quickly followed as she thought of Will and the burden of his own transgressions, which he had carried alone throughout his long life. What good had come of his staunch views of what could and couldn't be forgiven? How was he any better off now than a hundred years ago?

A week after her grandmother had been released from the hospital, Erin decided that it was time to begin repairing her relationship with her father. The more she thought about it, the clearer it became that although it was her father's act of adultery that had started the tear, it was Erin's perpetual negativity toward him and her total unwillingness to entertain the thought of forgiveness that had caused that tear to grow over the years until it had practically severed them from each other.

So, Erin sent her father a short text message.

Do you want to have lunch with me on Tuesday in uptown?

Almost immediately, she received his response.

Yes. Just let me know when and where to meet you.

Erin smiled to herself. She was doing the right thing. Hating her father had never made her feel good about herself. She had felt justified, but not good.

Returning her attention to her father's question, she remembered taking a flyer earlier that week advertising a new restaurant that had opened just a couple of blocks from her office. Reaching for her purse, Erin started rummaging through it to see if she could find the advertisement.

Holding a collection of receipts, pen caps, and tiny

squares of paper with random notes scribbled on them, her purse was like a bottomless pit, a repository for all sorts of things she threw in there when there was nowhere else to put them. Finally, her hand landed on a folded-up piece of paper, and she took it out to examine it.

It wasn't the flyer, though. It was an envelope. It was the envelope that held a non-existent check that her grandmother had insisted Erin mail to her handsome landlord in Boston. It was the envelope on which that wonderful landlord's address was neatly printed, in her grandmother's elegant handwriting.

Erin looked at the envelope for a moment. She had promised her grandmother she would send it, hadn't she? And she couldn't break a promise to her grandmother.

Chapter Twenty-Five

Boston, Massachusetts
September, Modern Day

Will caught himself pacing his bedroom for the third time in less than an hour. He couldn't remember what had distracted him from reviewing the previous month's expenses for his New York units, but now he couldn't seem to focus on anything, let alone columns of numbers.

Realizing he couldn't be productive in his current state, Will decided he would try to walk off the restless energy and headed to the front door, grabbing his jacket off the back of a chair with one swift motion as he walked out of the apartment.

Although almost officially fall, the weather was mild and the leaves had only just started turning. Between the elegant brownstone buildings, the colorful foliage, and the sun-warmed air, it should have been the perfect afternoon for a walk on Clarendon Street. For Will, though, nothing could ever be perfect again—not without Erin.

He had to stop thinking about her. It was doing him no good to replay in his mind every moment he had spent with her, every word they'd spoken to each other, and every kiss they'd shared.

And yet, he couldn't stop himself.

He had tried to stay away, hadn't he? He had tried to do the right thing, to protect her from the cancer of his existence. But he couldn't avoid her completely, and, like a cancer, the feelings inside him had grown to take over every rational thought, until he could do nothing but succumb. When Erin had discovered his secret, it was like an answer to a prayer.

Even still, Will had known all along how it would end. The problem was that it had been so easy to love Erin completely. It had been so easy to think it was okay, that he wouldn't be hurting her if he didn't have to hide his past.

How could he have been so foolish?

Turning right, Will crossed the street and walked faster, trying to run away from his thoughts. It did no good to dwell on what he had given up by leaving her. It did no good to think of the fleeting happiness of those weeks with her. Erin had filled his life with a joy he didn't think he was capable of feeling, a joy he certainly didn't deserve. He wasn't meant for happiness.

Will had awakened from his dream when Erin had announced her birthday. She wasn't a stagnant pond, as he was. She was a flowing river, cutting her path through the world. He would only hold her back.

He turned again, walking toward his building. Will had been through this same string of thoughts every day since he had left her, and he always came to the same conclusion. Erin deserved more than he could give her. He had done the right thing. The pain in his heart now—the emptiness—was no less than he deserved.

Turning right once more, Will closed the loop and walked the last few blocks back to his building at a brisk pace. Despite the pleasant scenery, he kept his eyes trained on the sidewalk in front of him and sucked in deep breaths to try to clear his mind. But even as he tried to think of nothing, Erin's face appeared each time he blinked, her lips curling into a sweet smile, just for him.

A woman's nearby laughter sent a pulse straight through him as he approached his building. Instinctively, he looked up, hoping. But of course, it was not Erin. He watched as two young women walked by, and the woman he had heard laughing a few moments earlier tossed her head back and laughed again.

Somehow, Will's heart sank even lower.

Walking up the drive, he spotted a postal worker on foot, coming from the direction of his tenants' mailboxes. "You have some mail today, Mr. Abbott," the woman said cheerily as she moved past him. A brief nod and a weak smile were the only response he could muster.

Will reached into his pocket for the keys as he approached the mailboxes. Opening his own, he pulled out five envelopes and two newsprint flyers, which he moved to the back of the stack. Then he locked his box and continued up the path to the building, examining each envelope to see who it was from, and knowing full well he was wishing for the impossible.

Only steps away from the front door, he stopped, his eyes glued to the familiar handwriting on the front of the fourth envelope. Despite the lack of a return address, he would have recognized that penmanship anywhere. No one wrote like Mrs. Dovetree did anymore, with such long, elegant strokes.

He warmed at the thought of the old woman with the youthful spark in her eyes and stubborn matchmaking ways. And, somehow, holding the old woman's letter in his hand made him feel that Erin was just a little bit closer to him than she actually was.

As he stood there staring at the envelope, Will wondered what the old woman could have possibly sent him. It was too early yet to be receiving October's rent. Was it unreasonable to think she might be sending news of Erin?

Gripping the stack of letters tightly, as though they might fly out of his hand of their own accord, Will entered the building. With trembling hands, he unlocked his apartment door and continued inside. He removed his jacket and tossed it onto the chair by the door, along with the other mail, but somehow managed to keep the envelope from Mrs. Dovetree in his hands the whole time.

Will's steps were slow and deliberate as he moved through the bedroom and into the office, his eyes quickly spotting the letter opener on his desk. Steadying his nerves, he flicked open the envelope from Mrs. Dovetree. When he unfolded the two pages he pulled out, he was surprised to see very different handwriting. Instead of the long strokes of cursive on the envelope, the letter bore small, neatly printed words. His breaths grew quicker as he turned over the pages and looked at the signature to confirm his suspicions.

Yours, Erin.

The letter was from Erin. Will couldn't believe it. His first instinct was to start reading, but then he thought better of it. No good could come of reading Erin's words. She loved him—of this he had no doubt—but he had removed himself from her proximity for the sole reason that he knew he could not resist her. How could he expect himself to read those loving words, hear her sweet voice in his head, and not give in to the urge to rush to her side? It was too much—he just couldn't risk it. For her own sake, he had to stay out of her life.

Resolving to destroy the letter, he folded it back onto itself and stepped quickly out to the living room, heading for the large, brick fireplace. He hadn't used the fireplace since his return, but a pack of matches was sitting on the mantle, waiting for him. His hands shook again as he plucked the box from the shelf and, tucking the letter under his arm, hurriedly took out a match, dropping a couple onto the floor in the process. Striking the match against the box, he lit it and put the rest of the matches back on the mantle. Watching the orange flame dance at the end of the match, he slowly brought the letter closer to the flame. Then he paused.

What if there's something wrong? What if she's hurt? What if she needs you?

Will shook his head slowly from side to side, trying to ignore the thoughts that grew louder in his mind. He knew the questions were self-serving, a last-ditch effort by his subconscious to stay his hand. And he knew what would happen if he read that letter. But his subconscious had won the moment, and as the small flame crept down the match toward his fingers, he tossed it into the fireplace, where it could do no harm.

His resolve was gone. There would be no other match lit. He had to know what was in that letter.

Stepping away from the fireplace, Will shuffled back into his bedroom, looking only at the folded-up letter that he had almost destroyed. As he lowered himself into the leather armchair by the window, a warmth spread all through him. His mouth curved into a smile without a conscious thought as he surrendered himself to read the pages in his hands. As his eyes scanned the pages, he heard Erin speak the words to him.

Dear Will,

I hope you are well. There are a lot of things in my head and in my heart that I want to say to you, but I told you I wouldn't come knocking on your door, and that's not the purpose of this letter. So, I will just say that I miss you very much and my feelings for you remain, as I told you they would.

Almost two weeks ago, my father took my grandmother to the emergency room. She had been battling the flu, and that particular evening she was having trouble breathing. Don't worry, my grandmother is home now and is just as well as can be. But over the course of the three days that she was in the hospital I spent a lot of time there with her, and with my father.

You know I haven't had the best relationship with my father. Ever since I was a teenager and he cheated on my mother, I've been harboring this festering hatred of him, and I've wanted nothing to do with him. He hasn't helped the situation over the years, either. You saw what happened at Easter. He's difficult to get along with, set in his ways, and has no filter when it comes to speaking his mind.

Anyway, on the first evening my grandmother was in the hospital, my father and I were kicked out of her room while she was attended to by the nurse. We went down to the hospital cafeteria, and after sitting there for a while, not saying anything, my dad brought up the subject of my mother.

I was furious at first. How dare he even speak her name to me? He proceeded to tell me about how he felt, about why he cheated on her so many years ago. It was almost more than I could bear, but I had nowhere to go, and, in a way, I was frozen, listening to him go on whether I wanted to or not. He tried to tell me the reasons for why he cheated. He told me about how he confessed his actions to my mother when she confronted him, and how my mother had forgiven him and continued to love him, despite what he had done.

I was fifteen when my father cheated on my mother. When I asked her about it, she told me what had happened in simple terms. But she always made a point to tell me how good my father was, and how no one was perfect. She told me she and my father had forgiven each other, and I think that actually made me hate my father more. It was as though I had to make up for my mother's seeming indifference by being staunchly against him. I hated him for betraying her trust, and I hated him even more for making her forgive him.

I didn't say much in reply to my father that night in the cafeteria, but I thought about what he said over the next few days. I'm thinking about it still, and as I'm thinking about it, I'm trying really hard to get over my issues with him. I've even asked him to go to lunch with me this week. Can you believe that?

I'm telling you all this not because you need to know about what my dad did or why he did it. What you need to know is that I was wrong.

Do you remember when you called me up to your

apartment that first time, when we had tea, so many months ago? I asked you if some things were unforgivable, and you said yes. I agreed with you then because that's what I thought, too—some people just don't deserve to be forgiven. Well, after going through all this with my father, after thinking about it non-stop for over a week, after finally actually trying to forgive him, I've come to a slightly different conclusion.

None of us deserve forgiveness, Will. But we need it. We need to give it and we need to receive it. If we don't forgive others and if we don't forgive ourselves, we become these seething vessels of anger and hatred. And that's no way to live.

I guess what I'm saying to you is that you need to forgive yourself. Just let it go. I know that God has forgiven you, and I'm sure Bessie has, too. All that's left is for you to accept that forgiveness. Accept the fact that you don't deserve it, and you can never earn it. All you can do is be grateful for it.

I told myself I wouldn't say this, but I can't write you a letter without telling you that I love you very much. As I put aside this grudge I've held against my father for so long, I think I am able to love you even more. And I am grateful for that.

Yours,

Erin

Will sat in the armchair for a while, staring at the letter, rereading certain portions, then the whole thing, until finally he laid the letter down on his chest and leaned his head back, closing his eyes.

What was he supposed to do now, with her voice in his head and her love in his heart? She spoke so simply, yet what she was asking him to do was impossible.

Just let it go.

He didn't know how. He had held on for so long, regretted for so long, and hated himself, Robert Cox, and even at times Bessie for so many years that he no longer knew how to live without those feelings. They were a part of him, inextricable.

Without warning, another voice echoed in his mind—a voice from several lifetimes ago:

Live, love, and be loved. Even if you feel yourself undeserving, know that it is what you are meant for.

Martha had said the same thing, hadn't she? She had wanted Will to be happy, to let go of his sadness and his anger.

Will rose and stepped quickly to his desk. He opened the bottom file cabinet drawer as far as he could and pushed the various folders and papers to the front to make room, reaching to the back of the drawer. His fingers grazed the wood of the box he had been looking for, and he carefully lifted it out of the drawer, holding the files out of the way. Then he let the drawer slowly slide closed.

Placing the box on top of the desk, he opened the lid and pulled out Bessie's bundled stack of letters, placing it on the desk next to the box. Then he reached for the two envelopes that he always kept under Bessie's letters and set them in front of him.

Picking up Erin's letter, Will read it one more time, then folded it back up and placed it at the bottom of the box.

Finally, he picked up one of the two envelopes that had been kept in the box—the one that was addressed to him—and unfolded the letter that was inside, turning it over to read it, even though he could have recited it by heart.

It was from his sister, Martha.

Chapter Twenty-Six

Charlotte, North Carolina
June 1881

"I'm so happy you are home, William. Even if it is only for two short weeks."

As cold and dead as his heart was, Martha's loving smile as she walked leisurely down the street with William produced an ember of warmth within him.

"It is good to see you again, Martha. You and all my sisters, although it seems that my sisters have made it a habit to become wives of late."

"Well, Jane's marriage to Mr. Porter can't possibly come as a surprise."

William looked at her in earnest. "As a matter of fact, I was very much surprised to receive Jane's letter requesting my permission for her marriage to Mr. Porter. I had rather thought you were quite fond of him, and he of you. I confess bearing some guilt in giving my blessing without having that point resolved first."

Martha's smile softened but did not lose its warmth. "Do not worry about me, William. I admit, I did have notions at one time of how nice it might be to be married to Tommy, but it is better this way. He and Jane will be happy together. They will have a beautiful family, and they will be together for a long time."

"So, you are not upset at how things have turned

out, Martha? They are not yet wed—I can revoke my blessing if there is something amiss, or if you have been hurt in any way. If Mr. Porter has lied to you or misled you, then he will no doubt do the same to your sister. I cannot allow that."

Martha quickly hit his arm, a look of shock on her face. "William! The wedding is in five days' time! You will do no such thing! Besides, Mr. Porter has been upright and honest in all his dealings with me and with Jane. He will be good to her. I am sure of it."

William had a feeling there was more Martha was not telling him, but the kindness in her eyes left no room for any doubt that she honestly believed the marriage between Jane and Mr. Porter was good and right.

More concerning than what had passed between Martha and Mr. Porter was the nagging feeling that something had changed in Martha since William last saw her. The evening before, upon his arrival home from Boston, William had been struck by how pale and fragile Martha had appeared to him. Today, walking in the summer sun, she did not seem so tired, but still there was a dullness in her eyes that William had never seen there before.

Martha sighed, still smiling, as she gently passed her arm through his. He bent his arm to support her as they continued walking.

"Are you happy, William, being in Boston?" she asked finally, looking up at him.

He tilted his head in her direction. With each stride, her arm grew slightly heavier in his as she put more of her weight on him. Perhaps he had been walking too quickly, for it seemed she was getting tired. Looking ahead, he saw a bench they could sit on for a little while to rest.

"What do you think, Martha? Am I happier?"

They approached the bench, and William motioned for her to sit next to him. He noticed the relief on her face when they sat down.

"'Happier' is a relative term, William. I believe you are happier, but I do not believe you are happy."

"I am as happy as I can be, Martha, and happier still having you here with me."

"Do you still think of Bessie?" she asked, bluntly.

The sound of Bessie's name spoken aloud sent an arrow of pain straight through William's heart, but he held fast to his indifferent expression. "I do. Every day. I cannot help it."

Martha nodded, but he could tell she disapproved.

"Do you think of our dear father every day?" she asked after a brief pause.

He thought about his sister's question for a moment before answering. "Not consciously, but he is on my mind. Sometimes I will say something, do something, or look a certain way, and it will give me the feeling that our father is near. Perhaps I am turning into him."

She giggled at his explanation. "It is the same with me. I can even hear him scolding me sometimes over things I am thinking of doing but have not even done yet!"

William chuckled. "He was a fine man and an excellent father."

Still smiling, Martha nodded again. "Those are good thoughts to have William. Remembering the dead in that way, it is good."

He could hear the reprimand in the words his sister left unspoken. "You are implying that the way I am remembering Bessie is not good?"

At this, Martha looked him squarely in the eyes, and William steeled himself for the impending reproach. "I'm implying nothing, William—I'm telling you plainly that it is not good. There is a difference between keeping someone's memory alive in your heart and dwelling on that person every waking moment until their death begets yours."

Even as the words left her mouth, Martha's expression and her voice both softened. "I realize it has been very difficult for you, William," she continued, "but I do not like seeing you this way. When you entered the parlor last night, I thought you would be my old William, returned from the edge of despair. I prayed you would be, but you are not. Instead, you are the very picture of despair. I can see it plainly, even if others cannot."

What could William say in response? His sister was right, after all. The sorrow and regret he felt the day he said goodbye to Bessie was with him still. It permeated his body. It filled his soul. In many ways, he relished it and made a home for it there.

"It is what I needed to see," she continued, her fingers reaching for the gold chain around her neck in a gesture he noticed had become a habit for her. "I wasn't sure before, but now I know. I know what I want most in my life, William, and it is for you to find your peace. Because no matter how long a life I have, or how many joys I experience, knowing that you suffer under the weight of despair will render all such blessings meaningless. I would choose a brief moment knowing that someday you will regain your peace and let love reside in your heart over a lifetime knowing that my selfishness has doomed you to wallow in misery for the rest of your days."

William sat there for at least a minute, staring at his sister and puzzling over the meaning of her strange words. It was almost as though he had been a witness to an inner dialogue rather than an active participant in a conversation. Unable to come to any reasonable conclusions on his own, he was about to ask her to explain when Jane's boisterous voice came calling from several feet away. They both turned to look in her direction as she came bounding toward them, carrying a box.

"Martha, Martha! You must come home with me at once!" Jane cried, stopping in front of them and grabbing Martha by the arm as she tried to catch her breath. "I've just come from Mrs. Jenkins' shop, and she has done such a wonderful job with Mother's veil! It looks like new! Come back to the house with me so that I may show it to you. I should wear my dress with it, as well, so that you can see how lovely it all looks together."

"Jane," said Martha, her face transformed from the contemplative expression of just moments before, "this may well be the twentieth time you've put on that dress in half as many days." Martha looked at William with a feigned look of exasperation at her older sister's enthusiasm, and it was as though their last few minutes of conversation had never taken place.

"But you've not seen it with the veil!"

"Yes, you are correct," sighed Martha with a smile, defeated by her sister's exuberance. She stood up to walk back with her sister, and William was pleased to see her rise so easily. Perhaps a brief rest was all she had needed. Jane was likely keeping her up late each night with preparations and gossip. Perhaps that was the reason for the odd monologue he had just witnessed.

As Jane pulled her toward the house, Martha looked back at William and grinned. "Are you coming, William? You have seen neither the veil nor the dress."

"I should like to keep it that way until the wedding day," he replied with a bow, "so that I may be hit with the full effect of its beauty and weep like a baby at the sight of our lovely Jane, just as our mother will."

"As you wish, William. Come on, Martha!"

The two sisters giggled as they hurried back to the house, and William was left alone with his thoughts.

With each passing day, it seemed more people descended upon the Abbott family home. Relatives from near and far, friends and well-wishers, and additional servants borrowed from neighboring households to help with the festivities filled the house with laughter and a great sense of excitement.

William tried to immerse himself in the general feeling, but as he watched his mother and his sisters run around tending to the final preparations, he experienced a twinge of sadness at having missed his sister Mary's wedding over a year ago. It was one more thing to add to the pile of regrets that weighed him down. Had William come home for Mary's wedding, things would certainly have been different. Bessie might already be his wife, and the two of them might have been observing this whirlwind of activity with a knowing smile as they recalled the excitement of their own wedding day. They might have even had children of their own by now.

At this, William's thoughts turned to the poor child that had been growing in Bessie's womb when she died, the babe's life extinguished before it could even take its first breath. The misery of their fate, mother and child, took the breath from his lungs, but only for a moment. As William took another breath, and then another, he realized that he would not be relieved of his insufferable existence so easily.

The day of Jane's wedding arrived, and, but for the agonizing thoughts that plagued him, it was a beautiful day indeed. The weather was perfect—warm, but not too warm for the second week of June—and the sky was an endless sea of blue without a single cloud to interrupt it. Jane was, as William had predicted, a vision of beauty and joy as she stood beside her soon-to-be husband and they each took their vows.

As husband and wife embraced each other for the first time in front of the minister and the guests, William glanced in Martha's direction. Martha was standing with her sisters next to the newlywed couple, facing the congregation, her finger wrapped around the gold chain about her neck. She was smiling adoringly at the two of them, and the smile was genuine in every way. But, for a reason he could not quite articulate, William found something bittersweet in the curve of Martha's mouth. Was it a foreshadowing of how the two sisters, who had been inseparable for so long, now had to lead two distinct lives? Or was the sense of loss reflected in Martha's eyes not caused by the loss of a sister, but rather the loss of hope that one day she would have a love of her own—the love of the man her sister had just married?

William prayed it was the former, for Martha had other sisters, and her relationship with her now-married sister Jane would never go away. It would only change, as it had to. At the same time, he could not help but worry about Martha and what would become of her. Perhaps a trip to visit him in Boston would be beneficial, regardless of the reasons for the look in Martha's eyes.

William spent the following week visiting with family and friends in Charlotte and taking care of various chores that his mother and sisters were ill-equipped to handle in his absence. The week passed swiftly and, but for the nagging concern regarding his sister Martha, as pleasantly as could be expected.

On the morning he was to return to Boston, all five of his sisters, his two brothers-in-law, and his sole nephew, whom he adored, gathered just outside the front doors of the house to see him off. His newest brother-in-law, Tommy, had his arm around Jane's waist, and William could not help feeling again a prickle of sadness for Martha, who stood alone, her kind smile unwavering.

One by one, they each embraced him, wished him well, and stood back to let another member of the family say good-bye. Last by design was Martha. She stepped forward and wrapped her arms around her big brother.

"Oh, how I wish you could stay with us, William," she said as she released him.

"I will be back," he replied, still holding her hands. "I will see you again soon. Perhaps Mother will let you come visit me in Boston. I will write to her in a few weeks' time and mention how many handsome and wealthy young men are looking for suitable wives in Boston." He glanced over at his mother, who was arranging his sister Abigail's hair and smoothing her skirts as his sister tried discreetly to move away. "I believe that should do the trick."

He could see tears begin to form in Martha's eyes as she nodded. "That would be nice."

Martha moved toward him and they embraced once more. She held him for what seemed a long while, and when she finally moved away, she whispered in his ear, "Promise me, William, that you will be happy and that you will not let the weight of the past hold you down. Promise me that you will live and love, no matter what happens. Do you promise me that?"

With his hands on Martha's shoulders, William moved her so that her face was directly in front of him. The whites of her eyes seemed somewhat yellow to him, and she looked tired. He would have asked her then if there was something wrong, if there was something she wasn't telling him, but at that moment she said again, "Promise me, William, or I shall not be able to rest."

He found her choice of words odd and unsettling, but he nodded. "I promise."

His sister smiled approvingly, making him forget that there could be anything at all not right, and then brushed her lips against his cheek.

Squeezing her shoulders once more, William finally let her go.

Chapter Twenty-Seven

Boston, Massachusetts
Modern Day

Will looked at the tattered paper in his hand for several minutes, thinking of Martha and remembering her warmth and kindness. When he had left that day, after Jane's wedding, it had never occurred to him that he would not see his sister again. He could almost feel their last embrace and hear her last words in his ear.

The letter in his hands had arrived only a few weeks after his return to Boston. He had read every word over and over again, confused and afraid of what the letter might mean. Two days later, his mother's letter had arrived, which sadly put all doubts to rest.

He brought his eyes back to Martha's letter and began to read, the sound of his sister's voice resounding in his head.

My Dearest William,

I have thought about this letter for several weeks now, and yet I still do not know how to begin.

I suppose it is best to start simply. I love you, Brother. With my whole heart and soul, I have loved you and always will love you, in this life and the next. It is because I love you that I have not been completely honest with you or, until very recently, our mother and sisters.

It seems that the good Lord above is calling me from this life, and the hours I have left here are few. I have been ailing for some time now, but I thank God it has not been unbearable until only a few days ago.

As my last hour draws nearer, I think of my life, and I am content. I have had many blessings—in my faith, in my family, in my friends. And I must now give back to God what was His all along, as we all must do someday.

But even as I pass from this life, I think of you, and I take great comfort in knowing that you, unlike me, have the whole expanse of your life before you, spread out like the ocean, endless in every direction.

Remember your promise to me. Live, love, and be loved. Even if you feel yourself undeserving, know that it is what you are meant for.

Your loving sister,
Martha

Will held the paper in his hands when he had finished, rubbing his thumbs gently over the corners of the worn page, the pressure of unshed tears building behind his eyes.

What would his sister think of him if she could see him now? The same man who had held her and promised her that he would live and love, who had actually found love again after so many years, and who had rejected it just the same. What would she think?

She would be cross with him, he thought with a smile. Very cross. Even though she had done the same when she had turned down Mr. Porter's proposal of marriage for the sake of her sister's happiness.

But she had done so knowing she was dying. Will knew he was not.

Setting his sister's letter back down in the box, on top of Erin's, Will walked over to the large windows of his office. The sun was bright outside. There was no hint of death or sadness in its light or the objects it illuminated.

No, the sadness came from within himself. And maybe it was time now to put it out. Maybe it was time to let it go and, finally, keep his promise to his sister.

Will walked back over to his desk and picked up the bundle of letters he had received from Bessie lifetimes ago. He had kept each one, as a reminder of the love he thought they once had, of the life they never got to share.

Carrying the letters in both hands, like an offering, he walked slowly out of his office to the living room, the wood floors creaking quietly with each step of his solitary procession. Standing over the fireplace, Will looked from the matches on the shelf to the letters in his hands. Then he gently pulled the ribbon off.

Erin was right—he didn't deserve forgiveness. And Martha was right—he didn't deserve to be loved. But perhaps that didn't matter. Perhaps it wasn't about what he deserved, but what he was given.

He had been given time. Years and years of time, to think about what he had done, and to become a better person.

He had been given love. His parents had loved him, Martha and his sisters had loved him, and even Erin, knowing his sins, had loved him. Didn't that mean that, somehow, God loved him and that He had forgiven him?

Will had loved Bessie. He hadn't meant for her to be hurt. He hadn't meant for her, or her child, to die.

Perhaps Bessie knew that now. Perhaps she had forgiven him, too.

Taking the matches off the shelf, Will knelt in front of the hearth and placed the stack of letters and the ribbon down before him on the bricks. He struck a match and watched it glow for a moment before picking up the first letter. It was folded in half, and part of him wanted to open it and read it one more time, but he didn't. Holding his breath, Will set the flame to the dry, brittle paper and cast it into the fireplace, watching as it burned.

It was time to let go.

He picked up the next letter and set it on top of the one burning in the fireplace. Then he took the next one, and the one after that. He watched as each letter caught fire and turned to ash, and, as his eyes followed the rising smoke, he felt himself rise with it.

When Bessie's letters were gone, he picked up the ribbon. It was her ribbon, one of the ones she had used to tie her hair. She had given it to him a few months before he had left for California.

For a moment, Will considered keeping it. He could just put it back in the box. But he knew that was not what he needed to do.

Before the small fire he had created went out, Will tossed the ribbon into the flames, then watched as it burned, too.

He was done. It was all gone.

And now there was only one more thing left for him to do.

Chapter Twenty-Eight

Charlotte, North Carolina
Modern Day

"It sounds like someone's knocking on your door."

Erin had heard the knocking, too. "I don't know who it could be," she said, getting up from the couch. She walked down the steps of her apartment to the front door. The man she saw out the peephole had his head down, and she couldn't see his face. The streetlamps outside cast odd shadows on the man's form, and it was hard to discern even what color his hair was or what he was wearing.

Normally, she wouldn't have answered the door without knowing who it was, but Blake was upstairs, and a quiver of anticipation ran up her spine that she couldn't ignore. So, Erin unlocked the deadbolt and opened the door.

The man looked up. "Hi."

Erin couldn't believe her eyes. She opened her mouth to speak, but nothing came out.

Will didn't wait to be invited in. He surged toward her and pulled her body into his, finding her mouth and kissing her as though he had been holding his breath for the last few months and was now finally able to breathe. She wrapped her arms around him, and all thought left her mind as she focused her attention on his mouth and the feel of his tensing muscles as he held her even closer.

"Erin, who is it?"

Will pulled away abruptly at the sound of Blake's voice.

She knew what he was thinking, how it must seem to him. He had expected her to be home alone on a Friday night. And having a man at her place close to eight in the evening could only mean one thing.

The blood had drained from Will's face, and Erin was suddenly afraid he might turn and run. Grabbing his hand with both of hers, she pulled him further inside her small entryway, kicking the door behind him shut with her foot. She was not going to let him get away.

Erin looked Will in the eyes as she spoke. "Everything is okay. Just come upstairs with me."

The stairway was too narrow for both of them to ascend side-by-side, but she moved her hand to just behind her hip as she went up first, pulling Will gently behind her.

Blake was standing at the top of the stairs with his trademark grin on his face.

"Will, right? Good to see you again, man."

He held his hand out to Will, and Will reluctantly reached out to shake it.

Just then, the sound of running water coming from the bathroom broke the awkward silence, and Erin couldn't help but smile as she saw relief slowly relax Will's features.

"Blake and his fiancé, Susan, are getting married in a couple of months," Erin explained. "Somehow I got put in charge of designing the programs for the wedding ceremony, so I invited them over to look at what I've come up with so far."

Erin pointed to the coffee table in the living room, and Will turned his head to the mess of paper, string, and ribbons.

"Wow, I picked the wrong time to take a potty break," said Susan, standing between the bathroom door and the dining room, rubbing her hands on the front of her jeans and smiling. "You're Will, right? Nice to see you again."

Will smiled warmly, all signs of panic gone, and took a few steps toward Susan to shake her hand, as well.

"I hear congratulations are in order," Will said, still shaking her hand.

"Yes, I suppose they are. Thank you," Susan replied.

Blake sighed dramatically. "I told Susan, I said, 'Babe, I'm not getting any younger. It's time to stake your claim and take me off the market. I mean, I can't resist Erin's charms forever—I am only a man.'"

Susan laughed and punched him, rather hard, in the shoulder. "I don't know why I put up with you," she said, tenderly.

"It probably has something to do with my sexy facial hair," he replied, rubbing his chin for emphasis.

As though remembering that they were not the only ones standing there, the two of them looked over at Will and Erin and said, almost simultaneously, "We should go."

Erin couldn't even pretend to object.

Susan gave Erin a quick hug, and Blake gave her a longer one, whispering, "I told you he'd come to his senses."

Erin smiled and whispered back, "No you didn't."

Blake let go and grinned mischievously. "Well, I was thinking it, and I was right. You two have a good night. Remember, tonight is not a school night, so feel free to stay up as long as you want. Or go to bed as soon as possible. Whatever floats your boat."

Susan took her fiancé by the arm and pulled him down the stairs to the door. "You have absolutely no filter," she said quietly to Blake, just before calling over her shoulder, "We'll let ourselves out!"

Erin could hear the two of them fumbling with the lock, then the door opened and closed and the apartment was suddenly quiet.

Will was staring at her, and she couldn't quite read his expression. His eyes were wide, his brow was smooth, and his lips were slightly parted. He almost looked—at peace.

She smiled cautiously, reaching for his hand. "So, are you in town just visiting, or do you have other plans?"

"Other plans," he replied, the corners of his mouth hinting at a smile.

"I see. And what might those other plans be?" She spoke softly, feeling shy all of a sudden under the intensity of his gaze.

He grabbed her other hand and brought both hands to his lips, closing his eyes. The only thought in Erin's mind as he pressed his cheek to the backs of her hands was that he loved her with the purest of hearts. And it was almost overwhelming.

When he opened his eyes again, he lowered her hands from his face before stepping in closer and dropping his head so that their foreheads touched. "I got a letter from a beautiful young woman a few weeks ago that made me rethink my entire life, all one hundred and seventy years of it."

"She must have said something pretty important," replied Erin, breathless, her knees starting to feel like jelly as Will began dropping kisses on her cheek, by her ear, and down her neck.

"She did," he whispered into her hair. "She made me realize that even though I don't deserve her, somehow, for some reason, despite everything she knows about me, she has chosen to give me her love. And for that, I am, and will always be, eternally grateful."

Happiness washed over Erin, making her feel so light that she wouldn't have been surprised if her feet had left the ground. The empty feeling that had almost crushed her over the past several weeks was gone without a trace, and in its place was only joy and relief and hope for the future. For their future, together. There was nothing else she wanted. Nothing else she needed. She was complete.

The feeling of utter contentment was even greater than the desire that grew hotter as Will's kisses rounded her shoulder toward her chest, and Erin surprised herself by interrupting the advancing kisses to pull him into a hug. She held Will firmly against her, her cheek against his chest, his heartbeat strong in her ear, and his arms tightened around her. He was here, and he was hers, and she never wanted to be apart from him again.

They held each other in silence for a long time before she asked in a whisper, "So, what are you going to do now, Mr. Abbott?"

He pulled away from her slightly so he could look

at her face. "I will accept this woman's love. I will cherish it and hold onto it always." He dipped his head closer to hers. "And I will make every effort to deserve it a little more, each day, for the rest of my life."

As he spoke these last words, his lips met hers in a long, gentle kiss.

When they parted, Will stroked her hair and smiled. "For a moment, when I heard a man's voice up here, I thought I was too late. I thought I had lost you."

"I told you I would wait for you to come around," Erin replied, wrapping her arms around Will again and resting her head on his shoulder.

"I know, but no one waits forever."

She laughed against his shoulder, then tilted her face up to look at him. "It's only been three months."

"But it felt like a hundred years. Believe me, I would know."

Her arms tightened around him. "Oh, Will, I've missed you, too. Was it really my letter that changed your mind about us? To be honest, I don't remember exactly what I said, other than telling you about me and my father."

"It was your letter, and my sister's letter, and the fact that I just couldn't live another day without being with you."

His sister's letter? He had mentioned the letters Bessie had written while he was in California, but never any letters from his sister. "Your sister wrote you a letter?" she asked. "About us?"

Will nodded. "Years and years ago, just before she died. And yes, it was about us. I just didn't realize it at the time."

His mouth drew closer and he began kissing her

again, his hands moving up and down her back. Almost in answer to her thoughts, his fingers found her skin, slipping under her shirt and rubbing small circles everywhere they went. Her skin warmed and tingled everywhere he touched, and a small sound of pleasure escaped her covered mouth as their kiss intensified.

As close as they were to each other, she wanted to be closer, to feel more of him against her, everywhere. She wanted Will, all of him, in a way she couldn't explain or even articulate. And suddenly she understood.

She untucked Will's shirt in the back as they kissed and slid her hands against his skin. He was so soft and warm, and she could feel his corded strength beneath her fingertips.

Will pulled her against himself, somehow holding her closer, kissing her more deeply. She was drunk with the feeling, and her every thought centered on how to be closer to him still.

Suddenly, Will stopped. He brought his forehead to rest against hers once more, and she could feel his chest heaving with each deep breath he took. Still holding her, he almost growled, "I want to take your clothes off."

A jolt of electricity ran right through her as the words hit her ears, and she replied without hesitation, "Okay."

Will's grip on her tightened. "I'm going to marry you," he added.

"I know," she replied, breathless. Waiting.

Wanting.

He was still, and all Erin could hear was his quiet and steady breathing. Her heart was racing with anticipation, her core tightening in expectation, and she tried to calm herself by matching her breathing to his.

"If I take off your clothes, I will not be able to...protect your virtue."

This time she hesitated, but only for a second. "I don't want you to protect my virtue anymore. I just want you."

Will sighed as he moved his head away from hers a little so he could look at her. There was a battle raging behind his warm brown eyes.

"We should go to your grandmother's."

She raised her eyebrows at him. "My grandmother's? Right now?"

"Yes." He smiled, and it was the most beautiful smile she had ever seen. He had never smiled like that before. There was only joy in his eyes. It was pure and radiant and boundless, and it held no trace of pain.

"May I ask why, at this very moment, you would wish to see my grandmother?" Erin smiled now herself, his joy spilling into her, despite the prick of disappointment that his mouth was speaking instead of kissing her.

"Let's just say I'm a lot less likely to rip your clothes off in the presence of your grandmother."

"I thought you said you weren't going to protect my virtue anymore."

Erin walked over to the couch, pulling him behind her, and they sat down.

"Believe me," he sighed, "I don't want to, but I would feel bad messing up the perfect record you've maintained all these years. Well, I probably wouldn't feel *that* bad at first, but eventually I would. Besides, we're going to have the rest of our lives to do all those things I want to do to you right now."

"Are we?" she asked whimsically, resting her head on his shoulder.

"Yes. That's the other reason we should pay your grandmother a visit."

Erin sat straight up and looked at him. "What's the other reason?"

"To announce our engagement."

She smiled coyly at him. "I don't recall you proposing to me. And I'm pretty sure I would remember something like that."

"I suppose I didn't actually frame it as a question earlier, but rather as a statement of fact." Will cleared his throat. "Allow me to rephrase, Counsellor. Would you condescend to marry an undeserving man such as myself?"

"Marry a man such as yourself—no. But marry you—certainly."

He shook his head, laughing. "You're making this too easy. Aren't you at least going to ask me for a ring, like this one?"

Will pulled a black velvet box out of his jacket and handed it to Erin, who stared at him in disbelief.

"You mean, you're actually proposing to me? The real thing? It's happening right now? This is a ring?"

He laughed again, nodding. "Well, go on and open it. See if you like it."

"I love it," she replied, holding his gaze, the box still sitting closed in the palm of her hand.

Will sighed with teasing reproach as he took the box back and opened it for her.

"Oh my—it's beautiful!" she exclaimed, putting a hand over her mouth. "It's just beautiful. I can't believe this is happening right now."

Erin's eyes welled with tears as Will took the ring out of the box and slipped it onto her finger. She held her hand in front of her, fingers extended, just staring at the princess cut diamond mounted on a platinum band. It was simple and elegant. It was timeless, like Will.

He laughed as he wiped away her tears, then pushed the numerous stray hairs that had escaped from her ponytail back behind her ears. "I hope those are tears of joy," he said.

"Pure, unadulterated joy. Thank you." She hugged him, squeezing as hard as she could, as though she could freeze this moment, this feeling, if she could hold him tightly enough.

When they separated, he moved his hands to her shoulders and, keeping her squarely opposite him, said, "I'm the one who is thankful for you—for your persistent, unquestioning, undoubting love. I was so wrong to think that God was keeping me alive all this time as a punishment. He was keeping me alive so I could wait for you."

As though unable to maintain any distance between their bodies, he stood abruptly and pulled her off the couch, bringing her crashing into him as his lips sought to cover hers.

Erin looked at her hand again. "It looks brand new."

"It is. I bought it last week." A wrinkle of doubt appeared between his eyes. "Is that okay?"

She laughed. "Of course it's okay. I guess I just figured you would have some very old heirloom ring."

"I want to let go of the past," he replied, looking at her with a breathtakingly serious expression. "I want to start my life anew with you."

"We will both start over," she replied. "And our life together will be wonderful. Because we'll be together."

He looked down, sighing.

"Hey, what's wrong?"

Will chuckled under his breath. "Nothing's wrong. I just feel bad. I'm sorry I didn't do anything fancy for the proposal. No doves or balloons or sky-writing airplanes. You didn't even get dinner out of this. After all these years, I just didn't have the patience to wait."

"It was perfect," said Erin, and she meant it.

"Are we really going to my grandmother's right now?" Erin asked, letting Will drag her to the stairs.

"Sure, why not? It's only eight-thirty. You think she's asleep?"

"She's probably getting ready for bed, but not asleep just yet. Besides, she would want to know about this, even if we have to wake her up."

As he helped her put on her jacket, Will chuckled to himself. "I hope your grandmother's not too disappointed."

"Disappointed? Why would she be disappointed?"

"Because," he replied, pulling her closer and kissing the tip of her nose, "as of tonight, her favorite landlord is no longer on the market."

Erin laughed, cupping Will's face in her hands. "It's not my grandmother you have to worry about. It's her neighbor across the hall."

"Ah, Mrs. Myer. I had forgotten about her."

"You can be sure she hasn't forgotten about you."

Erin grabbed his hand and pulled him down the stairs behind her.

"She'll direct her efforts elsewhere once she finds out I only have eyes for one woman, and she just happens to be the kindest, wisest, and most beautiful woman in the world."

Erin gave him a quick kiss on the cheek as she passed through the door he held open for her. "You're going to make a very good husband."

Chapter Twenty-Nine

Almost exactly six months after Will came back into her life, Erin and Will were married. The wedding day (and, more specifically, the wedding night) couldn't come soon enough—they had exhibited an extraordinary amount of self-control leading up to that night, and Erin couldn't wait to put an end to her perfect record. From the look in Will's eyes as they stepped into the wedding suite, Will was looking forward to it, too.

They were both quiet as Will helped Erin step out of her wedding gown and removed the hundred pins that held her hair together.

"What are you thinking?" she murmured as the last pins were pulled out and her hair fell down around her shoulders. She was wondering why he hadn't removed her strapless bra and white stockings yet and why he was still wearing pants and an undershirt.

"I'm trying to calculate how much of an increase in rent I need to charge my New York tenants to pay for a kitchen remodeling project I have in mind."

She grabbed his arm as he turned away from her, making him meet her gaze. "That's really what you're thinking right now?"

"Well," he brought his mouth close to her ear, his breath warm on her neck, "if I wasn't thinking about that, you would already be naked, and I wanted you to

323

have something before we start doing all the things I've been waiting to do with you."

"In that case, hurry up and give me this present of yours," Erin's lips curled, "so that you can finish unwrapping *your* present."

"Good grief, woman. You're going to give me a heart attack before I even have a chance to touch you."

She giggled as she watched him move to his suitcase and take a thick envelope out of the zippered side pocket.

"This is for you," he said, handing it to her.

Erin looked at the lovely handwriting on the front. The ink was faded, but it was clearly addressed to "Mrs. William Abbott." The return address was there, too, but there was no name for the sender.

"Who sent this?" she asked, looking back up at him.

"Open it. You'll see."

Sitting on the edge of the bed, Erin carefully opened the envelope and withdrew a single sheet of paper that was folded into a lumpy rectangular packet. Unfolding the paper, she withdrew another packet from within, this one made of tissue paper. The sheet of paper was covered in writing, done in the same beautiful cursive as the envelope. She looked to the bottom of the handwritten page and found the signature.

"Martha Abbott? This is from your sister Martha?"

A terrible thought occurred to her. "Were you married before, Will?"

"No!" he answered quickly. "It's for you. My sister addressed the envelope to you. Somehow, she knew I would meet you, and I guess there was something she wanted you to have. Something she wanted to tell you."

"The envelope was sealed. You've never read the letter? You don't know what's in this tissue paper?"

He shook his head. "She didn't want me to read it. She meant it for you."

Although curious as to what was inside the tissue paper, Erin turned to the letter first and, with one more glance at Will, started to silently read it.

As she passed her eyes over the first paragraph, shivers ran up her spine.

"This can't be true," she whispered. Then she looked up at Will. How could she doubt Martha's words? Wasn't he living proof that anything was possible?

She read on, with Will standing nearby, waiting patiently. When she was done, she handed the letter wordlessly to him, then unwrapped the tissue paper.

****

Will's eye caught a flash of gold as Erin carefully peeled away the layers of tissue paper to reveal a length of chain with a gold ring on it—a man's ring set with three distinctive blue stones, one above the next.

"Martha's ring," he muttered, suddenly remembering his sister wearing it around her neck, the end tucked into her bodice. "One of our servants gave it to her. Radka was her name. She told Martha it was a family heirloom."

"According to Martha's letter," Erin said, pointing to the page in his hand, "it was much more than that."

"Why? What did Martha say?"

Even as he asked the question, he began reading his sister's letter. They were only words on a page, written a very long time ago by a woman long since gone, but still, as his eyes took in each phrase, he could feel Martha's presence. He could see her in his mind—young and happy, full of joy and kindness. Full of life. And he remembered.

Radka did not purchase this ring, his sister had told him. *It was handed down to her by her father, and he had received it from his father upon his twin sister's marriage. At least that's what she told me. It's a special ring. You wouldn't believe the stories that go with it.*

"Did you know the ring grants wishes, Will? Did Martha ever tell you that?"

He shook his head. "Not in so many words, but I remember her saying it was special."

Martha had never elaborated, though. She'd never said what was so special about the ring. Perhaps Radka had asked her to keep the information in confidence. More likely, Will had been too preoccupied with his own sadness and misfortune to bother inquiring.

"She made her wish for you, Will. How could she not tell you that?"

Will sat quietly down on the bed beside Erin and laid the letter on his lap. "I think she did tell me, only I didn't understand it at the time. But she did—she told me what she was going to do, and then she did it. And then she told me what I had to do to hold up my end of the bargain, only I didn't. Not for a long time. Not until you."

I know what I want most in my life, William, and it is for you to find your peace. Because no matter how long a life I have, or how many joys I experience, knowing that you suffer under the weight of despair will render all such blessings meaningless. I would choose a brief moment knowing that someday you will regain your peace and let love reside in your heart over a lifetime knowing that my selfishness has doomed you to wallow in misery for the rest of your days.

According to what Martha had written in her letter, all Martha had to do was wish for the thing she most desired, and the ring would grant it. The idea seemed absurd, but Will's whole existence had been absurd. How was a wish any more unbelievable than his life had been? Wasn't a wish just a prayer—a request for a miracle?

Then another thought entered his mind. Radka had given his sister a way to have what she most desired. What if Martha had made a different wish? What if Will had come home to Charlotte having achieved the peace Martha so wanted him to have? Would she have wished for her own health? Would she have told Tommy Porter she was in love with him? Would Tommy have married her instead of Jane? Would she have had the life she deserved?

Will knew he would never have the answers to those questions, and, really, it didn't matter. Martha had chosen his happiness over her own. She had told him as much when they had spoken before Jane's wedding. His wellbeing was what she wanted most. That fact was almost as unbelievable as the ring itself.

Looking over at his wife, half-undressed, her hair a mess, and her eyes wide with wonder, Will sighed. Martha's wish had been granted, for all Will felt now was peace and, more importantly, love.

Seeing Erin's hands nervously fumbling with the ring and the chain Martha had given her, Will asked, "Are you okay?"

She looked at him incredulously. "Me? Of course, I'm okay. I'm worried about you."

He almost laughed and put his hand on hers. She was, in many ways, like Martha—always concerned about everyone else. "Why are you worried about me, sweet wife?"

Erin's lips curled into a smile. "I like how that sounds."

"Me too." He brought her hand to his lips and kissed it. "Tell me what you're worried about."

She let out a long breath. "I just want to make sure this new information," she tilted her head in the direction of the letter he still held in his lap, "is not going to cause new guilt."

He nodded slowly. "You mean because if the ring really could grant my sister any wish, if she had wished to be healthy, she would have lived? And if I hadn't been so perpetually miserable, she wouldn't have wasted her wish on me?"

"Something like that," she replied softly, a tender concern in her gaze.

Tracing her cheek with his finger, he gave her a lop-sided grin, and he could see the relief in her expression almost immediately. "I'm done with guilt, Erin. Martha made her choice, and her choice was meant to give me a chance at happiness. Lord knows I didn't deserve it, but I am thankful for it. I am thankful for many things. And the only way to express my thanks is to love you, with all my heart and soul."

"I like how that sounds, too." Reaching for his hand, Erin smiled at him, and his heart was filled with pure joy.

Will picked up the letter with his free hand. "There is something I don't understand, though," he said, reading the words once more. "Martha's letter says that the wish only lasts as long as the person has the ring. If that's true, then how could the wish outlive her?"

Erin frowned. "Let me see the letter again."

He handed her the page and watched as she reread it. He could almost see her lawyer's mind working on the puzzle.

"That's not exactly what she says." Erin pointed to a paragraph near the end of the letter. "She says Radka told her that the person who has the ring keeps the wish until she gives the ring to someone else. If Martha gave the ring to Mrs. William Abbott, well, there was no Mrs. William Abbott until today, when I married you. So, I think she was able to keep her wish alive until now." Erin grinned. "I think your sister was a genius."

Will laughed. "Martha certainly was a lot of things. Kind, sweet, lovely, clever. You would have loved her."

"I know," she replied softly.

Without another word, Erin placed the letter on the nightstand nearby, along with the ring and chain. Then, covering Will's cheek with her hand, she drew him to her for a kiss. As they kissed, her hands slid beneath his shirt, and any philosophical musings that had lingered in his mind were quickly displaced by more carnal thoughts.

He released her mouth just long enough to throw off his shirt, then turned his attention to the thousand clasps on the corset she wore. Standing up, he pulled her to her feet and kissed her neck as he undid the clasps, one by one. She reached for him, her chest heaving with each breath as he finally freed her from her undergarment.

As they relieved each other from the last of their

clothing, a single thought remained in Will's mind.

He was her husband, and she was his wife. They were one.

Epilogue

Nine Years Later

Erin put the last of the dishes into the dishwasher and finished wiping off the counter after dinner. She couldn't help smiling as she heard the girls' laughter flow from the family room into the kitchen, and she stopped for a moment to survey the scene, unnoticed by its participants.

The three girls were playing "salon" with their daddy. Poor Will had has legs extended in different directions, socks removed, and his hands were placed palms-down on a large hardcover book that the girls had balanced on his lap. Martha, the eldest of the three at seven years old, was pretending to paint her father's fingernails by dipping a paintbrush into a small plastic cup of water. Like her namesake, Will's sister, Martha had always been Erin's happy baby, the one who rarely fussed and always seemed to have a smile on her face, even as an infant.

Jamie was two years younger than Martha, and, unlike her sister, was a high-maintenance little girl. As a baby, she liked to sleep all day and cry all night. Now, at five years old, she had finally outgrown her nighttime fits of screaming, thank goodness, but she had also found other ways to be high maintenance. She loved all things pretty, sparkling, or pink and had "convinced" her sisters that it was her turn to be the head stylist. Erin watched as Jamie stood on the couch cushions on one side of Will and pretended to style her father's hair with a hairbrush and some of her pink bows.

The youngest of the sisters was Paige Rose—Paige for Erin's mother and Rose for Erin's grandmother. Erin's grandmother hadn't lived long enough to meet Paige—she had passed away peacefully in her sleep at the ripe old age of ninety-two only weeks before Erin found out she was pregnant again.

Paige was their playful one, their jokester. Everything was a game with Paige, and a fun one at that. From waking up in the morning and bounding down the stairs to bestow full-body hugs on her mother and father to hiding from her mother when it was time for bed, it was all laughter and fun for Paige. It was no surprise to Erin that the three-year-old had chosen to "paint" her daddy's toenails, as she took every opportunity to tickle Will's feet in the process and found the whole thing incredibly amusing.

Erin's heart was filled with joy at the sight of her beautiful family, and she thought to herself that she could not possibly love Will or her girls any more than she did at that moment.

"Daddy, I love how sparkly your hair is. I hope my hair is this sparkly when I grow up."

Erin shook her head and quietly laughed at hearing her prima donna Jamie's comment. In the other room, she could hear Will chuckle. "Why on earth would my hair be sparkly, Miss Hairstylist? Are you putting pretend glitter in my hair?"

"No, Daddy," Jamie replied. "It's just naturally sparkly. Mommy, come see how sparkly Daddy's hair is. But don't be sad. I like your hair, too, even though it's a boring brown."

Curious, Erin put down the washcloth in her hand and stepped out of the kitchen to see what her daughter was talking about. She ran her fingers through Will's hair and her heart caught in her throat. Suddenly, she understood what the little girl was saying. The "sparkles" were the strands of silver hair that were scattered throughout Will's head of thick, dark hair.

"It is beautiful, Jamie. Daddy will have to look in the mirror so he can see for himself tonight before bedtime."

Will turned to her, looking for some sort of explanation, but Erin just smiled, dropping a quick kiss on his lip. Then, looking at her watch and seeing what time it was, Erin clapped her hands three times. "Does anyone know what time it is?"

Martha raised her hand and waved it enthusiastically. "Oooh, oooh, I know!"

Jamie, on the other hand, simply shouted out, "Time for dessert at Grandpa's house!"

It was their Saturday night tradition—an early dinner at their house followed by a visit to her father's apartment a few miles down the road for dessert.

"A little bird told me that Grandpa has ice cream sundaes for us tonight!" said Will enthusiastically as he pulled his socks back on.

"Was that little bird Mommy?" asked Martha earnestly.

Will laughed. "Maybe."

"Okay, come on, let's go! Get your shoes on, girls, and put on your jackets. It's a little chilly tonight. Hurry up, let's get moving! We're wasting ice cream eating time!"

****

Later that night, when the ice cream had been washed out of their hair and the girls were finally sleeping soundly, Will pulled Erin close to him as they settled into bed. He was tempted to slip his hands under the pajama top she wore but contented himself for the moment with having her snuggle against him, despite the clothing that separated them.

"You know what it means, right?" she asked him, her voice already sounding sleepy. He knew she was talking about the silver hairs Jamie had discovered that night.

"It means I'm getting older. It means we're really together, going through life side-by-side."

"We've always been together, Will. But yes, I think you're right."

She touched his face with her hand, and he found it increasingly difficult to content himself with snuggling.

"Do you think it started on our wedding night, when I opened Martha's envelope?"

"That was your theory back then, that when you became Mrs. Abbott, the wish would be gone." He slipped his hands under her shirt and wrapped his arms around her, finding the smooth skin of her back. "I think you were right."

"Mmm, our wedding night," she murmured as he began kissing her neck. "That was a good night."

"Was it? I don't remember," he teased, pulling her shirt off.

Erin ran her fingers down his bare chest and laughed. "Then allow me to remind you."

****

Later, Will put his arm around his wife and moved closer to her as she turned her back to him and settled into a more comfortable sleeping position. He could feel her body relax against his as she hugged his arm to her chest. Just a minute later the slow rhythm of her breathing told him that she was already asleep.

He loved Erin with all his being, and that love had flowed over to create three beautiful, joyful, amazing little girls. He, a man who had caused the loss of hope and had extinguished life, had now become a source of joy and a co-creator of life. How had he deserved such an honor? How had he deserved such a life?

The truth was he didn't deserve it at all. But there was a certain peace that came with realizing that, although he had done nothing to earn the many blessings in his life, all he had to do was to accept those blessings and be thankful.

Will kissed the back of his sleeping wife's head and closed his eyes. His sister Martha would have been proud of him. He had finally granted her wish. He was living his life again. But even though he was getting older and death was once again inevitable for him, or perhaps because of that, he knew he had a lot more living to do.

And he looked forward to it.

A word about the author…

Winner of the Georgia Romance Writers' 2020 Maggie Award for Excellence in the Unpublished Historical Romance category, Kathryn Amurra is the author of sweet and sensual romance stories with mystical and historical elements. Her newest series, Heart's True Desire, revolves around a ring and a necklace from generations past, each of which has the power to grant the bearer his or her deepest desire. Amurra is also the author of the independently-published Soothsayer's Path series set in Ancient Rome. An intellectual property attorney by day, some of Amurra's best writing takes place between the hours of 10PM and midnight (or later), when she has "logged off" from her day job and her hubby and three girls are asleep. https://www.kathrynamurra.com